12/14

Look Behind Every Hill

Look Behind Every Hill

A Western Duo

Steve Frazee

Five Star • Waterville, Maine

First Edition
First Printing: July 2006

Published in 2006 in conjunction with
Golden West Literary Agency.

Set in 11 pt. Plantin.

Printed in the United States on permanent paper.

Library of Congress Cataloging-in-Publication Data

Frazee, Steve, 1909–
   [Secret of Kansas gulch]
    Look behind every hill : a western duo / by Steve Frazee.
— 1st ed.
     p. cm.
   ISBN 1-59414-402-8 (hc : alk. paper)
   1. Frazee, Steve, 1909– Secret of Kansas gulch.
  II. Title: Secret of Kansas gulch. III. Title
  PS3556.R358S425 2006
  813′.54—dc22   2005033748

Look Behind
Every Hill

Table of Contents

The Secret of Kansas Gulch

I

Much farther apart from the camp of Poverty than his 100 yards of isolation gave him, Jay Meade sat on a stump before his tent and listened to the hosts of thunder beat their mighty drums. Black clouds came in silently to smother the mountains and a wind began to test its strength. The last to be enveloped was a massive ridge black with timber, lower than the snow-veined peaks beyond. The storms of centuries had clutched ineffectually with wet hands at that mountain. On the eastern end of it a great thrust of granite made a bell-like muzzle that slanted upward—Old Bugle. Around it stood tremendous peaks yet nameless.

Old Bugle held Meade's secret well. He smiled at it almost affectionately. Let the storm come raging. When it was gone, Old Bugle and Meade would still be here. When Poverty camp was gone, they would share their secret.

Meade was a tall man with a shoulder span that caused his shirts to rip down the back when he bent to a shovel on the creek; so now he was wearing loose buckskin secured by trading sugar to a Ute. His face was golden brown from the high-altitude sun. His hair was thick and sandy, carrying reddish glints when the sun was out. It was no one's business that his face had once been sweated pale from walking behind a plow in the sultry heat of eastern Kansas. All else about his life on the Kaw was no one's business, either.

There was in his expression something that fell just short of aggressiveness, a sharply defensive look that said to the world: *Do not expect me to help carry any of your burden. I have my own affairs.* He watched the sullen sky come down on Old Bugle, and then he looked, with a bunching at one corner of his mouth, at the scurrying of men below in Poverty. Their uncertainty and their quick changes of mind carried up the hill to him as clearly as their gabble. They ran about like hogs before a storm, and there was no direction or unity in their excitement.

Situated in the narrowest part of the gulch, the camp straddled Feather Creek with no plan except each individual's desire to be on his claim and within spitting distance of water. Lean-to shelters, bough huts, tents, dirt-roofed cabins of aspen logs—what did it matter where a man threw down his body after a day upon the creek? The song of gold reached a whining pitch of madness. All else, including politics and slavery, was subject to it.

Largest of all the tents was Billy Bland's saloon. Scalloped edges, limp and faded now, spoke of the days when the canvas had helped shelter a circus that went belly up in Independence. If food was sometimes short in Poverty, whiskey never was.

Men came from the saloon and looked at the sky. A few bustled away. "It's rained before," a miner said. "We're still here, ain't we?" He was one of those who went inside again.

The squat and burly Mercer brothers, Ed and Harvey, brought a bottle with them when they came out to see about the weather. They drank and wiped their mouths on their sleeves and laughed at the sky. They caused Meade a faint stirring of dislike, animosity striving to grow without real sustenance. Active dislike of them was too much trouble, just as positive friendship for anyone involved conditions that Jay Meade had tried to eliminate from his life some time before. Like and dislike were nets that men throw around themselves, and then they struggle bitterly and howl for succor after becoming enmeshed.

Ed Mercer said: "Move your tent, Phillips, if you're in such a fret about a little water."

Ban Phillips was a hulking man, long-armed, stoop-shouldered. His grizzled beard spoke of age that was out of place among the residents of Poverty. He was from a hillside farm in east Tennessee. "I ain't so worried about the tent," he drawled, "but I don't want to see about three feet of stuff washed on top of my placer. I jest got my sluice. . . ."

"Move your claim, too." Harvey Mercer laughed. He held the bottle toward Phillips. "Drink up, grandpa, and let it rain in peace."

Ban Phillips turned away and went down the crooked street, walking with the awkward-looking stride of a mountaineer.

"If you're worried about your daughter," Ed called, "me and Harv'll be glad to come down and move her!" Both Mercers laughed.

Phillips did not look round. He went on to his tent, halfway down the street. Meade watched him duck inside. *Ellen Phillips Greenaway,* Meade thought. She tried to contain her thoughts, looking out impersonally upon the men of Poverty, but deep behind her eyes were things known and remembered, and sometimes they crept to the surface when she talked to Meade. She was a widow. Her son was about six, there with her and Phillips in the tent. The four married women of Poverty said the camp was no place for a child. Of course, they had no children themselves, not yet, but when they did, it would not likely happen in some forsaken place like this.

Meade smiled. He could watch the antics of Poverty and take no part in them. Therein, he was sure, lay his strength. Entanglement was failure. Ellen Greenaway could prove just that, but still he kept thinking of what he had seen in her eyes, of the full bloom of her strong body when she helped her father at his sluice.

Annoyed at himself, he glanced toward Old Bugle, forgetting that the clouds were down. Wind with the cold of rain running in it pushed against the blackened folds of his buckskin shirt. The chill touched one section of his chest more sharply than any place else. He folded his arm across that side, aware of his action, also knowing that he would not do so when close to men where the act might be marked by shrewd eyes.

It was then that he saw Bennet Mercer ride out of the timber and come up the gulch at a trot. He came, Meade thought with cold distrust, from the general direction of Old Bugle. Ben Mercer, half brother to the other two, rode about the mountains while others worked. Yet he had a remarkable talent for appearing to do as much as any man in camp. He was like the acrobat in the troupe of five or six, who moves on the stage, giving short shouts, banging his hands together, doing nothing, but covering his inactivity skillfully while the audience is engrossed in the feats of his mates. Most naturally the drone acrobat must take his bows with the others.

Meade was pleased with his comparison. He had no quarrel with Bennet Mercer; rather, he admired the man's ability to let others do the chores.

Mercer was in a hurry, but he stopped when Stella Kinnison hailed him from the doorway of the tent in the pines on the hill to his left. There were four others like Stella in the tent, and they plied an old profession. They did not own a claim in the gulch, but they shared an interest in almost every one.

From the saddle of his nervous sorrel gelding Mercer imparted a certain air of elegance to the bow he gave the madam of the brown tent. He did that with an urgency upon him, with a storm poised like a lance above him.

Stella said: "Shouldn't they be moving some of those tents, Mister Mercer? Right there in the gulch bottom and all. . . ."

"I'm going now to see about it"

"If any of the women want to come up here, they're welcome, but I don't suppose. . . ." Stella Kinnison let her thought die in the muttering sky.

"That's most kind of you," Mercer said. "I'll pass the offer on."

The mayor, the *Burgermeister,* the gallant leader who did no work. Muscles bunched at the corner of Meade's wide lips. By God, you had to hand it to the man, at that.

Mercer rode on up the street, pausing here and there for a few words with men hustling around their possessions. Four men were carrying sections of their sluice to high ground. Mercer pointed out a good place to them. A woman came from her tent with a bundle of clothing. She looked around wildly, and then she darted up the hill and tied the bundle to the branch of a huge yellow pine tree.

Closer now the thunder slammed the tenpins of its sounds. The wind died and the air was charged and waiting. If the head gates of the mountains chose to direct water toward the gulch, there would be nothing to impede the flow once it struck the half-mile area where trees and brush had been cut largely away. Evidence of former floods had been here for anyone to see, and that was why Meade's tent was on the hill. He watched Ban Phillips and his daughter run from their tent. They began to trench around it frantically, as if the thought had just come to them. That, Meade thought, would be as ineffectual as the puny dikes farmers used to throw against the brown roll of the flooding Kaw.

Bennet Mercer stopped a moment to speak to the woman and old man. His voice was cheerful in the heavy air. "It may not be as bad as we expect, Missus Greenaway, but it's well to take precautions, of course."

Ellen nodded. She pushed a strand of hair away from her face and went back to work. Ban Phillips had not paused. A stubborn man, Meade thought, pitting his stooped back and shovel against a sky full of water, a typical man setting himself against forces that he could not beat.

Four men were playing cards on a broad stump in front of a bough hut. If the water came, they had nothing to take to safety but themselves and a few tools. They laughed and made their bets.

Ben Mercer had a word for them, also. He left them laughing louder when he rode on.

Mercer lost his easy manner when he stopped in front of Billy Bland's saloon. Without dismounting, he cursed his half-brothers from outside. "Get the tent and everything else up on the hill!"

Ed and Harvey looked at the sky. They grumbled like the thunder, and then Ed said: "Why don't you help?"

"Because I've got to see about others who need help." Ben was patient, but he was also loud. "Now get a move on, boys."

Ed and Harvey lumbered down the street. Meade had never seen them disobey their half-brother, and he supposed he never would. That was as it should be. Some men were stupid and frenzied. Others were born to profit by that. Jay Meade was thankful that a bullet had taught him a few such basic facts while he was still young.

His tent was trenched; his tie ropes were securely staked; there was plenty of dry wood inside for his tin stove. A haunch of venison hung from the ridge pole inside. There was $1,000 in dust in soft leather against his belly. Let all kinds of storms descend; he could look with mild amusement on the scene below.

Before long the first big drops of rain would come. Meade stood up to go inside and build a fire. When the fools got washed out down there, some of them would have to come to his tent to warm themselves.

"Oh, Jay!"

Ben Mercer was riding up the hill. Trotting ahead of him was Luke Reardon, one of the Negro miners. They reached Meade's tent almost together. Reardon waited for Mercer to speak first.

"You've heard of the cow and the flat rock, Jay?" Mercer's white teeth made a streak as he looked up at the sky.

Meade grinned. "That's what it looks like, Ben."

Mercer swung down. His movements were as graceful as his manner. He was a slender man with a clear, olive skin. His face was sharp but not quite aquiline. French, he said. His family owned an entire cotton county in Mississippi. Although he himself had never told Meade so, it was hinted that Mercer had little need of gold, that he had brought his half-brothers out here after they had become involved in a dueling scrape with an international flavor.

He was, it was said, protecting them against further difficulties until the three of them could return home. The story, real or fancied, gave Ben Mercer a mantle of gallantry and boldness that completely missed Ed and Harvey, the prime participants. Only occasionally did Ben's public treatment of his half-brothers as inoffensive black sheep slip to the point of allowing him to curse them as stupid dolts. Meade thought there must have been one hell of a difference in the off-side parent behind the Mercers. As close as he allowed himself to like any man, Meade liked Ben Mercer. They shared something in common—a desire to let others do the burdensome things, the unselfish work.

Mercer said, looking into the gulch: "I don't suppose there's anything much to be done, unless they follow my suggestion and move their traps out of there."

Luke Reardon cleared his throat. He was a stocky man, powerful. His clothes always seemed too small. His face was chocolate-colored, his chin and cheeks entirely beardless. Sometimes the proverbial suffering patience of the Negro was not with him. There were five in his tent. Two of them, blacker than Reardon, claimed to be part Cherokee. Reardon claimed to be a Negro. "I was thinking . . . ," he began.

"You suggested moving up the hill, did you?" Meade asked Mercer.

The Frenchman shrugged. "I spoke of it to some, yes. They stared at me. Back home"—he glanced carelessly at Reardon—"ones like these, and others, too, move only when their houses float away."

"I was thinking . . . ," Reardon began again.

"Now look at that." Mercer pointed. His half-brothers had moved their tent up the hill, and now they were walking around the pile of canvas, kicking at it. "If they get it up at all," Mercer said, "it will be upside down." He spoke with an exasperated tolerance, as one would speak of the fumblings of small boys. "Do you have any of that fine brandy left, Jay?"

"I think so. Come in." Meade turned at the tent flap and said to Reardon: "What was it, Luke?"

"There." Reardon pointed to two towering yellow pines above the aspens near Meade's claim. "They set some slantwise in the gulch, Mister Meade. If you was to get all the men to put logs between them and brush and stuff, maybe most of the water would turn away from our claims."

"Oh, hell!" Meade said, but he looked. The upper end of the gulch was wider than the lower and at one time Feather Creek had wandered off to the right, against the slope. The simplicity of Reardon's idea caught him. The man was right. By throwing a sturdy buffer on the anchor of those deeply rooted pines, any sudden burst of water could be diverted toward the old creekbed.

"We could save about half the claims that way," said Reardon.

That was probable, but the idea was an intrusion on Meade's hard code of self-sufficiency. He said: "Your claim is clear down the gulch, Luke. It wouldn't help you any."

"I know."

The unspoken meaning behind the simple words ran on in Meade's brain, disturbing him, making him half angry.

"Would you do it, Mister Meade?" Reardon asked. "We ain't got much time."

"No. Why should I? My ground will catch as much wash as the next claim. Let every man take care of himself."

The Negro looked steadily at Meade. "That don't always work, Mister Meade."

"With me it does," Meade said curtly. He did not dislike Reardon as an individual, or feel obliged to pity him as a black man. That much had carried over from the days when Meade had thought slavery was an issue demanding action. What he did not like about Reardon at the moment was the stubborn way the man stood there, expecting Meade to share a common problem.

"Everybody came here for himself. Let him take care of himself." Meade turned away.

"Someday that Old Bugle up there is gonna blow big and mighty against what you just say, Mister Meade." Reardon was pointing toward the mountain. The clouds were riding deeply below its spine now, but he pointed as if he could look through the clouds and see the great granite bell slanted toward the sky. "She's gonna blow someday, Mister Meade."

Reardon went down the hill. He left Meade standing with one hand on the tent flap, frowning, caught momentarily by the solemn mystery of the words.

Inside, Mercer laughed. "You don't know black men very well, do you, Jay? Leave them where they belong and you have something. Out here they get ideas. You're a Kansas man, aren't you?"

"I live in Colorado Territory, Mercer."

"That's a handy answer, but someday it won't do." Mercer was seated at the table, his trim black boots thrust past one leg. He shook his head. "Have you ever been South?"

"Kentucky." Meade took a drink of brandy. He kept thinking of the gigantic muzzle of Old Bugle buried beneath the clouds. The tent still held the heat of morning. Everything was in place, neat and orderly. Meade took another drink, and then the vague dissatisfaction began to leave him.

"Kentucky is not the South," Mercer said lazily. "You have to go deeper than that to appreciate our problems, this thing that some Northerners call slavery."

"I've never been South and I'm not a Northerner," Meade said. "You can't talk politics to me."

Mercer smiled. "That puts you in a peculiar position.

Right here in this miserable gulch we have all the elements of the North and South. It's fortunate, also, that we have gold to make them forget their backgrounds. I've sometimes wondered what might happen if someone like that crazy man back in your state, John Brown. . . ."

"He'd stake a claim and forget politics, if he had any sense at all."

Mercer laughed. "I believe he would. That's what we've all done. I'd like to see it kept on that basis, but sometimes I worry about the explosive elements of the camp, men like that old Phillips and Johnny Creston. For a hill country Tennessean, old Phillips has some powerful feelings about Yankee dictation."

"I don't worry a damned bit, Mercer. I just want as much gold as I can dig. Let fools fight out their politics somewhere else."

Mercer rose. "What we need is a larger gulch, or fewer men. Neither being likely, we'll take what we have." He stepped to the door. "You know, it might not rain after all. I suppose by now my brothers have trampled half my clean clothes into the earth. Thanks for the drink, Jay." Mercer stepped outside. He called his horse and it walked to him. He rode away, humming.

Meade looked at the two big pines. Reardon and the other Negroes were carrying logs to make a diversion wall.

The first few drops of rain came down softly. *I'm not responsible for the welfare of stupid men who do not know enough to keep their shelters out of a gulch that has flooded before.* For one sharp instant Meade remembered old man Brown back in Kansas, bitter, brooding, intense Osawatomie Brown, with his stained Bible in a dirty linen coat, and his talk of a violent God calling for the punishment of those who held men in bondage. Meade had crossed the swamps and drifted through the trees with Brown and his gigantic sons and their two-edged sabers. He had listened over campfires deep in the groves. One course is eternally right and one is wrong. Meade had believed, half in reverence, half in awe, before the burning power of the great fanatic. Brown was still fighting, but Meade no longer believed in anything but himself, not after that morning on the limestone bank above the Wakarusa.

He twisted his mouth at the men and problems of Poverty camp. He turned from them and went into his tent. Steady now but still not violent, the rain was sucking all the trapped heat from the shelter. He built a fire and lay down on his cot. He was a man on a hill above trouble, snug, secure.

II

After a short time he was restless. He went to the flap again. Like field mice the residents of Poverty had dived to cover. Bland's saloon was full of sound. The smoke from fires was curling down to blend with the mists on the cooling ground. After a fashion the Mercers had raised their tent, the brown canvas drooping toward the center pole. Only the Negroes were left now, still working on the log wall. Their clothes were tight against their bodies. They carried logs and brush, building their barrier slowly. They were singing, deep and low, in the icy rain.

Somewhere on the mountains there came a jarring burst of thunder. It was the last. As if it had signaled the storm forces, the rain increased suddenly. It hissed down, slanting into the gulch, swaying the branches of trees, bouncing from the soaked earth, then gathering in tiny rivulets to trickle toward the creek. The surface of Feather Creek danced to the frenzy of it.

During his two years in the mountains Meade had seen storms like this before. They struck with utter fury, and wore themselves out quickly, settling then to a sober steadiness or ending entirely. This storm did not slacken. After a while he could scarcely see the men working on the barrier. They did not stop. The idiots!

Meade yelled through the hissing murk: "Reardon! Let it

go! Come up and get warm!"

Staggering, slipping as he helped carry a log, Reardon replied: "No, thank you, Mister Meade!"

Through the sheets of slanting water Meade saw Ban Phillips, coatless, bare-headed, cutting an opening in the dike before his tent. The berm, designed to turn away rising water from the creek, had so far served only to trap falling water behind it. The inside of the tent must be flooded already.

More men ran from their shelters, some sprinting toward the saloon, others carrying blankets and gear up the slope toward the doubtful shelter of the larger trees. One man stepped on a blanket, dragging behind a running miner. They both fell down and rolled in the mud of the streaming hillside. Their cursing carried up to Meade.

Now the ditch was gurgling strongly where it came to a V in front of Meade's tent door, and he knew that all the hills were gathering their little streams, and that the long miles of slopes back to the mountains were running with water that had come too quickly to sink into the humus of the forest floor.

For twenty minutes the sky came down. The rain ended as abruptly as if a gigantic head gate had been lowered. Feather Creek was roily, but scarcely any higher than it had been before. The little trickles wound crazily down the slopes and stopped. Men crept from shelter and held their hands out, palms upward.

"It's stopped!" they cried. "She's over!"

Let them find out, Meade thought, but he did call down the hill to the Negroes, who had stopped their work. "You've got about a half hour to build that wall, boys! And when you hear a roaring in the gulch, you'd better hightail for high ground!"

Others heard Meade's advice.

From in front of the saloon Ed Mercer said: "Old know-it-all up there in his mansion house. He thinks it's going to rain some more."

"I can see a patch of clear sky," someone said. "It's over. Hell, what was we worried about?"

"You sure about that, Mister Meade?" Reardon asked.

"I'm sure."

Reardon tried to keep his companions working, but they kept watching larger patches of light appearing in the sky, and soon they all went back to their tent.

Phillips began to remove the dike around his tent. Ellen came out with her skirts pinned up, wading barefoot in the trapped water around the tent. Her legs gleamed white against the brown of the wet ground. Ben Mercer came out of his tent. He brushed his sleeves and straightened his hat and went down the hill to talk to Ellen.

Men went back to the claims to work. Poverty camp was normal. Poverty camp was full of idiots, Meade thought. The water was gathering far up the gulch. They had heard what he yelled at Reardon. Meade built up his fire and set a frying pan on the stove. He cut himself a venison steak an inch and a half thick.

The first distant rumbling sound came while Meade was turning his steak to salt it. It was a rushing and a roaring, the growling of the mountains over a burden they could not hold.

Someone in the gulch yelled: "Oh, my God, boys!"

"Washout!"

It came boiling down the long gulch, a mighty fluid fist that smashed and tore. It was a confined surge built from a million trickles, sweeping the turns, slamming high where rock obstructed it. Uprooted trees and brush and débris, scoured from the forest, twisted in its grip. A wall of water built by the violence that had come and passed. There was time to yell and time to run, and that was all. The water struck with savage force against the low barrier the Negroes had built before the light patches in the sky betrayed their purpose. Brown spray shot high. The logs withstood the shock and more dead timber piled upon them, turning the flood toward the old creekbed.

No longer yelling, possessions forgotten, the miners scrambled up the slopes, sprawling in the mud, crawling higher while they strove to get their feet under them to run again. They all got clear because fear was the whiplash.

The flood twisted back upon the camp below the joining of the old creekbed with the present one. Tents crumpled. Their white became the color of the power bearing them. Bough huts and lean-tos tossed upon the water. The aspen log cabins bumped and twisted, and then they came apart. Their dirt-covered roofs fell when the walls came down. In a jackstraw mess of leaping timber they all went down the gulch. Logs cracked and broke and their splintered ends shot on with the flood, straight toward the part of the camp still standing. Then all of Poverty was gone in seconds.

Like the violent rain that had spawned it, the flood died quickly. Feather Creek was over its banks, a racing sluice of dirty brown laced with slapping foam. Near higher ground the pools were quiet. They would dry up in a few days. There was mud upon the claims and scattered logs and slime and branches half buried in the wash, but the earth was gravel and rocks, unhurt. The gold was still there; it would take a little more digging, that was all.

One tent was left in the gulch bottom, twisted in the snags of a huge dead tree that had become lodged in the rocks. That, and the three tents on the hill, made the camp of Poverty now. They would troop down the gulch to salvage their possessions. Some would quit, but not too many. The sooner Poverty was dead the better Meade would like it. But most of them would set up again, right in the gulch bottom. Men learned just what they cared to learn, which generally was not much.

"Mister Meade." Ellen Greenaway and her son were at the tent flap.

Meade strode across the room. "Come in, Ellen." He grinned. "Save anything?"

"We carried a few things up the hill after we heard you yell that last warning." Her eyes were Scotch gray, calm, but the hunger was back of them, and it was something that the married women of the camp must have seen, for Ellen Greenaway did not get on too well with them. Meade lost himself for a moment in her look. She was a woman in the full bloom of maturity, with all the rounding parts now clearly outlined by the dampness of her dress. Her hair was curling from the wet, rich brown hair caught with a single grosgrain ribbon at the back of her neck. She was carrying a pair of her father's trousers and a linsey-woolsey shirt.

Ripley, her son, was a red-headed boy, husky, blunt of features. He was already showing some of the tough-grained fiber of old Ban Phillips, Meade thought. His father had died of fever six months after marriage with Ellen. Little Johnny Creston, the Abolitionist, had once said: "The man showed mighty poor judgment, I'd say, dying off like that so soon."

Someone had answered: "Maybe he just wore out."

Ripley began to tell Meade all about the flood. "She was a hundred feet deep, a-bellering and a-roaring. . . ."

"Never mind, Rip. Mister Meade saw it." Ellen dropped the pants and shirt on a camp stool. With her back to

Meade, she stood at the stove a moment, warming her hands.

Meade's gaze was on the contours outlined by the damp dress. Strength and beauty mingled there. She weighed, he guessed, perhaps a hundred and thirty pounds, not much for a tall woman. Those things were surface facts. His mind went on from there. She turned suddenly and he knew by her expression that she realized and understood his interest, and maybe she had provoked it deliberately.

"I don't like to disturb your meal, Mister Meade, but I was wondering if I could change my clothes in here. They're fixing Ben Mercer's tent for the women, but. . . ."

"Of course." She did not want to be around the other women, Meade thought. He took Rip outside with him.

Men were untangling the tent wrapped around the gnarled tree in the gulch. Johnny Creston's voice was loud. "By God, anybody can tell it's mine. Look at the patch right there near the peak."

"How can you tell with all that mud on it? Ours had a patch near the peak, too." Hardin Clements was a Virginian. He bore no love for Johnny Creston, the Ohio man who said that slavery was a curse upon the land. A time or two they had nearly come to blows in Bland's saloon.

"I say it's mine, and that's the end of it," Creston said. He was a wiry little man, with all the fire and cockiness that go with smallness.

Clements said: "We'll see about that."

Men rallied to both sides at once. Watching from the hill, Meade thought sardonically how clearly the issue split, not over the tent, but over politics. The Mercer brothers shouldered in. "Who says this ain't Hardin's tent?" Ed challenged.

"Here's four of us that say so!" Ora Sammons waded

over, with three Free State Kansas men behind him. A tremendous man, rough-spoken, Sammons stood a head taller than anyone in the group around the disputed canvas. His shirt was plastered against the bulging muscles of his back. Through a rip a long slash of red undershirt showed like a streak of blood. His hat never seemed to fit completely over a bulging mass of blond curly hair.

"Why, hell, yes," he said, scarcely glancing at the canvas, "that's Creston's tent."

The Mercers moved apart. They fought that way, one circling to the back or coming in from the side. Watching them closely, Meade felt his vague dislike of them growing.

He doubted that the two of them would care to tackle Ora Sammons openly, but the crowd was growing. Loy Blaisdell came trotting up with his five Missourians, drawn by the loud voices and the prospect of a fight. Blaisdell was not as tall as Sammons, but he was a heavy man, rawboned, flat of muscle, a long-jawed stretch of wildcat in a brawl. "What are the damned nigger-lovers looking for?" he yelled.

"Anything you've got to offer, you pro-slavery bastard!" Creston shouted. He was like a fice among a pack of mastiffs.

There were the makings of a first-class dogfight down there, Meade thought. His amusement was tinged with bitterness as he watched.

Ban Phillips came kicking through the mud, thrusting men aside until he reached the center of the commotion. His voice was louder and deeper than all the shouts and so he made himself heard. "What's going on here? You sound like a herd of storm-bound bulls!"

Someone more inclined toward reason than fighting told Phillips what the trouble was.

"Untangle the tent and lay it out," Phillips said. "We'll see whose it is."

"To hell with the tent!" Creston said. "Blaisdell came over here looking for a fight."

Two men made a half-hearted attempt to pull the tent off the snags, and then they stopped. The line between the two groups became quite clear, each man sizing up a probable opponent. Sammons was in the forefront on the Free State side.

Blaisdell and the Mercers stood a little in advance on the pro-slavery side, Blaisdell with his shoulders hunched, with his black beard dripping in the rain as he stared at Sammons.

There were weapons on both sides, but, unless the thing exploded into complete insanity, they probably would not be used, Meade thought. All fighting in the camp so far had been with fists and teeth and feet. In a moment the damned fools would start brawling wildly, over issues they did not understand, over the future of black men they had never seen.

Ban Phillips walked between the two groups, waving his long arms. "Now, look here, boys. . . ."

Ed Mercer tripped him, and, when he stumbled, the other Mercer brother shoved him. Phillips made a long splash in the muddy water. He came up cursing, pawing mud from his face, his rôle of peacemaker left where he had fallen. Whether or not he understood who had tripped and shoved him, his politics became clear. "Ye miserable 'Bolitionist scum!" he roared. He made a mighty swing at Sammons.

The blond giant caught the flailing arm and flung Ban Phillips back into the Southern crowd. "Let Blaisdell start it," he said. "Let's see if his weight is as big as his mouth."

Ellen darted from Meade's tent. "Pa!" she yelled. Her voice was lost on those below. She grabbed Meade's arm. "Stop them! He's an old man. He'll get hurt!"

"The others aren't old men," Meade said.

Ripley was jumping up and down. "Bust 'em, Gramps!"

Ben Mercer strode between the two groups. He was a slight figure, standing between Sammons and Blaisdell, but his voice was the cracking of authority that expects obedience. "Stop it," he said. "Stop it now. With everything in camp gone, this is a strange way to settle our troubles. You, Blaisdell, you, Sammons . . . what's the matter with you fellows? This camp has got to work together now or everything here is lost for good." The words were old and worn, but Mercer gave them force. "Ed and Harv, you're making me gray-haired. Now get down the gulch and help folks find their stuff."

Ed and Harvey Mercer walked away. The fringes of the two groups began to break up. Ben Mercer kept on talking.

"Yankee nabobs," Phillips growled. "They'd like to rule the world." He went floundering down the gulch.

Sammons and Blaisdell were the last to turn away. Their support was gone. Their hatred of each other was still alive. When he passed the tent, Blaisdell grabbed a torn seam. He ripped it wide open and laughed. "There's your damned tent, Creston!"

In splinter groups the men of Poverty went toward the cañon to salvage what they could. The torn tent lay still snagged in the tree. No one went near it until Luke Reardon and the Negroes waded out and began to untangle it.

Ellen gave Meade an odd, questioning look. "How was it you didn't get into that? You're a Kansas man, on one side or the other."

31

"I came from Kansas, that's all. Let them have their petty fights."

It isn't a petty fight," Ellen said. "You saw right there what this whole nation is going to split over someday."

Meade grinned. "Even the women in Tennessee are brought up on politics, huh?"

"Not politics, just the facts you have to live with." She kept watching his face. "Aren't you going down the gulch to help?"

"Why should I? I haven't lost anything."

"I see."

"It's fine that you do, Ellen."

Meade watched her walk away in her father's turned-up pants and flopping shirt. *Damn her!*

The coldness of his delayed meal was not entirely the reason for its tastelessness. Afterward, he sat at the table smoking his pipe, one hand toying absently with the bulge of his money belt.

He went outside. The Negroes had set up the disputed tent, right in the gulch bottom again. The peculiar rounded opening at the flap told Meade the tent was Reardon's. One man was trying to patch it. The other Negroes were going down the gulch.

Before Mercer's tent the married women were huddled in the rain, all four of them trying to start a fire. So far they had white smoke.

Meade went down the hill. Oatis Peek, one of the Negroes who claimed to be part Cherokee, was patching the seam Blaisdell had ripped, punching holes with a knife, lacing with a piece of tent rope.

"The old dam didn't hold much, did she?" he said. There was no accusation in his tone, no suggestion that Meade had failed to do his part. That irritated Meade.

He said: "You know what the Cherokees do when one of their women makes a slip with a Negro, don't you?"

Peek turned his broad face toward Meade. There were a few short whiskers on his chin and lower jaw. He nodded.

"Then why do you keep saying you're part Cherokee?"

Peek showed no surprise that the subject had come up so abruptly. He blinked at Meade, considering the question. "I don't know, Mister Meade. It never was no help. I just got in the habit. I hear folks claim to be part this and that . . . I just don't know."

"Do something for me when you've finished your patching." Meade nodded toward the smoke. "Start that confounded fire for them if they insist on cooking outside. Tell them they can have my tent if they want to. Give them anything out of it they need."

Peek nodded. He seemed to realize that the indirection was based on Meade's desire to save face before this weakening of his detached attitude toward Poverty.

"You do that then, Oatis. Between you and me you're the oldest son of a Mingo."

"I ain't, Mister Meade. Maybe I won't say so no more."

"Don't feel sorry for yourself!" Meade said savagely. "You're a man, a freed man. This isn't Virginia. You don't even have to face a guardian any more." Pat words from Osawatomie Brown's talk came to Meade's mind, but he did not say them. He walked down the gulch.

Oatis said: "You just ain't no Southerner, Mister Meade. I been wondering. Now I know."

Just inside the cañon Meade saw his first group of men. They had recovered a slab of bacon and a keg of Bland's whiskey. Before a fire under an overhanging cliff they were cooking the bacon on sticks and drinking from the broached keg.

33

Bough-hut men, the card players. That marked them. Kickapoo rangers from the swamps. Tomorrow they would have big heads. The next day they would try to sell their claims or trade them for a handful of food and leave. A few less in camp, that was all to the good.

On a sandbar where the trees came down to water through a break in the cliffs Billy Bland was sitting by a fire near two kegs of whiskey he had found bobbing in a pool.

"Still in business, I see," Meade said.

Bland shook his head. He was a beefy, moon-faced man with a roundness of body that belied the smooth flow of muscles that could drag a balky mule off its feet. "It's free," he said. "It's all a man can do to get out of here, without trying to carry kegs on his back." He pointed to a tin cup on the unbroached keg. "Help yourself."

Bland, as far as Meade knew, had no politics. That in itself was a recommendation. Meade took a drink. The flood had not improved the quality. He said: "You could just dump it in the creek and save yourself waiting for free customers."

"I thought of that, but it's still whiskey. They'll need something to warm themselves when they come crawling back up the cañon."

"Maybe it will also help to find your tent," Meade said.

"Yeah, I mentioned that to them." Bland grinned.

He was no fool. He took care of himself. A man would always know where Bland stood; he would never lose his head over suffering humanity somewhere in the South.

A few adventuresome men who had tried to penetrate the deep drop of the cañon were hauling themselves out of it when Meade reached the main group in a wide spot where the walls were broken by great chimneys. Loy Blaisdell and Ora Sammons were standing chest-deep in a

34

pool, straining to lift a snag around which someone's tent was fouled. Others were trying to free the canvas. Ben Mercer was directing the operation from the shore.

"Heave your end higher, Blaisdell," Mercer said.

"It's already higher'n his!" Blaisdell glared down the snag at Sammons.

That was one way for them to demonstrate their strength and cool off their politics, Meade thought, but it would not last.

"Give them a hand," Mercer said to Ed and Harvey. "One on each end of the log."

"I'm half drowned already," Ed grumbled. He looked without enthusiasm at the half dozen men trying to free the tent.

"Go on," Mercer told his half-brothers. "We've all got to work together. Get out there."

Ed and Harvey obeyed. Johnny Creston laughed. "I'd do it, but I'm too short for that place."

Ellen was leaning on a rock, wet to the waist. She had made large pleats under the belt of her trousers. The heavy garment gave her a shapeless look. Meade went over to her.

"Your tent?" he asked.

She shook her head. "We found ours and laid it on a rock upstream." She studied Meade a moment. "I thought you said you weren't coming."

"Changed my mind. Where's the boy?"

"With Miss Kinnison."

"My God, you could have left him in my tent."

"I could have."

Ben Mercer said: "Want to get out there and help a little, Meade? Some of those men are pretty chilled."

"I like your end of it better, Mercer."

Creston laughed.

"Somebody has to direct things," Mercer said. His composure was undented, but before he turned back to the work in the rushing stream, he gave Creston a slow, speculative look.

Clements, the Virginian, said: "You showed up a little late, Kansas man." His tone was an insult. He was a dark-haired man, dark-browed, a thin mouth and a tight, hot look when anything he said was questioned. It was rumored that he had been involved with too many wives of too many prominent men in Virginia, and so his family had shipped him West.

Meade said: "I came just right to suit me." He ignored Clements then and took Ellen's arm. "Let me help you out of here."

She hesitated, looking at Clements, who said: "Never mind, Kansas man, I've already volunteered."

"I've changed my mind," Ellen said. "I believe I will go back with Mister Meade." She turned away from Clements's bitter, surprised look and told her father she was leaving.

Men were already going up the cañon ahead of Meade and Ellen. Most of them stopped when they came to where Bland was waiting at his kegs. "That happen to be my tent?" he asked four strapping Ohioans, who were half dragging a huge bale of canvas. They dropped the burden. Bland nodded toward the kegs. "Help yourselves."

When Meade and Ellen came to the Phillips tent, Meade made a roll of it and draped it on his shoulders. It was dusk when they reached the gulch. The fine, cold rain was still falling.

Stella Kinnison called from her tent at the edge of the pines. "The boy's fine, Missus Greenaway. He fell asleep a little while ago."

"Thank you. When I can get my tent set up, I'll come after him."

Mrs. Pingree and Mrs. Ledbetter came out of Mercer's tent. Amelia Pingree's question pointedly ignored Ellen. "What's happening in the cañon, Mister Meade?"

"About all that's going to," he said. "They'll be coming out pretty soon." He said to Ellen: "You'd better stay in my diggings tonight."

"Where will you stay then?"

"I've wolfed it out on the ground before, in worse weather than this."

Oatis Peek was dozing on the stool beside Meade's stove. He leaped up. "I kept the fire. I made some stew with what I didn't give the ladies of your meat." He started out. "If Missus Greenaway's going to stay here tonight, you welcome to sleep in our tent, Mister Meade."

"Thanks, Oatis, I'll do that."

"He's adopted you," Ellen said. She stood by the stove, shivering. "What side were you on . . . in the border trouble back in Kansas?"

"I'm on no side," Meade said curtly. "Change your clothes, Ellen." He went outside. While he waited, he saw a group of men just emerging from the cañon, and a little later he heard Creston say: "Ah, trouble, your foot, Reardon! They talk it big but they don't care to start it."

A fire bloomed in front of the Negroes' tent, and Peek called out to the men coming up the gulch. A handy man, that Oatis, Meade thought. He doubted that half the men of Poverty had the skill to start a fire in wet weather.

Ellen called and he went inside. She had changed to her dress, and now she was trying to smooth the wrinkles with her hands. She had used her brush and comb. Her hair was gleaming in the lamplight, and the warmth was turning it into curls. He realized how cold she must have been when he saw that color was returning to her face. She stood a moment, smiling at him. "Your turn, Jay." She caught up his canvas jacket, spread it over her head and shoulders like a hood, and stepped outside.

Meade threw his sodden clothes into a corner. He put on boots and a suit he intended to wear someday when he rode from the mountains a wealthy man.

Afterward, for a while, he seemed out of place in his own quarters, sitting idly on the cot while Ellen made coffee and dished up the stew.

"There are men down there cold and hungry," she said suddenly.

With their bellies full of whiskey and their minds filled with a senseless fight, now that gold was not immediately before them to hold attention. "Too bad," Meade said. "I can't feed them all." One glance around the tent had told him that Peek had been liberal with his supplies. "And they should know enough to build fires."

The tin stove threw comfortable heat. The rain pattered gently against the canvas. They ate slowly, their glances meeting with apparent casualness across the narrow folding table. Now and then voices came up the hill as if in quarrelling, but that was all outside, where it belonged.

Peek hailed the tent, not loudly. He stood just outside the flap. "Missus Greenaway's father send word he not going to climb out of that cañon in the dark. A lot of folks staying in that place tonight."

"All right, Oatis," Meade said.

"Luke tell me to say they's going to be some trouble at our tent maybe. That Clements and Johnny Creston arguing about things."

"Let 'em argue."

38

"That Clements, he big and mean, Mister Meade, and not many of Johnny's fellows come out with him. That Clements. . . ."

"Tell Reardon it's their fight, not mine."

There was a pause. "Yes, sir." Peek tramped away in the mud.

Ellen said: "Clements is mean, Jay, and little Johnny. . . ."

"Has a big mouth. He's been talking Abolition enough to have had a hundred serious scraps. Now let him have one."

Meade rose to pour more coffee. That done, he stood a moment behind Ellen. He put his hands on her shoulders and the warm, firm feel of the flesh came through her dress to him.

"I really should go see about. . . ." She stood up slowly, turning to face him. She was in his arms an instant later, strong and pushing hard against him. Their mouths came together with a fierceness that sought heightening and escape.

Together they moved away from the table, their shadows one great splotch on the tent wall. Meade leaned back and blew out the lamp. The flame ran hard and urgent between them then. They did not hear the rain, and the rising voices of men somewhere near the Negroes' tent came but dimly.

This, Meade knew, was the moment that must have been lying in his mind from the time he offered to help Ellen from the cañon; it must have been there longer, too, from the time she had let him first glimpse the lonely hunger in her eyes.

Down the hill someone shouted savagely, the sound of anger breaking free of unproductive bickering. Loy Blaisdell's heavy voice roared: "Kill the Yankee rooster, Clements!"

Other voices yelled, and it was all confusion in a moment. Meade raised his head to listen. Ellen's hands
reached up his neck and pulled his head down once more.

Johnny Creston yelled in anger and pain. A shot boomed
in the rainy night. "No more of that, you Free State
bastards! Stay clear and let 'em fight it out!" That was
George Unruh, one of Clements's friends. "I'll gut-shoot
the man that interferes! Kill him, Clements!"

Meade raised his head again.

"What's the matter with you?" Ellen asked. "You said it
was not your fight." Her fingers dug hard against his
shoulder blades.

"I. . . ." What was the matter with him? He had buried
this idiots' fight in Kansas. Creston had asked for whatever
he was getting. Creston was a little man, and a little man
should keep his mouth shut, or be handy with a knife or a
pistol.

"That's it, you've got him, Clements!" Blaisdell bellowed.

"There's nothing wrong with me." Meade pulled Ellen
against him again. In the dark warmth of the tent they
moved toward the cot. Her mouth was a darting flame.

"Put the boots to him, Clements!" That was a new
voice, either Ed or Harvey Mercer's.

The Free State men were outnumbered down there, and
Creston was taking a beating against a man twice his size.
The memories from Kansas were not buried after all.
Meade pulled away from Ellen and went to the door. "I'll
be back," he said.

She cursed him from the darkness. . . .

The crowd was near a huge fire in front of the Negroes'
tent. Meade ran down the hill through rain that was now
only a coolness against his face. Johnny Creston was on his

feet, but that was all. One arm was hanging limply. He was pawing blindly with the other hand, still trying to stagger toward an opponent he could not see.

Reardon and the other Negroes were in one group, the firelight bleakly dark upon their faces as they watched. George Unruh, a lean, red-bearded man with snags for teeth, was grinning wolfishly as he held a pistol on four of Creston's friends.

Clements was grinning, too, merely waiting for Creston to stagger close enough to be knocked down again.

Ben Mercer was warming his coattails at the fire, looking unemotionally at the scene.

One of the Missourians said: "He's over there, Creston." He gave Creston a shove toward the fire and nearly spilled him in it. "Over that way," another man said, and banged Creston with his shoulder. The little man stumbled toward Clements, who knocked him down.

"Put the boots on him," Blaisdell grunted. "The Free State bastard."

From the corner of his eye Ben Mercer saw Meade arrive. "That's enough," Mercer said crisply.

Creston got to his feet and staggered once more toward Clements.

"Separate them," Mercer said to his half-brothers.

Ed Mercer pushed Creston back. "Go on, you damned banty." The little man struck weakly at him. Ed Mercer doubled his arm and swung his elbow into Creston's mouth. "Stop it now. We got to have some peace around here."

Unruh put his pistol away. He grinned at Clements, and then he inclined his head toward Meade. Creston was down now and not moving. Ed Mercer's elbow had taken the last of his will to fight. The Free Staters knelt beside the injured man. "If I hadn't lost my pistol," one muttered, looking at Clements.

Silent, like wolves that had not tasted enough, the crowd looked inquiringly at Meade. His anger was a hell inside him that left him white and shaking.

"Roll him on his side," one of the men beside Creston said. "He's gagging on them teeth and blood. The other side, you damned fool! That's his busted arm."

Blaisdell laughed.

Ben Mercer said: "Creston finally got himself a fight, Meade. We kept it fair, and that was all we could do."

"Like hell," Meade said.

Mercer shrugged. The faces watching Meade were vicious, waiting. He had plunged against this sort of thing before, welcoming it.

Hardin Clements said loudly: "I hear you used to be with old John Brown, Kansas man."

That was bound to come out someday, Meade had always known. He was getting control of himself. He was wondering why he had made a fool of himself, rupturing the careful way of his living, and wondering how best to step away from the situation.

"Step up, Meade," Clements said.

Two years before Meade would have smashed a man like Clements in a matter of moments. He could do it yet, but . . . no, he could not risk a fight, when there was no reason for it. He had let anger rush him into this.

"He don't want to pick on a little feller like you, Clements," Blaisdell said. "Try me, Kansas man."

Meade turned suddenly and started up the hill.

"By God!" Blaisdell roared. "A brush-pile rabbit, a Lawrence mealy-mouth!"

The last face Meade saw before he stumbled into the

darkness was that of Oatis Peek, and Peek's mouth was open and he was looking at Meade with pained surprise.

Jeers and curses followed Meade. He went away with his anger a mighty force against himself. He almost ran against the figure standing in the darkness part way down the hill. It was Ellen.

She said with biting calm: "I see you settled things."

"Look, Ellen. . . ." He took her by the shoulders. She knocked his hands away. "Look, Ellen, back in Kansas a rifle bullet hit me. . . ." He stopped, and the explanation he had sought to give seemed weak against the stiff thrust of her silence. "To hell with it," he said. Down at the fire they were still laughing about the way he had run.

"You were shot," Ellen said. "I wonder where?" She walked away, going toward the women's tent.

III

On an aspen ridge a mile east of Poverty, Meade fired his rifle twice at nothing. That much for hunting; that much for those who might be wondering if he really was hunting deer. The echoes rolled from ridge to ridge. He went directly northwest then, toward Old Bugle.

The way was rough, leading down across the lower reaches of the cañon, then over cliffs, and into a tangle of timber killed by fire before the memory of white men in the mountains. The difficulties of his path seemed to make his secret more secure. He never used the same route twice going or coming from Kansas Gulch. Before, he had always gone there to make sure that no one else had done so. This time he was going to reassure himself that not only the gulch was safe, but that no stain of change had touched Jay Meade's philosophy.

Driven by sweating urgency, he came at last to the broad, brush-choked flat that lay between two waves of granite on the side of Old Bugle. The heavy undergrowth had held yesterday's rain so well that the ground was still soaked, but there had been no washing. Kansas Gulch. Meade would let the name be known and the location be known only after there was nothing left here for others.

He wriggled through the brush toward his cache of tools in a little cave. The stream that ran down the middle of the gulch made endless S marks. Even now it was clear while Feather Creek was still fouled with mud. Although the stream was only three feet wide, it ran that deep in places, twisting slowly over yellowed gravel. Trout with crimson-slashed throats cruised by in schools. Almost as much as anything about the gulch, the stream pleased Meade. It would provide all the water he needed to become a wealthy man.

He went on to the cave and got his tools, and then he went to a section of the gulch where he had not dug before. The overburden was light. His shovel went down into sand and gravel. Fifteen minutes later he was squatted by the stream looking at a long string of coarse gold in his pan.

Seven dollars' worth, he estimated, and he had panned in haste. On top of that, he was not even an expert man with a gold pan, like Peek and the other Negroes, who had learned from Cherokees in Georgia. Kansas Gulch—Midas Gulch. Wherever a man touched the gravel under the centuries of growth, there was gold. At bedrock, perhaps four feet down, no telling what there might be. Meade had not wanted to risk digging a hole that big.

He flipped the gold into the stream. He went back to the test hole and refilled it carefully, replacing the damp overburden, sweeping a piece of branch over the finished job. He could not completely hide the impress of his boots. That worried him. There was always a chance that someone from Poverty would stumble onto the gulch.

If that happened, Poverty would be deserted in a matter of hours. Everyone would come storming over here. Meade would not be the original locator then, under rough mining law. He would not be entitled to two claims as the founder. Not even that. The place would be dug up in no time, the brush cut away, the stream diverted to run in a dozen directions—with constant bickering over the water supply—and Meade would be left with one claim.

Afraid and angry, he looked at the gulch. It was at least a half mile long and 200 yards wide. It was, he guessed, about the richest piece of land in America. It was his now, every bit of it, but, if anyone else ever found out, he could not hold it.

He returned to the cave and put his tools away. Shielded by bushes, he sat looking down on a peaceful flat underlaid with gold. All at once there was no satisfaction in the sight, and he was filled with a bitterness and a yearning that went back to the days in Kansas when issues were clear, when his young eyes saw a world split by right and wrong, with God surely on the side of those who were right.

Jay Meade had walked with old John Brown, and had been inspired by the fearful strength of the old man's narrow vision. Meade was not with the Browns when they killed the Doyles and Dutch Henry and Allie Wilkinson. Men called it murder, but from a distance Meade saw it as the wiping out of evil.

Hosea Sprague and Willie Shoemaker showed Meade the blood of border warfare on a bitter winter night across the Missouri line. Hosea was a little man with a crinkly beard and tiny, hot eyes. He was fond of speaking John Brown's words, but they always came out as curses instead of pronouncements of a man moved by the Lord. On an old farm horse Meade rode with Hosea's Abolitionists across the Missouri line to a farm near Pleasant Hill, there to strike a blow for the freedom of black men.

In the cold, clear night they came to the edge of the trees and looked across a weedy field at farm buildings.

Shoemaker said: "That ain't the place, Hosea."

"It'll do," Hosea said. "There's horses in that barn. No telling what we'll find in the house."

"But I thought we came to free some slaves," Meade said. It was cold under the bare trees. He held his rifle tightly. "You said. . . ."

"They're all slaves over here," Hosea said.

They led their horses along the bank of a sandy ditch that angled toward the buildings. They roused a watchdog that came savagely, a large dog that was not afraid to close with a man. Shoemaker ripped it open with a knife. It scrabbled on the frozen ground, snarling, biting at the manure pile. Someone smashed its head with a rifle butt.

Meade helped lead four horses from the barn. Six men crept up on the house, moving in low toward a windowless side where weeds had been blown against the boards. Hosea told Meade to stay with the horses.

In the pigpen shoats squealed. Someone said: "Don't worry, Tom. They've heard us already in the house. Get two we can carry easy and kill the rest."

Meade heard a door scrape open. A moment later two men with rifles came around the corner of the house. They fired and Meade's breath was torn from him. He reeled against one of the horses. Holding hard to the tie ropes of the halters, he was hauled across the yard when the animals began to plunge.

The men crouched near the weed pile killed the two farmers when they ran toward Meade. A moment later a woman screamed in the house. Joe Bruton laughed.

Meade felt his strength going. The horses were quieting down now, and there was no more firing. He called to the men in the pigpen. They came past him on their way to the house, trotting. He cried out again.

"What's the matter?" Tom Penning asked irritably.

"I'm hit."

"Oh, hell! You're scared, that's all."

Meade's hands slipped down the ropes and he fell.

The two men came over to him. Penning turned him over. "He's busted, all right. You'd better hold the horses, Paynter."

"While you run free in the house, huh? To hell with that, Penning."

The laughter in the house was louder now. There came the sound of breaking wood, and the woman screamed.

"Put the horses in the barn then," Penning said.

The two men did that. And then they pushed the door shut and ran to the house. Meade thought they were going for help, but no one came. He lay on the ground with one side numb, with blood freezing on his clothes. He was afraid to feel his side, but at last he did. The lower part of his ribs were blown away, and he felt bone splinters sticking in the fabric of his torn coat.

He cried for help. The laughter from the house mocked him. He tried to rise. He was on his hands and knees when the blackness came.

Meade was dimly aware of events later when they lifted him up and tied him in the saddle. The house was burning then. Hosea was in a great hurry to be gone. Someone took a woman's garment from a sack of loot tied to a saddle. Shoemaker stuffed it under Mead's shirt, against his shattered ribs.

"You got to ride," he whispered. "Hosea won't leave anyone behind to give our names."

Meade rode with his eyes half closed, with his mouth slack, with pain from every movement of the horse ripping through his chest. When they stopped in a grove on the

Kansas side of the line at sunrise, Shoemaker and Hosea looked at the wound.

Hosea said: "It's not bad at all, Meade." His hot little eyes slid sidewise to his men. They were trading items looted from the house.

"Don't leave me."

Hosea looked back the way they had come. "Now you know we wouldn't do anything like that, boy."

Out of an agony as great as his physical hurt Meade said: "They didn't have slaves."

"They favored slavery," Hosea said. "The woman said so. Didn't she, Shoemaker?" He laughed.

Shoemaker did not answer. He lifted Meade on his horse. By the next afternoon nothing mattered to Meade; he no longer recognized a conscious will to live, but he clung to the horn and kept going. He roused a little when Penning galloped in from rear guard to report ten men on their trail.

"How close?" Hosea asked.

"Damned good and close. Fast horses, too. It looks like some of Dave Atchinson's bunch."

Hosea cursed. "If it's them, they'll follow us almost to Lawrence." He studied Meade for one tight moment. He reached to his waistband for his pistol.

"Not while there's a chance he'll make it," Shoemaker said.

"He'll give our names!"

"We'll beat them, if we get across the Wakarusa first. This boy has got to have his chance."

Meade thought he did not care, but when he saw Hosea beaten down by Shoemaker's steady look, he felt strong enough to stay in the saddle—and live. That much was spirit; his body was past knowing.

The pursuers slid past the flank of the Free State raiders and cut them off from an easy crossing of the Wakarusa.

"Those bastards always got the best horses," Hosea complained. "There's a ford upstream. Come on!"

The scramble through the trees on the high bank above the creek was the worst of all. Meade had to duck low under branches, and that pressed bone ends into his body. The Missouri men were closing now. They came on without shouting, deadly determined.

Meade could go no farther. He stopped his horse. He slid off and fell on the ground. And now he really did not care.

Penning was still bringing up the rear. When he reached Meade, he leaped down and went through the wounded man's pockets. He took Meade's horse and rode away. Soon afterward Meade heard the slavers coming. He dragged himself into the bushes. Some of the Missouri men, their faces dark and intent, went by him moments later, and then he heard gunfire and shouts. The sounds were hard and brief at first, and then they broke with a great burst, and later they swirled away into silence somewhere far ahead in the trees. Meade crawled out of the bushes. He tried to rise, but he could not do it. He huddled on the ground, knowing that everything was done now.

So this was the glorious cause that old Brown had talked about across the campfires, when there was no pain or cold or thoughts of dying. Better that 100 evil men should die than one Godly man. Meade remembered the woman's screams, and the rifles' crashing flame, and firelight from the burning farm touching the ragged beards of the Free State men while they hurried in silence to leave their work behind them. There is evil and we must crush it. All men must walk in freedom.

On a frozen hill above the mud banks of the Wakarusa, Jay Meade, then sixteen years old, knew that he would be free before the night came. The burly Negro came padding from the leafless forest like a great cat. He was carrying two rifles, three pistols in his waistband, and a sack of clothing from which protruded the top of a boot. "Another one," he muttered, half eagerly and half afraid.

He knelt by Meade, tugging at his boots, talking to himself to bolster purpose. "Awful young, this one."

Nothing the wounded man did told the scavenger that this one was not dead, but suddenly the jerking at Meade's legs stopped. The Negro was silent. Meade opened his eyes fully. The big round face was close to his, staring.

"Help me," Meade whispered.

The Negro stared.

"I'm Free State."

"You're dying. You're dying, hear me? Like the rest up there in the trees. And jest a young one, too."

"Take me to a doctor," Meade whispered.

The man went back to the boots. He pulled them off and put them in his sack. He searched Meade's pockets, and then he went away.

Terrible anger against all mankind roused strength in Meade that he did not know he had. He began to crawl, sobbing. Some time after dark a dog was sniffing him, jumping away, stiff-legged, when Meade reached toward it. The dog stayed with him, barking, until a man came stumbling through the trees.

This time Meade expected nothing. The man lifted him and carried him to a wagon that jolted Meade into unconsciousness before it went 100 yards.

Jupe Markham was neither Free State nor pro-slaver. He was a former New York City horse-car driver who had come to Kansas to raise hogs and sheep.

In the spring Meade was walking, helping Markham around the farm. He was careful not to bump the void in his side that was covered only by skin. He fell into the habit of holding his elbow over it.

Meade never returned to his uncle's farm on the outskirts of Lawrence. Old Jethro Meade was almost as fanatical about slavery as Osawatomie Brown himself. Jay Meade was done with his crusade; let black men, and all other men, take care of themselves.

"I'd go out West if I was you," Markham said.

He gave Meade money along with the advice. Meade returned the money when he washed his first gold from the mountains. Long afterward Meade heard that Jupe had been killed, either by Free Staters or pro-slavers. He had been the only man in the world to whom Meade felt any obligation, and that had been based on more than money.

Now Jay Meade owed obligations only to himself. He was not as bitter as he might have been because there was Markham to remember, and even a few things about Willie Shoemaker.

IV

He made a long arc below the mouth of the cañon and eventually came to the same aspen ridges where he had fired his rifle earlier in the day. He moved swiftly but with caution. If he could pick up a deer, it would give his absence the proper color.

From the top of a rocky escarpment he saw Ed and Harvey Mercer in a vale below him. They were walking at a moderate pace with lowered heads. They could be trailing a deer, but Meade did not think so. He shifted his rifle to both hands. Once more he was gripped by a sharp emotion of mingled fear and anger at the thought of having his secret discovered.

At the moment the Mercers' course was north, not toward Old Bugle, not even toward the cañon. Meade went crashing down the hill. The Mercers spun around to watch him. In the bottom of the little valley he saw no fresh deer tracks, but he saw his own boot marks. The Mercers had been trailing him, sure enough.

"Any luck?" Meade asked.

The brothers shook their heads. They stared at Meade, and there was something in their eyes that reminded him of Hosea Sprague.

"I missed a big buck not far from here this morning," Meade said.

The Mercers looked at each other. "Yeah?" Harvey said.

"Just two ridges east." Meade looked at the sun. "There's always deer over there. If the three of us make a little drive, we should be able to pick up one, at least."

The Mercers were shrewd but they also had the inflexibility of mind that goes with slyness. They could not smoothly extricate themselves from their rôle of deer hunters.

"We'll just about have time to make it over there and get our shooting and get back to camp before dark," Meade said.

The brothers hesitated, and then they followed Meade. "You don't generally miss twice in a row," Ed said.

"You heard the shot?"

"Yeah," Harvey said. "We heard."

Near the ridge that Meade had mentioned they jumped five deer. Each man got one. Meade reloaded his rifle quickly.

Ed and Harvey exchanged glances. "You must have reloaded faster than that to get two shots before," Harvey said.

"I can generally get two shots, if the country is some open and they don't light out too fast."

"One shot suits us." The brothers grinned at each other.

Meade hated them now. They had followed him. If they ever found out about Kansas Gulch, his days of walking the mountains in security were done. He said: "I'll stand on one shot when I really need it."

The Mercers sized him up carefully. Ed smiled from the corner of his mouth.

They gutted the deer and carried them back to Poverty. Meade intended to take half his meat to Ellen and her father, but Ben Mercer was already at the Phillips tent. His boots were clean and shiny. Meade wondered whose hands had set up the tent.

Ben waved his arm at his half-brothers. "Bring one of those over here for Missus Greenaway." He gave Meade an enigmatic look. "I see you and my brothers work well together."

"Very well." Meade looked at Ellen. She nodded. Last night might never have been, and yet it was the reason for her reserve now.

Ben Mercer saw the coolness between her and Meade. It pleased him. Still smiling, he glanced at Meade as if to say: *You'll never have another chance, my friend.*

"You'll stay for supper, Ben?" Ellen asked.

Mercer bowed. "Why, thank you. I will."

He took Ellen's arm and they walked into the tent.

Meade started toward his own quarters, and then he turned around and went the other way, up the hill toward Miss Kinnison's tent.

"I thank you, but we can't use a whole deer," the madam said. She was a lean woman with a thin, tight mouth. Seen on a city street, she would have passed as a housewife on her way to market. "Why don't you give Missus Pingree and Missus Ledbetter . . . ?"

"They've got husbands. Let them shoot their own meat," Meade said. "Do you want it or not?"

"Of course. Don't snap at me, Jay Meade, because Ben Mercer is making you look like an open-mouthed farm boy. I have eyes, you know."

"You also have a tongue, Stella." Meade grinned suddenly. He could get along with women like Stella Kinnison because the obligation between them was only momentary.

He ate with Stella and her girls, and he stayed a long time afterward.

When he went past the Phillips tent on his way home, Ben Mercer was still inside. Meade heard him laugh at something old Ban said.

Meade hated all the Mercers, and he knew it now. He wondered if Ben had sent his half-brothers out to trail him. It seemed most likely.

On a cot in the Mercer tent Ed and Harvey sat and sweated while Ben paced before them. The flaps were tied wide open. Down in the gulch the sluices were going again. Poverty had picked up from where the flood had left it. There were more huts and lean-tos now than tents.

Ben Mercer said: "You think he caught on that day the three of you came in with deer?"

"He's an idiot if he didn't," Harvey said. "We were right on his tracks."

"And he didn't say anything about it?"

"No." Ed scowled. "But he hasn't been away from camp since. He must have caught on."

Harvey said: "What makes you so sure he's got something, Ben?"

"He's taken too many hunting trips. Long ago he had enough gold under his belt to be gone from here." Ben swept his hand contemptuously toward the gulch. "Two or three dollars a day down there is the best anybody is doing now. Meade's not that kind of fool. He's found something, and he's waiting for the rest of us to clear out."

"Let's get out of this damned tent," Harvey said.

"In a minute." Ben went to the flap, looking down at the miners on Feather Creek. They were instruments he could use to hurry the death of Poverty, and at the same time he could wipe out a few Yankees. But it must be worked to keep Meade alive until Ben knew his secret.

Filthy Northerners, Ben thought. River men had been the first Yankees he ever saw. All his later impressions of Northerners inevitably faded back to that first memory of men who had insulted him and tossed him around like a beanbag when he started to draw his pistol.

Ben had come West because rumor had it that gold was plentiful for the picking. He had, of course, Ed and Harvey to do the stooping. About all that was left of plantation heritage was a love of luxury and a contempt of all things Northern, excepting women.

"Maybe Meade ain't got . . . ," Ed began.

"He's holding out something, somewhere," Ben said. "I've read too many faces. From now on you two will follow him whenever he leaves camp."

"If we used the horse . . . ," Harvey said.

"No" Ben shook his head. "I tried that. He took me into timber where the horse couldn't move. He did it deliberately. That's more evidence that he's hiding something."

"If we find it, we shoot him, huh?" Ed asked.

"Of course not!" Ben Mercer always recoiled at the thought of direct violence. Like other unpleasant tasks, violence was something that could be shifted to others.

"What'll we do with him, then?" Ed asked.

"I'll tell you when the time comes." Ben had told his half-brothers enough. He wished sometimes they were intelligent enough to appreciate how wide and complicated his planning was, but their minds moved in short straight lines. Ben prided himself on being able to manage a dozen details at one time.

He had started already. Billy Bland, who had gone out for whiskey, was carrying a letter to a man named J. C. Barto, last seen by Ben in Denver. For the $200 Ben would give him, Barto could raise more sparks among the fiery elements in Poverty than a dozen Crestons or Clementses. It would be too bad if Southerners suffered as much as Yankees, but above all Poverty must be deserted. Then Meade would make a move, but Ben Mercer planned to be well head of him by then. Gambling at a table had always given Mercer great satisfaction. He was not a cheat, and yet he won more often than he lost because of a shallow but effective insight into the characters of individual players. Now Mercer was taken with a feeling of satisfaction far above ordinary gambling. He was playing men against each other, and he knew exactly what he was doing, while only one of the others was aware of the stakes.

There was, at one glance, something strange and prophetic in the figure of the little man who rode into Poverty on a white mule one evening just as Meade had stepped from his tent to throw out his dishwater. The man rode with the reins draped on the saddle horn. He was reading a book. On the back of his neck was a discolored straw hat, held by a chin thong. His hair hung to his shoulders. His face was pink and shining. At intervals he raised his head to the sky as if to confirm some passage just read in the book.

A wandering spell-binder, Meade thought, full of hell-fire and the coming of destruction on evil men. The mule, he observed, was in good condition. It picked its way across the creek and started toward the camp. The rider closed his book and dropped it into one of the pockets of a bulging coat.

He raised both hands toward the heavens. "The evil is upon us!" His voice was a great booming sound that carried up and down the gulch. He kicked the sides of the mule as if to make it gallop into camp, but the mule plodded on at its own pace. "We have brought the evil upon us!"

There would be moaning and wailing in Poverty tonight,

Meade thought, and then someone would have to feed this wandering preacher. He went back into his tent.

But a few moments later he came out again. He had caught a shouted word to bring any man running.

"War!"

The little man had stopped near Billy Bland's empty tent. Late workers were leaving their sluices, running toward him. Others were coming from their cooking fires before their shelters.

"War!" the rider shouted. "War has come between the states!"

Stella Kinnison ran from her tent. She turned and shouted excitedly, and a moment later her girls were running down the hill behind her. Ban Phillips plowed up the street awkwardly. Red-headed Ripley broke away from his mother when she called to him, and he was one of the first to reach the man on the white mule.

War, Meade thought. Well, it was bound to come some day, and 1859 was just as good as any time, for those who were interested. He saw the Mercers duck out of their tent and plunge down the hill. Then Meade, too, was running toward the saloon.

The rider was at once enveloped by a roar of questions. He did not get off his mule. He sat there with his arms upraised, with his eyes closed, and his round, pink face turned toward the sky.

"Where?" they bellowed at him. "When?"

The little man opened his eyes. They were small and bright. He bowed his head. "May God forgive me for bearing such evil tidings to honest men."

Johnny Creston, with one arm in a sling, with his mouth still swollen, shouted fiercely: "Stop mumbling. What's the news?"

"War!" the rider cried. "May the Lord help us."

Hardin Clements said: "Give us the paper."

"There's none. The evil tidings came just as I was leaving Denver."

It was Ben Mercer who at last brought order out of the yelling. "Let the man talk. Let's hear all of it."

"Evil upon evil," the rider said in his deep voice. "Our fair land trembles, and the voices of our patriots call from their graves. The love of brothers is forgotten, and they tear at each other's throats, and there is no end and the end is come. The Abolitionists have marched on Richmond. The streets there run with blood and the flames of the buildings are red against sullen skies."

"Richmond!" Clements yelled. "The Yankees marched on Richmond?"

"Who gave you the news?" Meade asked.

"Dispatch riders from the East came as I left Denver. The news was then two weeks old, and now more time has passed, and the grappling of brother with brother has spread like fire across the prairie."

Suddenly the rider had no more to say. He bowed his head, as if in prayer. There was an unhealthy silence on the crowd of miners, and Meade noticed that there had been a shifting of positions, so that now there were two distinct groups, with others standing in the middle ground.

The Free State men had gathered with Creston and Ora Sammons. The Southerners were grouped with Clements and Blaisdell. Ban Phillips, stooped, staring at some deep thought, was alone with his daughter, and the Mercers were apart. The women, married and unmarried, had drawn together unconsciously.

The crowd began to break up in little groups. Mrs. Pingree and Mrs. Ledbetter realized that they had been standing with Miss Kinnison's girls. The married women withdrew hastily.

Ben Mercer came over to Meade. "What do you think, Jay?"

"I think it's true."

"So do I," Mercer said in a low voice. "But I'm afraid of the effects, even right here. Do you suppose one of us should ride out and see if we can get any more news?"

"What for? The damage is done." It had not started here, or even back in Kansas, but here was where the trouble must be dealt with—by those who thought they had a stake in it. Meade went back to his tent.

There were two meetings that night. The Northern men met on the hill near Miss Kinnison's place of business. They built a huge fire and went into a solemn session. The Southern men met in the gulch. They were noisy and full of oratory. Meade heard part of their meeting. Clements suggested that all loyal Southerners leave at once to join the fighting, but Blaisdell and George Unruh protested on the ground that the Northern men would stay in Poverty and take all the placer claims.

"The ground is worked out, anyway," Clements said.

"Maybe," Blaisdell said. "Let's stay and see what the Yankees do."

On the hill the Northern men were no doubt coming to the same conclusion, Meade thought. Meetings, speeches— a way to let off steam, but, remembering Kansas, Meade wondered how much further the situation might develop.

He did not hear the voice of the man who had brought the news, nor did he see Ban Phillips around the Southern fire. Ed and Harvey Mercer were there, but Ben was visiting in the Phillips tent. Meade had seen the lantern light from inside fall on him when he went in. The Negroes' tent was dark, but they were at neither meeting.

After quiet had come, deep in the cold night, Meade heard alarmed shouts. He tumbled from his cot and looked out. The Negroes' tent was in flames. The occupants were running around it, shouting, throwing dirt with their hands. Men came with shovels and threw more dirt, but the tent was gone in minutes.

Johnny Creston's voice lashed out: "That slaver bunch did this, you can bet!"

"You lie, little man!" Clements called. "Do you care to back up that statement?"

A pistol blasted. Someone answered with a rifle. There were two more shots and then everyone near the burning tent was diving toward the darkness. Confused shouting followed as the camp became fully aroused. Only Luke Reardon stayed in the light of the flames, throwing dirt on burning blankets and other gear.

Ben Mercer shouted: "What's the matter with you damned fools?" From the sound of his voice Meade knew he was sprinting down the hill. "Stop that shooting! Have you all gone crazy?"

Mercer strode up beside Reardon. There was no more shooting. Out in the darkness men muttered and called to each other. They discovered that no one had been hurt. Creston, Meade thought, must have fired the first wild shot toward Clements. Both sides had heard gunfire and it had jarred sense into them for a moment.

Ben Mercer yelled to his half-brothers to bring down some blankets. He told Reardon to use Bland's tent for the night.

Dawn fell on a camp that was sullenly divided, and now every man was armed.

Late that afternoon Billy Bland returned with a new supply of whiskey. Men left their work and ran to him to hear more news about the war.

"War?" Bland's moon face was incredulous. "There ain't no war I heard of." He was three days from Denver, and he said he had traveled rapidly, and, when he had left, there had been no news of war, or even rumors of it.

The fact went down hard. Meade observed that there was scarcely any relieving of the tension, except among the women.

"Didn't I advise you boys not to get excited until we knew for sure?" Ben Mercer asked. "Now let's all have a drink and forget this foolishness. That J. C. Barto was a crazy man, that's all."

Meade drank with the rest. "Barto, huh? So that was the fellow's name?"

"That's what he said." Mercer shook his head. "Crazy as a loon, Meade."

The camp of Poverty drank Bland's whiskey. The splinter groups eyed each other with hostility. Perhaps there was no war after all, but all the sources of it still existed, and last night there had been burnings and shots fired in anger. These things would not be forgotten.

Loy Blaisdell and Ora Sammons got into a fight when Sammons said the Missourians had burned Reardon's tent. They were both huge, rugged men. They battered each other unmercifully in front of the saloon, with the adherents of both sides not cheering much, but watching each other narrowly. Before it was over, Sammons chewed off Blaisdell's ear and broke his front teeth and left him lying helpless.

The Northern men crowed then. Johnny Creston jumped around like a rooster, patting the pistol under his belt. The Southerners withdrew, carrying Blaisdell with them.

Maybe there was no war back East, Meade thought, *but it had started here.*

On his way home Meade brushed against Ban Phillips coming from one of the Southern tents. He spoke to Phillips and stopped to talk to him, but the Tennessean gave him a glowering look and passed on without speaking.

Luke Reardon called softly from inside Meade's tent as the owner approached: "We're in here, Oatis and me."

It must be something secret and important, Meade thought, or they would not have gone into his quarters while he was not there.

"Maybe you'd best not light no lantern," Reardon said. "We'll bother you just a minute. It's this. They's quite a few men figuring to leave this place." He named some of them. They were indifferent miners, and none of them had any stomach for the trouble brewing in Poverty. "We're wondering, would it be all right to buy their claims?"

"Why ask me?"

"You're a good gold man, Mister Meade," Peek said. "You know about placers."

"How much do they want for their claims?"

"About seventy-five dollars, I guess," Reardon said. "Johnson say his worth more, maybe."

"Any claim here is worth that, all right," Meade said.

The Negroes were patient workers. They extracted more from the ground and worked longer hours than the average miner. They knew as well as he the value of the placers, so there must be a larger reason why they had come to see him.

"The thing is, how will folks feel about us buying that many claims?" Reardon asked.

"You're wondering what white men would think about you owning that much ground, is that it?"

"Yes," Reardon said.

"Buy the claims."

"You mean that, Mister Meade?" Reardon's voice was soft.

"That's my personal opinion. I don't speak for the camp. Sure, there's going to be men who won't like it a bit." Those who had not worked hard enough to have money to buy extra claims, and those who had gambled their gold away, or drunk it up at Bland's saloon, and those who thought Negroes had no right to property.

"You could buy some of those claims, too," Reardon suggested.

Meade considered. It was not a bad idea toward reducing the number of men in Poverty. "When are these fellows leaving?"

"Day or two," Peek said.

"Let's go see them now," Meade said.

He bought four extra claims and the Negroes bought eight, and then the news spread. The results were not entirely what Meade had expected. He had not realized how shrewd a miner the camp considered him to be. At first, the Negroes' part in the transaction was overlooked; Jay Meade had bought several extra claims. Therefore, there must be a great deal of gold yet in the gulch. Men who had considered leaving now decided to hang on a while longer.

There was a subtle shifting of attention that amazed Meade. Political trouble submerged to smolder beneath the surface. Gold was once more the major issue, but there was not going to be gold enough to satisfy everybody, so that problem would intensify in time.

Among those who most resented the fact that Negroes

had stolen a march was Johnny Creston, the Abolitionist. "It ain't fair for anybody to hog everything," Creston said for public consumption. "Especially niggers."

"You're getting halfway smart," Loy Blaisdell told him. "You might even change your tune in time."

"I never will!" Creston shouted. "But it ain't right for anybody to hog claims, just because they've got the money to buy them!"

Meade saw Creston in a new light. The man had not changed at all. He said he was an Abolitionist, but like a lot of ranters his own noise deceived him. If Johnny Creston had been born in Virginia instead of Ohio, his voice would have been loud for slavery. In either case, the human issues would not have concerned him greatly. At least, old John Brown was deadly sincere, Meade thought.

Within a week there was another drifting away, as those who had stayed beyond their time on a quick upsurge of hope realized that gold was just as hard to dig as ever. This time it was Ben Mercer who bought the bulk of the claims for sale, and he got them for less than Meade and the Negroes had paid per claim. Meade wondered again if what lay in Ben Mercer's mind was just the same as what lay in Meade's. Meade decided to make a test. He went deer hunting again.

He went directly away from Old Bugle this time, with no intention of circling around to Kansas Gulch. He made no effort to make his trail hard to find. In the park country far south of Bugle Mountain, he waited to see if anyone had followed.

Ed and Harvey Mercer came out of the thickets, searching for signs of his passing. They found them, and came on slowly. Meade made a circle to be sure. Within an hour the Mercers were in sight again, from where he crouched in the edge of the aspens.

In a moment of great anger he made a mistake. He raised his rifle and shot into the grass between them. They ran back to cover. Meade cursed himself for a fool. There was no way now that he could retrieve the situation and make them think that he had fired close to them as a joke or because he did not like to be trailed on general principles.

That one rash move, made in rage and fear, had set solidly in the Mercers' minds the thought that he had something to conceal. Meade vowed not to go anywhere close to Old Bugle now as long as there was a man left in Poverty.

Two hours later he knew the pair were still on his track. They made no more rash crossings of open spaces, but he doubled back on his trail and came behind them. There in the damp mold underneath the aspens he saw the boot marks of the Mercers. The persistence of the two squat men struck him forcibly. He was uneasy and angry again, and he kept thinking of Kansas Gulch.

It helped his mood very little when he shot a deer a short time afterward.

He took one half of it to Ellen. She was alone in the tent, mending clothes. "I hung a peace offering in the tree," Meade said. He waited uncertainly until she invited him in.

"You feel the need of a peace offering?" she asked.

"Well, I . . . about that night, Ellen. . . ."

"We'd best forget that, Jay."

"I've missed talking to you, Ellen."

She smiled faintly. "I've been here all the time."

"In that case, I'll come by again. Tonight?"

"If you wish."

He could not tell whether she was mocking him or not. He covered his thoughts with a grin, and backed out of the tent. A hell of a place to go courting, he thought, what with

Ripley eyeing every move and expression, and old Ban sitting there like a brooding mother hen. But if he did not get a move on him, Ben Mercer would walk away with Ellen one of these days.

The Mercers—Meade's worries about Kansas Gulch came back. He saw Ben Mercer near the creek, examining a sluice on one of the claims he had bought. Meade went down to him.

"Hello, Jay. How are your new claims looking?"

"Fair enough. Tell me something, Ben. Every time I go hunting, your brothers are hot on my track. Why?"

"They are?" Ben's expression was frank, surprised. "So that's where they sneaked to this morning." He shook his head. "I don't know, Jay. You always bring in game. Maybe the boys sort of like to trail your good luck."

"I dropped a shot between them today, Ben. I don't like to be trailed."

Mercer nodded sympathetically. "I can understand that. Of course, just out hunting deer. . . ." He spread his hands. "I'm sure they had nothing more in mind than seeing where you get all your meat."

"Speak to them, Ben. Today they didn't stop trying to see where I get my meat even after I warned them off with a shot."

"They're stubborn, all right." Mercer smiled. "They probably thought it was a good joke, that shot. You wait and see, I'll bet they'll be laughing about it tonight."

If Ed and Harvey laughed about the incident, Meade was not around them to hear. After supper he went to call on Mrs. Greenaway, encountering the obstacles that he had expected.

In the evening shadows Meade and Ellen walked on a ridge above Feather Creek. The scent of the long-leaf pines was about them. The rocks they sat on were still warm from the heat of day.

"What happened to you in Kansas?" Ellen asked.

Meade told her briefly. "A doctor told me afterward that one good punch there"—he tapped his side where nothing but skin lay over the lung—"might kill me."

"Couldn't you wear something over it?"

"Sure." Meade laughed. "I could strap a board there, or a piece of a washtub. It's much simpler not to expose myself to trouble."

"But it isn't just the ribs. I can understand that, but you've lost all interest in other people. You don't care anything about their problems."

"Sure I do, as long as their problems affect my own."

"I never knew you before you came here, Jay. I can't tell whether you were selfish before or whether you've tried to change yourself since that trouble in Kansas."

"Does it matter?"

"Yes, it does."

"I'll have money, Ellen."

"Many selfish men do." She shook her head gently, studying him in the half light. "I don't mean that you wouldn't be generous with material things. You are now, when it occurs to you, but I don't know if you could give any part of yourself to anyone."

"I could to you, Ellen."

She was still doubtful. "I don't know, Jay."

She would not have gone so deeply into the matter if she didn't have a strong feeling for him, Meade thought. He could change her doubts in time because he himself had no doubts about Jay Meade. "Just give me a chance. . . ."

"You have a chance, every day you live."

"I don't quite understand."

She frowned at the darkening gulch. "We'd better go back now."

He kissed her before they started down. By her response, which was not based on the logic she had thrown at him, Meade thought he knew more about Ellen Greenaway than she knew about herself.

V

Seated on a stool near the doorway of his tent, Ben Mercer observed with annoyance that there was dust on his boots, and he had not been outside yet. Ed had forgotten to dampen the floor again. Ben reached to one of the cots and took one of Harvey's shirts to dust his boots.

That done, he gave his mind to other matters that were annoying him. Problem one: the political hostilities of the camp had not achieved a sustained pitch. There were fewer men now, but still too many. He would give that problem consideration later. Problem two: Jay Meade. How to manage him once his secret was discovered. Any stupid thug could dispose of a man by violence. Ben had never killed a man and did not intend to do so, or allow his half-brothers to do so. If he could not win the possessions of others, including their lives, by devious means, then there was no satisfaction in winning. Problem three: Ed and Harvey could not be used any longer to trail Meade. They were willing enough, too eager, in fact. That could be settled easily. Hereafter, they could search on their own for Meade's secret.

As for Jay Meade himself, let there be a plan developed to wipe him from the picture once his secret was known. Ben Mercer was scarcely welcome any more in the Phillips tent. Even old Ban was getting sour, a change that Ben could not understand in any other terms other than he favored Meade's attentions to Ellen over Ben Mercer's. In a moment that was rare to him, Ben's reasoning suffered, and he was surprised to experience a touch of murderous anger. He began to work out a plan, complicated, tangled in the emotions of men, so intricate that even Ben Mercer was pleased by it. It gave him satisfaction to think that he was shuffling human beings, using them like a deck of cards.

He went down to the creek, stopping a moment to chat with Meade, and then he went on to where Ed and Harvey were sweating at the sluice.

"Are you ever going to work?" Ed asked. It was a rhetorical question.

Ben smiled it away. "That first day Meade caught you on his trail . . . where were you?"

"Maybe a mile east of camp," Harvey said.

"And his trail was then leading toward the cañon?"
"Yeah."

"And not directly toward Bugle Mountain?" Ben asked. "Don't stare up there, you idiots!"

"He was going sort of with the cañon," Ed said.

Ben nodded. In every case Meade had gone in any direction but toward Bugle Mountain when he left Poverty. Ben said: "Tomorrow, before daylight, you two light out for Old Bugle. Go up and down it and all around it, if it takes three days. Pay particular attention to any place where you find water enough to wash gold."

It was a wild chance, based on reasoning that might be faulty, but Ben had lived his life close to sharp gambles built on hunches that he never allowed to be hunches, but rather insight into human character.

His ego did not allow him to show his eagerness two days later when Ed and Harvey came back after dusk to report that they had found a broad gulch, bisected by a stream, in the folds of Old Bugle.

"Any sign of him being there?" Ben asked.

"No." Harvey shook his head. "We went up and down it. The creek's too narrow for a man to pan right in it and then hide the marks. He'd be bound to break the banks down."

"What kind of ground is there beside it?"

"Gravel."

"Did you test it?"

The brothers looked at each other. "We didn't have any tools."

"Couldn't you have scratched up enough out of the creek to bring back here for panning here?"

Ed spread his hands. "We didn't think of that. There's no marks of anybody digging over there, Ben. We don't think it's the place at all."

"I'll have a look myself," Ben said. "You two be on the sluice tomorrow. We don't want him any more suspicious than he is. Now tell me exactly how to get to this place."

The sun was just striking the creek when Meade, on his way to work, saw Ben Mercer ride away. His half-brothers came down to their sluice and went to work. Johnny Creston, his arm still in a sling, was lecturing on the unfairness of too few men owning too many claims in a gulch where gold was none too plentiful to begin with. He was finding support in scraggly-toothed George Unruh and several other Southerners. It was Unruh who, not long ago, had drawn a pistol to prevent Creston from getting help while he was being beaten by a bigger man, but now this meeting of minds by old foes was not odd at all, Meade thought absently. Gold could bring men together or send them at each other's throats quicker than anything he knew of.

He watched Ben Mercer uneasily. For two days the other Mercers had been gone. They must have returned some time during the night, and now Ben was hot-footing off into the mountains. Meade realized that he was concerned when any man left Poverty camp to go into the mountains, but he was extra sensitive when the Mercers made a move.

Oatis Peek came across the creek and stood waiting for attention.

"What is it, Oatis?"

"Lots of folks getting heated 'cause Luke and us got so many claims, Mister Meade. You suppose we could sell some of 'em?"

"That's your business, if you want to."

"That Luke, he won't do it. He say we bought 'em fair. He says they're ours. Couldn't you kind of talk to Luke, Mister Meade, maybe tell him it would be better if we don't have folks muttering at us?"

"I've got troubles of my own," Meade said. "I don't give anyone advice."

"But you could talk to Luke. You could say. . . ."

"No."

"Maybe he listen to you, Mister Meade."

"No. Don't bother me."

"I didn't aim to bother you." Peek went back across the creek.

"Damned niggers grabbing everything in sight," Creston said loudly.

Meade worked for an hour longer. He went to his tent, got his rifle, and walked on up the hill into the trees. He stood there uneasily, watched Ed and Harvey. They had paid no attention to him; they made no move to follow him.

He took a chance then and went by the shortest route to Kansas Gulch.

Before he reached there he saw the tracks of Ben Mercer's sorrel. When Meade came out of the trees and looked into the gulch, Mercer was walking slowly along the creek. He stood with his hands in his coat pockets while Meade walked toward him.

Mercer smiled. "You're a long ways from camp today. I've got my horse in case you want to pack in a deer."

"I haven't got a deer."

"Oh?" Mercer glanced up the gulch. The bulges in his coat pockets were caused by something larger than his hands, Meade observed. "Unusual place, this. I stumbled into it, never dreaming there would be a flat spot this big on the side of Bugle."

Until this moment Meade had not realized how heavily the secret of Kansas Gulch had ridden him. He was ready now to kill to defend the place. If Mercer made a move, if anything in his face changed a fraction. . . .

"I wonder if a man could pan anything out of here," Ben murmured. "I doubt that anyone has ever tried this gulch, don't you?"

"Probably not."

It was all Meade could do to keep from glancing toward the cave where his tools were hidden.

"Say there was gold here." Mercer shook his head. "It sure would cause a problem, wouldn't it, Meade? Every ragged miner in Poverty would run his legs off to get here. In a way, it seems unfair that fifty people should be let in on something that, say, two men could share."

"If there happened to be any gold here."

"Of course." Mercer smiled. "I was merely supposing." He shook his head again. "It doesn't look so good to me."

There was mockery behind his tone. "Still, if I had a shovel and a pan, since I'm here. . . . It would probably be a waste of time, Meade. You going on back now?"

Meade nodded.

"We may as well travel along together, then." They looked at each other squarely. "We could travel together quite a distance, Meade."

"If we could trust each other."

"Yes," Mercer said quite seriously. "That always is a problem among human beings, isn't it?"

He turned his back and sauntered into the willows to get his horse. *He's judged me to a T,* Meade thought, *he knew I wouldn't shoot him.* There was no illusion that Ben Mercer had been fooled about Kansas Gulch. He had guessed shrewdly, and later he would confirm his ideas.

When Mercer led the horse back, Meade studied the Frenchman's sharp, handsome features. He knew then that they were both alike, that neither of them would take less than all of Kansas Gulch.

They went back toward Poverty together. Mercer talked easily of everything but that which lay uppermost in Meade's mind. Killing would not solve anything for Meade; he knew that much about himself, even if he had been keyed up to shoot Mercer a short time before.

They reached Poverty in the middle of a tumultuous miners' meeting in front of the saloon. Standing on an empty whiskey keg, Creston was doing the talking.

"We make our own laws here!" he cried. "And we can change our own laws. When one group of men holds more claims than they're entitled to, it's time to change the rules. I propose that any man who owns more than two claims, no matter how he got them, be made to throw back for filing all that extra ground."

"You're damned right!" Unruh yelled.

Meade nudged Ora Sammons. "What brought it to a head?"

Sammons spat. "Unruh and Creston went over to jump one of the Negroes' claims. Reardon run 'em both off with a pistol."

"Let's put this matter to a vote!" Creston said.

Meade raised his voice. "Before we do, I want to know who pays back the money some of us paid for extra claims. You can vote all you damned please, but I own ground here that I intend to keep. If anybody wants it, decision of a miners' meeting or not, they'd better come after it with a rifle."

"It ain't fair for some to hog ground," Ban Phillips growled.

"I bought the ground," Meade said. "Reardon and his boys did the same. Ben Mercer did, too. Nobody's taking anything from me."

Meade sized up the chances. There were men here who did not like Creston. Some of them would vote against his proposal solely on that basis, but there were also Southerners who would vote against the property rights of Negroes automatically, and there were men who would base their action entirely on the have not principle. It would go the wrong way, Meade thought.

He went over to Ben Mercer.

"The more claims spread around, Ben, the longer there will be men here."

"I'm thinking of that." Mercer's eyes narrowed. "Make Creston the issue, Jay. He's not well liked."

"You do it. You're a better talker than me."

Mercer shook his head. "You've got their attention now, Jay. You've never spoken up before."

"Let's put it up for vote," Creston said.

"Just a minute," Meade said. "It's a fine thing when an Abolitionist can stand on a whiskey keg and tell honest men what to do. Creston went across the creek to jump a claim. He got run off. He's sore about that. He wants to drag all of you into something you don't want to do. I'll tell you what I'll do, and Ben Mercer will do the same. We'll sell any one of the claims we bought to any man here, for just what they cost." Those who wanted claims the most did not have money to buy them, and Meade knew it. "We'll sell you claims. You don't need an Abolitionist troublemaker to tell you what to do. You listened to the lies of one idiot who rode in here to tell about a war that wasn't so. Now you're listening to another crazy man who. . . ."

"That's a lie!" Creston jumped up and down in rage. He put his weight too close to the rim of the whiskey keg and it tilted. Ed Mercer was standing close to it. He shoved it with his foot and the keg went over. Flailing with his good arm, Creston spilled into the street.

There was a roar of laughter. Ben Mercer did not allow it to subside before he raised his arms and announced that the drinks were on him. Not everybody tried to get inside the saloon, but enough did to break up the meeting.

White with anger, Creston rose and tried to gain attention. He could not do it. He gave Meade a bitter look and limped away.

That night, when Meade went to the Phillips tent, Ban met him at the doorway.

"You ain't welcome here, Meade."

Meade stared at the Tennessean. "Why not?"

"That business at the meeting today. I've always suspected you was a hog, and now, by God, I know it. You'd take everything in the gulch, if you could, you and them Negroes and Ben Mercer."

For once, Meade thought, *Mercer was sharing the blame.* "Well, now. . . ."

"You even changed your tune and jumped on one of your own men, an Abolitionist like yourself. That shows what kind of a man you are, Meade. It's money with you and nothing else."

"Who's been talking to you, Ban?" Meade asked.

"I don't need anybody to tell me what's right under my nose to see."

Meade studied Ban's angry features. He decided that the old man was sincere, that no one had worked on him to put him in this condition.

"Now get away from this tent," Phillips said, "and don't hang around here no more!"

"I'd like to ask Ellen about that first."

"By God, I said it!"

Meade pushed the flap aside far enough to look past Phillips. Ellen was standing at the back of the tent. Her face was pale and she was biting her lip. Her son was beside her, frightened by the uproar, but showing the same stubborn look of his grandfather.

"What about it, Ellen?" Meade asked.

She hesitated, and then she nodded. "Yes, you'd better go away now."

Meade thought he could read her face and tone well enough to know that she was merely trying to avoid more trouble with her father, and not stating her own policy.

"All right," Meade said to Phillips. "You're wrong, Ban, and maybe you'll cool off later. But I don't care whether you do or not. You can't stop me from seeing Ellen when she. . . ."

Phillips roared his anger. He swung a powerful blow at Meade's face. Meade caught it on his arm, but there was force enough to make him step back hastily. He stepped on a rock, going backward, was thrown off balance, and fell to one knee.

"Stay away from here!" Phillips shouted. He backed into the tent and jerked the flaps together.

In the dusky street there was laughter. George Unruh said: "Looks like anybody can lick that big mouth."

Ben Mercer stood in Kansas Gulch with his mind so aflame with greed that he had no time to be annoyed by the muddy condition of his boots and clothes. The streak of gold in the pan he held was from the sixth test hole he had dug. He was an inefficient hand with a pan, but he knew the sight of gold as well as any man. He looked up and down the gulch. There was wealth here to make him a king in New Orleans. He could deck Ellen out like a queen, and he could live as he had always deserved to live.

Most carefully he covered up the last test hole. He hid his tools in the willows, and washed his hands, and removed some of the mud stains from his clothing.

When he got his horse to ride back to Poverty, he observed that the animal had suddenly taken on a scrubby appearance, and the saddle was a cheap thing for a man to put up with. All that would soon be changed.

He needed two fools now to do his bidding. One of them he saw from the hill, a stooped, grizzled man putting in an extra half hour of work at his sluice: Ban Phillips. The other—well, he would have to be most careful in his selection of the other.

Mercer went down to where Phillips was shoveling. The old man glowered at him. "Move over on your own ground, Mercer."

"I've been thinking of what you said to Meade the other

evening, Ban. I've come to the conclusion that you were right in one thing, at least . . . the claims. I'm going to take the loss on my extra ones and throw them back for filing."

Phillips stared at him suspiciously.

"It will be worth it for the good will and harmony of the camp. Of course, it will have to be done by lots, a drawing among those whose claims are the poorest."

"I don't want something for nothing, Mercer."

"Of course. I didn't have you in mind at all, Ban. I merely wanted to get your opinion of the idea."

Phillips scratched his chin on his shoulder. "Well, it sounds all right, I guess."

"It has to be worked out. We don't want to say anything for a while. Any advance notice might generate excitement that would ruin the whole thing."

Phillips jabbed his shovel into the gravel, scowling. "Just why are you aiming to do this, Mercer?"

"To forestall trouble that might wreck the whole camp, for one reason. And then, quite frankly, I think it might help my cause with Ellen." Mercer laughed, giving it the proper rueful shade. "I haven't been doing very well with her lately, you may have noticed."

"Meade or Reardon won't throw back any of their ground," Phillips said.

"Meade might. I intend to talk to him about it. He really can stand to better than I, you know. This gulch is only a flash in the pan compared to what Meade has farther back in the mountains."

"What's that?" Phillips was aroused instantly.

"Keep it quiet, Ban, utterly quiet. Meade has discovered, I'm sure, a very rich placer. Quite naturally he wants to keep it for himself. Wouldn't you?"

"Where is this place?"

"I don't know. I have seen him panning gold right here at the creek, some of the richest pans I ever saw, and the gravel was entirely different from anything we have here."

"Ah," Phillips said, "he goes hunting a lot."

"Why, sure," Mercer said. "He used to spend more time traipsing the hills than he did working his claim. That's what he's gone and done. He's found something and he aims to hog it all."

"Now wait a minute, Ban. I could be wrong, you know. Maybe when the time comes, he'll let the camp in on it."

"The hell he will. After the way he's done here?"

"Easy," Mercer said. "Don't let everybody in camp hear you. I might be wrong, as I said. If we knew for sure where Meade went when he leaves here, then we could tell everybody. That is, if he really does have some. . . ."

"You said you saw him panning stuff that didn't come from this gulch."

"Well, yes." Mercer was hesitant. "But unless we knew where he got it, what's the use of starting a big hullabaloo?"

"We can trail him."

"I've thought some of that. But you know. . . ."

"I'll trail him, by God!" Phillips said. "If he's trying to hold out something that ought to belong to everybody, we'll soon have it out in the open."

"When we're sure, but not before."

"Have you got any idea where it might be?" Phillips asked.

Mercer frowned. "A couple of times when my brothers ran into him accidentally while they were hunting, they noticed he was coming from the direction of Old Bugle."

Phillips pulled a mud clot from his whiskers. "Up there, huh? We'll see."

"Are you sure you can trail him?"

Phillips spat. "I learned from men who ran down Indians for fun, Mercer."

Mercer nodded. These uncouth backwoodsmen, they were like the half savages of the Mississippi swamps, bragging of abilities that any civilized man would scorn to possess. Mercer glanced up the hill. His half-brothers were cooking in front of the tent.

All at once he was revolted by the thought of the kind of food there would be. "I'd like to talk to you later about working out some fair method of spreading my extra claims around."

"Yeah."

Ban Phillips was not thinking now of that minor problem. His deep-set eyes were on Old Bugle. He was a rare kind of fool, Mercer thought. The man actually was simple enough to want to share untold wealth with his fellows. Mercer went toward his tent, pausing on the way to talk to groups of miners cooking before their huts. He needed a second fool now, one with no illusions of honesty whatever.

He talked to Northerners and Southerners alike. As a matter of principle, most of the Yankees did not like him, and he sensed that in their attitudes. But it pleased him to see the grudging admiration they gave him because he approached them openly and in a friendly manner. They prided themselves on being rough and uncouth, and they considered working with their hands a mark of honor, and yet behind that front they paid unconscious homage to anyone who dressed better than they and prospered without working. *Pigs and idiots*, Mercer thought. It was men like these who thought Negroes should be free.

Before he reached his half-brothers, Mercer knew who he could use as the second fool.

VI

Day by day Meade watched the Mercers. He knew that Ben had been gone all day, but now the Mercers made no move at all. The game of waiting was hard to bear. Meade no longer slept well. Sudden noises brought him from his cot with a pistol in his hand, and in his mind there was always a vision of Ed and Harvey Mercer waiting to kill him.

During sleepless nights and while he labored at his sluice, Meade tried to work out some plan to meet the issue before he was worn down with waiting. The answer was simple, but it was not one his mind could accept cold-bloodedly—kill the Mercers. If he were working Kansas Gulch, impossible as long as Poverty existed, and the Mercers came to take it from him, then he would be able to accept the obvious means of settling the affair.

He went to Kansas Gulch. It was just the same as before. He found Ben Mercer's clumsily covered test holes and was filled with murderous rage, although he had expected to find them. He searched out the tools Mercer had hidden in the willows. Meade took them to the cave, haunted by the fear that others could have found the tools, and wondered, and dug, and caused a stampede. He went back and dragged branches over the test holes Mercer had dug, and then he concealed the branches in the willows.

Now that he was here, he began to worry about what

miners would be thinking of his absence from camp. Maybe
there were others as shrewd as Ben Mercer. He left at once.

In Poverty he was never free of worry about Kansas
Gulch; in the gulch he was constantly in a fret about what
was going on in the minds of men in Poverty. Too many
times of late he had come directly to the gulch. Even now
he was starting back the same way he had come. He circled
away to the west, and then bore around until he approached
Poverty from the south, hunting as he went, but for once he
had no luck.

That was a bad omen, he told himself, and a moment
later he was cursing himself for becoming superstitious.
The sun was resting on the mountains when he reached
camp.

He went straight toward the saloon, feeling an uncommon need for some of Bland's strong whiskey. He
passed the hut where George Unruh and Loy Blaisdell
lived. Unruh was coming from the creek with a bucket of
water.

Unruh bared his rotting teeth in a grimace of surprise.
"Well, by God!"

Blaisdell was building a fire in a crater of blackened
stones. He made a quick motion with his hand at Unruh,
and then he rose and followed Meade.

Ripley Greenaway came out of the Phillips tent as
Meade was passing. He was crying.

"What's the matter with you, Rip?" Meade asked.

Mrs. Pingree's fleshy face appeared in the doorway an
instant. She stared in horror at Meade, and then she gasped
and disappeared.

"You ought to ask the kid what's the matter, you dirty
bastard, Meade!" Hardin Clements was standing behind
Meade with a pistol. With him were Unruh, Blaisdell, and a

dozen others whose huts Meade had passed. Their faces were all the same, grim, accusing.

"What's the matter, boys?"

"Drop your rifle," Clements said. "Or don't, if you feel lucky. I've always had a hankering to shoot you, Meade." After a moment Meade lay his rifle at his feet. Clements gestured with his pistol. "Get on up the street."

Men were coming from all directions now.

Ora Sammons said: "He had his guts, walking right in like this."

"Have you all gone crazy?" Meade cried.

"Sure," Blaisdell growled. "We're all crazy but you, you murdering son-of-a-bitch!"

"Murdering . . . ?" Meade stared around him. The hostility was like an evil odor.

"We don't need to even try him!" someone yelled.

Billy Bland battered his way through the crowd. "Oh, yes, we do!" His moon face showed equal anger when he looked at the speaker, and then at Meade. "There ain't going to be no mob running wild like a flood here."

"What is it, Billy?" Meade asked.

Expressionless, the saloon man studied Meade. "Somebody shot Ban Phillips."

"Old Ban?" Good Lord, how was Ellen taking it? Meade wanted to go to her at once. He took a step before he realized his position.

"You had trouble with him," Bland said.

"I . . . why, yes . . . a little argument. But I haven't even been here today."

"It didn't happen here," Bland said. "Somebody got him up there in the timber, about a mile away, with a bullet through the back of the head."

"It wasn't me."

"It wasn't him!" Unruh jeered. "He was the only one away from camp besides Phillips, and his tracks were right there!"

Ben Mercer slashed his way through the crowd. "I don't believe it, Jay. It looks bad, I'll admit. It appears that Ban was trailing you, and that you turned around and shot him. I don't believe it. We'll find some way. . . ."

"You won't find nothing!" Sammons shouted. "You're not running the whole camp yet, Mercer!"

"We're not a pack of wolves, Sammons," Mercer said. "Meade will get a fair trial, with all the evidence weighed carefully. I know myself that he wouldn't harm Ban Phillips, even if they did have trouble. I know. . . ."

"You don't know nothing!" Sammons said. "You're not going to smooth talk all the evidence away, neither!"

"Meade is entitled to all the defense he can get," Mercer said. "I myself am convinced that he is innocent, and I'll defend him before any miners' court."

Meade looked at the bearded faces all around him. With few exceptions, he saw death staring back at him in every case. Most steadily he looked at Ben Mercer. Mercer's expression was frank, concerned, and he, beyond all doubt, was death itself.

"No, Mercer," Meade said. "If I need any defense, I'll take Billy Bland."

Mercer shrugged, and turned away.

Bland nodded. "There will be no whiskey sold until this is over. Now, everybody clear away from my tent and let me and Meade talk."

"We won't clear away very far, remember that!" Unruh yelled.

Meade went inside with Bland. He wanted to go and see Ellen. She would know he had not killed her father; she would know at a glance, he was sure. And then he remembered the looks on the faces of the miners, and he wondered why he thought Ellen would know he was innocent.

"Where did you go today?" Bland asked. He took a drink of whiskey, and Meade saw that his hands were shaky. Bland was neither a drinking man nor a nervous one. His sudden deflection jarred Meade.

"Hunting," Meade said. Because it was a lie it did not sound sufficient, and so before he could stop himself he said: "I went hunting deer."

"All right," Bland said, and it was difficult to know whether he believed Meade or not. He started to take another drink of whiskey, and then he put the cork in the bottle and looked steadily at Meade. "Did you do it?"

Meade shook his head.

Bland's expression did not change. "I didn't think so. Now I'm sure. Who the hell would want to kill Ban Phillips?"

"Where were the Mercers, Billy?"

"The Mercers?" Bland turned his face until he was looking sideways at Meade. "You and Ben . . . and Ellen . . . no, no, Meade. Ben wouldn't go that far. Besides, all the Mercers were right here in camp all day."

"You're sure about that?"

"Darned good and sure, Jay. For once, Ben was working . . . a little. He piddled around the sluice with Ed and Harvey all day."

"Who found Ban?" Meade asked.

"The kid . . . Ripley."

"Oh, my God. What was he doing a mile from camp?"

"Phillips told his daughter he was going hunting. The kid wanted to trail along, and the old man wouldn't let him, so Ripley followed, anyway. He heard the shot and thought his grandfather had a deer."

"What kind of sign was there?" Meade asked.

Bland shook his head disgustedly. "Everybody rushed up there. They tramped in all directions. They got into arguments. The ones that were late started pointing out the tracks of the ones that had got there first. Blaisdell and Sammons damned near got in another fight. It was a mess."

"But my tracks were there, and Phillips was following me?"

Bland nodded. "That much was clear. Why would he follow you, Meade?"

Meade shook his head. Kansas Gulch was the only reason he could think of, but Phillips would not have known about that, unless Mercer told him. And why would Mercer tell him, complicating a situation that was already bad enough—unless, of course, he had planned all the time to put Meade in the very fix he was now in?

"Who was out of camp today?" Meade asked.

"John Ledbetter and me tried to figure that out. If any man had been gone all day or even half a day, we might have known for sure, but there were men dragging firewood off the hills, and some back a ways in the trees whipsawing sluice planks, and even a few prospecting along the edges of the trees. A matter of one mile and back in a hurry." Bland shook his head. "It might have been any one of a dozen men, or even two or three of them, for all we know."

"Rifle or pistol, Billy?"

"Rifle," Bland said gloomily.

"I didn't fire mine today."

"I saw it was clean. If you had killed old Ban, it would have been that way, wouldn't it?"

"Yeah." They were not getting anywhere, Meade thought.

Unruh shouted from outside: "No use to talk all afternoon, figuring up lies, Bland! We know who's guilty!"

Meade was sweating. Men die for obscure reasons, accidentally, killed by other men for reasons that are never clear. Maybe Phillips had died that way, and now Jay Meade stood a good chance of hanging because of it, and he would be just as dead as if he had killed Phillips, and Ben Mercer's interests would be as well served as if he had planned the whole affair.

"Did Ban ever have trouble with anybody that you know of?" Meade asked.

"He was surly and grumpy sometimes," Bland said. "But you're about the only man I can think of that he ever had trouble with in camp."

"That time after the flood, when there was the argument over the tent?"

"Ban was trying to make peace then, Meade. Nobody was sore at him. They just didn't want him stopping their fight."

The voices outside were growing louder. Meade took a drink of whiskey at a gulp. "You're not much help, Billy."

"I can't think," Bland said. "I'm sure you didn't do it, but I can't think of any proof. Can you?"

"No. But why should I kill him?"

"He told you not to hang around his daughter. You and her have been meeting around ever since."

"Are you defending me or not, Billy?"

Bland sighed. He took a quick drink and put the cork back into the bottle reluctantly. "I'm just trying to think of what they're going to say, that's all. It would help some if you were a little better liked, Jay, but you've been a lone wolf, and that isn't going to set well."

To lose his life just when he had all that gold at his fingertips. . . . He knew Bland kept a loaded pistol in the same box with his choice whiskey. For one wild instant, Meade considered taking it and fighting his way clear of Poverty. Ben Mercer would never tell about Kansas Gulch. Meade could come back later when the camp was dead and fight for what was his. So strong was the thought that he moved a few steps to go around the bar. He stopped. If he made a break, Ellen would be convinced of his guilt, if she now had any doubt, and throughout the entire territory he would be known as a murderer. He turned his back on the bar.

Bland's head was cocked so that he was looking sideways again. "That's right, Jay, it wouldn't have been any good at all. Let's go out and tell them we're ready as we'll ever be."

Miss Kinnison and her girls were the only women present. They stood on the hill above the crowd of miners, now almost silent as they watched Meade and Bland come forth. There was no bench or semblance of one. The judge stood in the street. He was John Ledbetter, a quiet workhorse of a man, never known to take a drink.

Johnny Creston was the prosecutor. He liked to make a noise, Meade thought, and he would not have forgotten the last miners' meeting when Meade ruined his program.

The jury was composed of all the miners, standing there with their minds already made up.

"This is a trial for murder," Ledbetter said. "By gosh, boys, we got to do the best we can to be honest and fair. We think Jay Meade killed Ban, but we don't know it. We'll listen to all the evidence there is, and then we'll try to come out with a verdict based on that. I want all talking done by one man at a time. Ora Sammons is going to see to that. He's got the authority of this court to crown any man that starts yelling out of turn."

No one laughed. There were the dignity and sincerity in Ledbetter's words that kept silence. Sammons, now that he was an instrument of the court, was not as belligerent toward Meade as he had been earlier. He kept punching at his woolly blond hair and staring at Meade, and he appeared to be remembering that they were from the same state, and, if they had not been friends, still they had always been on friendly terms.

"He's going to get an honest trial," Sammons said. "That means you keep your mouth shut, Unruh, unless somebody asks you something, see?"

There were sunburn scabs on Unruh's cheek bones. His red beard was unkempt. He twisted his mouth as he glared at Sammons. "Give a dumb ox five cents' worth of authority and. . . ."

"That's all!" Sammons yelled.

"We'll hear from Oatis Peek," Ledbetter said. "We're not going to try to swear anybody to the truth because we expect everybody to tell the truth. Step out here, Oatis, and start things. Tell us about the kid."

Peek edged out from the crowd. He looked around hesitantly. "I see the kid busting down past where we're sawing planks. I stopped him and say what's the matter. He say his grandpa done been shot dead in the trees. Then I told Luke and he told Mister Clements and some others, and then everybody goes hightailing up to where the boy says."

"All right, Oatis," Ledbetter said. "Clements, let's hear from you."

The dark-faced Virginian stepped out. His thin lips made their movements close to his teeth while he talked. "We went up there to see, Blaisdell and I and half a dozen others. The kid had been mixed up and we wandered around over two or three ridges before we found the place he'd tried to tell us. Phillips was lying face down, over a log. His rifle was under him. We could hear some of the others threshing around in the brush, so we yelled and fired a few pistol shots to guide them to us. Then we picked up Phillips and carried him back."

The crowd listened as raptly as if they had never heard any of the statements previously. Ledbetter said: "Anybody want to question Clements?"

"I do!" Creston strode into the open place in the middle of the street. The red bandannas that held his broken arm were a splash of brightness against the drab clothes of the miners. "You saw by the tracks that Phillips had been following Meade, didn't you, Clements?"

Clements stared with dislike at the feisty little prosecutor. He spoke to the crowd instead of to Creston. "Yes, Phillips had been walking in Meade's tracks."

"You know for sure that they were Meade's tracks?" Bland asked mildly.

"Peek said so," Clements said.

"I notice things like that," the Negro said. He glanced apologetically at Meade. "Mister Meade's the only man in camp who don't wear boots with the heels all run over on the edges or worn down to nothing. Him and Mister Ben Mercer."

"And Mercer was here," Creston said. "It's clear enough. Phillips followed Meade, who saw him doing so, and killed him. They had had trouble. It's clear enough."

"It sure ain't to me," Bland said. "Why was Ban trailing him in the first place?"

"That has nothing to do with it!" Creston cried. "A man has a right to go anywhere he wants to in these hills. Phillips might have been using the same route simply because it was the handy way to go where he was going hunting.

Meade saw him and killed him, for reasons we all know. I demand that the jury vote right now."

"You demand too damned fast, Creston," Ledbetter said. "We got to hear all there is to hear. Bland, have you got any evidence that anyone else besides Meade was close to where Phillips was killed?"

"There were a dozen men out of camp today, for a while," Bland said.

"Sure there were!" Creston said. "I was one of them. Right around noon I was a quarter, or maybe even a half mile up the hill looking for deer. Ledbetter was close to there, too, cutting spruce boughs for his bed."

The judge nodded. "That's right. A lot of us, like any day, were at least a short ways out of camp."

One by one Bland called seven men, who admitted being away from Poverty during the day. Each one had a reasonable explanation, and none admitted being more than a half mile from camp. They supported each other, and the dissident elements involved convinced Meade there could be no conscious lying. It was rather that they were sure they had the guilty man before them, therefore, they banded together, confirming each other's statements in order to make the case stronger against Meade.

While Bland was questioning them, Meade saw Creston conferring with the Mercers. An alliance there? Not likely beyond the extent that Ben was telling Creston something to use against Meade. There was the feel of a rope already around Meade's neck. He watched Ben with an arm around Creston's shoulder—and was afraid.

"I doubt no man's testimony just given," Bland said, "but I want everyone to consider this . . . Meade was not the only man out of camp. No one had any reason that we know of to kill Ban Phillips, least of all Meade. Someone did, and it could have been one of the men absent from Poverty for a length of time that we can't now prove. Meade walked into camp unconcerned. He didn't even know Ban was dead. His rifle was clean. Hardin Clements was the first man to examine it, and he can testify that it was clean. Meade intends to marry Phillips's daughter. There is no reason in the world, and no evidence to show for him even wanting to shoot Phillips."

Bland spoke in a low voice. There were points in his argument that were thin, but the whole of it had a sobering effect on the crowd, Meade observed. Maybe there was room for hope. But what was Ben Mercer telling Creston?

Bland stated his argument three times, in different words. He hammered it at the crowd and the jury. His sincerity made them see it as he saw it. For the first time Meade saw doubt on faces that had been charged with anger.

"This should never come to a vote," Bland said, "because there is no evidence at all to show who killed Ban Phillips."

Creston stepped forward, not speaking until all eyes were on him, until the miners were wondering how he would counter Bland's serious speech. And then he smiled.

Sammons whispered to Meade. "I'm for you now. I sort of got excited before."

"Where did you go today, Meade?" Creston asked.

"Hunting."

"You brought back nothing. Is that customary?"

"It happens. You didn't get anything either." There was a small ripple of laughter.

"I was only a short distance from camp," Creston said. "I didn't take out in one direction, spend a whole day in the hills, and come back from the opposite direction. Why did you do that, Meade?"

"Because I covered a lot of country"

"This coming in from a direction other than you went out has a guilty look about it, I would say."

"I do that frequently," Meade said. "Deer are where you find them."

"You don't object to other people hunting deer, do you?"

"Why, no. Why should I?"

"Then why do you shoot at any man who follows you?" Creston demanded.

"I don't."

"That's a lie," Creston said dramatically. "I want the court to listen carefully. A short time ago Ed and Harvey Mercer happened to cross Meade's trail while hunting. They went on it a short distance because it was the way they, too, were headed. Jay Meade deliberately tried to kill them. He fired three shots at them, didn't you, Meade?"

"No," Meade said. He could not afford to admit that he had fired at all.

Creston blinked. "You deny it?"

"I do."

"Step out here, Ed Harvey."

Pig-eyed. That fitted the Mercer brothers better than it ever had, Meade thought. They watched him intently.

Ed described the scene the day Meade had fired to warn them off his trail. "I think it was two shots," he said. "We were busy running across an open park, so maybe he only got in two cracks at us."

"And for no reason that you know of?" Creston prompted.

The brothers shook their heads.

"You still deny it, Meade?" Creston asked.

"I do."

"Come here, Ben."

Ben Mercer appeared reluctant to testify. "There's things about this that perhaps we don't understand."

"You're damned right!" Creston said. "Tell us what Meade told you the same day that he fired either two or three shots at your brothers."

Ben hesitated. "You understand, boys, that I don't think Meade killed Phillips, but. . . ."

"Just answer as I directed!" Creston said.

"Well, Jay came to me and said he'd fired a couple of times . . . I think it was a couple of times, didn't you say, Meade? . . . at my brothers because they were trailing him. He said he didn't like to be trailed. Now, personally, I think it was in the nature of a joke."

"That's all," Creston said. Ben stepped back into the crowd. "What do you say now, Meade?"

"It didn't happen," Meade said.

Damnation! Suppose he had admitted to the truth? Then what explanation could he have given? The weight of Kansas Gulch was killing him literally, and still he could not let anyone know.

"He says it didn't happen!" Creston waved his arm. "Three reliable men say it did. What reason has Jay Meade to fire on those who accidentally come upon his tracks? We don't know. He refuses to tell us. We do know that he fired at Ed and Harvey Mercer with murderous intent. And we do know that his aim was better when he fired one shot at Ban Phillips under identical circumstances!"

Creston was silent. His words hung in the air, and then they settled into men's minds and killed all the effects of Bland's previous argument. Meade stared at Ben Mercer, who returned the look without expression.

"Billy Bland has said that Meade's rifle was clean when he returned to camp. Why wouldn't it be, gentlemen? He carries with him the materials for cleaning it. It was said that he had no reason to kill Phillips. And yet Phillips, an old man in years, knocked Meade down one evening and forbid him seeing his daughter."

Creston went on, but what he said was little needed on top of the evidence of the Mercers. Meade looked at Bland, who was talking to Oatis Peek and Luke Reardon.

"I demand we vote!" Creston said. "The evidence is clear enough!"

"No, it ain't," Bland said. "Ben Mercer was sweet on Phillips's daughter, and then Jay Meade beat him out. And now Ben has rigged up this story about Jay shooting at his brothers. Ben keeps saying Meade is innocent, and yet he's the one that tries to bring the worst evidence against him. . . ."

"I had to obey the orders of the court," Ben said.

"Do you still say Meade is innocent?"

Ben hesitated. The pause was damning, and his statement afterward was worse. "In spite of evidence, yes."

Bland's expression said that he wished he had not asked his question. "One other thing. Both Peek and Reardon saw George Unruh a lot farther from camp today than he says he was. They saw him come across that old burn up there, and that's a lot farther than he admits he was away from camp. Come out here, Unruh, and explain."

Unruh looked viciously at the Negroes. "Yeah, I was up in the old burn, but that's west of where Phillips was killed. I was looking for raspberries. I'd forgotten."

"It's odd that you'd forget such a thing at a time like this," Bland said.

"There's one thing I didn't forget," Unruh said, still staring at the Negroes. "I didn't have no rifle."

"That's right." Reardon nodded. "We seen him with the glasses I traded for with one of the fellows that left. He didn't have no rifle."

Bland was undisturbed. "I was not accusing Unruh of killing Phillips. I merely wanted to make clear again my point that a great many men were a considerable distance from this camp today, including one who admits he forgot. How many more are there who have forgotten . . . one of them for a damned good reason?"

There was some strength in the point, but Meade weighed that against what the Mercers had said, and he saw that it was not strong enough. Bland and Mercer looked at each other.

"There's no busting hurry," Bland said. "We'd just better hold off until we find out who else forgot how far he was from camp, until we can search every inch of the timber near where Phillips was killed. There's the tracks of a third man there, some place."

"Sure!" Creston cried. "Let's delay until Meade has a chance to get away! Bland knows that everybody's tracks are all through that timber now! I demand we vote on the guilt of Jay Meade . . . now!"

John Ledbetter licked his lips. He gauged the attitude of the crowd. He was the judge, but that was a nominal title only. The vote would be judgment itself. He appeared reluctant to speak, but Unruh and Blaisdell were already laying a rope in the middle of the street. Men shied away from it, now that the issue was at hand.

"On the uphill side if he's guilty!" Unruh shouted. "That's where the handiest trees are! If you're a damned fool and think he didn't do it, get on the creek side!"

Unruh was the first to stand on the uphill side of the rope. Blaisdell joined him. His Missouri followers came up beside him. The Negroes went to the other side, and Unruh cursed them. All tight and dead inside, Meade watched the cleavage. Ed and Harvey Mercer stood on the guilty side. Ben made no move at all.

Sammons took the creek side, dragging two Free State men with him. The two stood there foolishly, as if they were afraid to be on the wrong side of where the majority was gathering. Men with their minds made up switched for their own reasons at the last second, a few veering toward the innocent side of the rope after staring uphill. The vote was clear enough already—guilty.

Not looking at Meade, Bland murmured: "Do you want to make a run for it?"

He was innocent, but his life was being voted away on the wrong side of a frayed rope. Only the thought of Ellen kept Meade from sauntering toward the saloon. He could get Bland's pistol, go under the other side. Both groups in the street were now so absorbed in making up their minds, in exhorting friends to join them where they stood, that there was a desperate chance to get away. Ben Mercer was watching Meade, and now there was a sardonic grin on the Frenchman's lips. *I'd better take the chance*, Meade thought.

It was then he saw Ellen coming up the middle of the street. Ripley was beside her. Mrs. Pingree and Mrs. Ledbetter were on the flanks.

During the moments Meade hesitated, Ben Mercer walked up close to him, standing there with both hands in his pockets.

The vote was there, and it was two to one guilty. Ledbetter could count it, and his sentence must be hanging, or the crowd would disregard him altogether.

Bland's moon face was white. He said softly from the corner of his mouth: "If he makes a break, Mercer, and you try to use those Derringers in your pockets, I'll break your pretty neck with the edge of my hand."

Gray and bleak, Ledbetter stammered when he said: "Well, you've voted guilty, boys. It's hanging, and I don't want no part of it."

"We can handle it!" Unruh shouted. He reached for the rope lying in the sand.

Ellen Greenaway said: "You're a pack of fools, all of you. He isn't guilty and I have the proof." Her face was puffed from crying. She stood with her arms around her son. The women beside her were pale, but from the little group there came a force of determination that turned all heads and left Unruh frozen in a stooping position with his fingers on the rope.

"Jay Meade did not kill my father," Ellen said. "He was with me when the shot was fired. We both heard it."

Mrs. Pingree said: "I heard it, too. Ellen and I had been picking raspberries, and she had left me an hour before to join Jay Meade."

Ben Mercer was one of the first to grasp the full significance of the women's statements. He was by then standing on the not guilty side of the rope, and he called attention to his position. "I said all along Meade was not the man!"

Unruh straightened up. "She's lying!"

Ora Sammons took two long steps and knocked Unruh into a heap. "I told you to keep your mouth shut!" Unruh could not hear. He was unconscious.

Ledbetter found his voice. "Does anyone care to dispute the evidence now?" he challenged.

Blaisdell said: "It wasn't Meade, but somebody is guilty!" There was a rumble of agreement. Meade stared at

Ellen. It amazed him to realize how briefly he gave himself to relief now that three determined women had marched up the street and blasted everything apart—and with a lie.

Ben Mercer put his hand out. "I'm glad I stood on the right side all the way, Jay."

Meade did not bother to look at him. He went toward the women, now going back down the street. "Ellen! Can I see you a minute?"

She waited while the two other women went on with Ripley. The marks of grief and shock were on her face, but her expression was remote when she looked at Meade.

"You saved my neck, Ellen. I. . . ."

"We prevented a hanging." Her manner took all personal feeling from the deed.

Meade said: "You know I didn't do it."

"I suppose not."

The shading of her statement jarred him. "You made a . . . look what you did to yourself before the whole camp." He meant to say it gently but the words emerged as a rebuke. "What I mean is. . . ."

"Shall I go back and tell the truth, Jay?"

"For what you did for me, I. . . ."

"The three of us did it because living here amid the filth and hardship and constant growling of a bunch of savages is bad enough, without having a hanging that would not have brought back my father. That's why we did it."

She was ready to break, Meade knew. "Before God, it wasn't me, Ellen."

"I know it wasn't."

He saw a longing in her eyes, a desire to give way and lean on his strength, but, when he reached out toward her, she backed away.

"Leave me alone."

She ran down the street. The married women put their arms around her and led her toward Mrs. Ledbetter's tent. Mrs. Pingree glanced back just once. Her contempt for Meade and all men showed clearly in the brief gesture.

Meade shrugged helplessly. Ellen had saved his life, and he had not even thanked her or said how sorry he was about her father's death. Something had gone wrong.

Bland came up behind him. "You're a lucky boy. They told a good story at the right time. They were out berry picking, and Missus Pingree was taking care of Rip. I was watching her face when she told that story. Yours and Ben Mercer's. What's between you two, besides the woman?"

"Isn't that enough?"

Bland was looking sideways. He shook his head. "You want me to guess?"

"Do your best, Billy."

"Before the trial, when you were depending on me for help I couldn't give, I wouldn't say it because the lever was too big. Now I'll say it. When you decide to open up that strike you've made somewhere, I'd like to have one claim. It could be that Ben wants more than that."

Meade eyed the saloon man steadily. "Around a gold camp it doesn't take much to start a rumor, does it?"

"You've got it, Meade. If you mixed with people easy, it wouldn't have stood out, at least to me. But you don't mix, so every little thing you do sticks out like a young coyote's ears. You've hunted too much, and you've worked too hard on your claim even when it began to peter out. A bit of advice, Jay. You and me and ten more like us couldn't outslick Ben Mercer. If he's got you foul some way, you'd better provoke a fight with him right here in camp . . . and kill him."

Meade was of the same opinion himself. And then there

would be Ed and Harvey to deal with, and Meade remembered the revulsion on Ellen's face when she spoke of violence and savagery. He had a feeling of being trapped, with Kansas Gulch grinding against him on one side, and the Mercers on the other.

Billy Bland walked away.

Meade went down to the Phillips tent. Burris Pingree was there alone, an angular, quiet-spoken man with a great black moustache. He nodded. The dead man was on a cot with a blanket over him. He had been a big man, but now there seemed to be little bulk to him.

Pingree said: "The women will be back pretty soon to lay him out. Funeral first thing in the morning, I guess."

Meade pulled back the blanket and looked at Phillips's face for a moment. He had been shot in the back of the head and the ball had ranged clear through. Meade swallowed a nasty, metallic taste. He pulled the blanket back in place, shaking his head. "I can't understand it, Pingree."

"It's harder for Ellen and the boy to understand."

Stella Kinnison stepped inside the tent. "What can I do, Pingree?"

"The women are running things."

"I'll stick around," the madam said. "At a time like this we're all about the same." She looked at Meade. "You'd better get down on your knees before Missus Greenaway, brother. I've heard of men keeping their big mouths shut to protect a woman, but I'll be damned if I've ever seen it, and I don't think I've seen it today."

Meade went out and walked up the street. Miners watched him pass and did not speak. If they now believed that he was not guilty of shooting Ban Phillips, they had replaced one hostility with another, Meade thought. They were wondering strongly now about his hunting trips, and they were remembering, too, that he had never been a true part of Poverty.

He stood in the tent doorway looking up at Old Bugle. *Someday that Old Bugle up there is gonna blow big and mighty against what you just say, Mister Meade.* A Negro could speak those words because he did not have the rights of white men and so must turn to prophecy and things mysterious for hope and comfort. A prophecy of hogwash. Self-determination would always rule men's conduct. But still Meade stood looking at Old Bugle until the sky grew dark around it.

Someone built a large fire in front of the Phillips tent. Miners stood around it, talking quietly. Meade saw Ben Mercer take Ellen's arm when she came down the hill to go inside. He escorted her to the doorway and stood a moment with bowed head when she disappeared.

Silently Meade cursed Mercer until the emotion left him hollow. Billy Bland was right. The straight and simple way to settle a large part of Meade's problem was to kill Ben Mercer.

The resolve already made was strengthened the next morning when Meade watched Ellen clinging to Mercer's arm at the brief funeral service. She was turning toward him because of grief, because of his false air of sympathy, Meade thought.

In a few minutes Ben Mercer would be dead. If his death cost him Ellen, that was something Meade would have to balance later against the fact that Kansas Gulch would be secure again—almost.

So Jay Meade stood like the rest, with his head lowered, but his coat was buttoned across a pistol under his belt. Burris Pingree read some words. He tried to pray, but the thought stumbled. He said—"Amen."—and closed the

Bible. The women took Ellen away. Dirt began to rattle into the grave from the shovels of four miners.

Meade unbuttoned his coat. "I want to talk to you, Ben."

"Why, yes." Mercer was already walking toward Meade. "I had something to ask you, too." His voice was pleasant and controlled. Men who had jerked around at Meade's harsh words now stared curiously.

"I have a proposition about our extra claims," Mercer said.

The miners began to drift away.

"Keep your hands away from those Derringers," Meade said softly. "I don't want to kill you beside Ban's grave." They were fifteen feet apart. They talked that way until they were near the first claim at the edge of the creek.

Mercer spread his hands away from his body. "Would I come armed to a funeral, Jay?" He smiled.

"Get armed then."

The miners were watching again. They could not hear the words, but they saw the tension. The four men filling in the grave leaned on their shovels, and then they went to work again when Mercer walked casually toward Meade. "Now my idea about the extra claims we own . . . ," Mercer said, and that was loud enough to carry.

"I think you had Ban Phillips killed." Meade kept his voice low. He could see the bulges of Mercer's Derringers in the pockets of his black coat. He wanted to insult Mercer, to drive him into going for his weapons. "I think you put him on my trail, Mercer, and had someone waiting for him."

Mercer's expression did not change. He came a few more paces toward Meade before he stopped. Meade cursed him then, calling him names to make him fight. A tightness that was close to blankness settled on Mercer's face. He shook his head. "You can't force me into anything, Meade. You're probably a good man with that pistol and I don't care to die."

"We'll see." Meade stepped ahead. He struck Ben Mercer with his open hand and knocked him down. "We'll see what it takes to make you fight."

On one knee, Mercer stared. His eyes were like black chips.

"Get up!"

"Touch me again, Meade, and I'll spread the news of your miserable gulch all over these mountains. You think I won't?" Mercer stood up. "Go ahead, you Yankee bastard!"

They threw their personalities and the force of their minds into the narrow space between them, and in the end it was Meade who began to give. The roots of Kansas Gulch were sunk so deeply into his brain that they strangled anger and purpose and left only the fear that Mercer was not bluffing.

"I knew you would try to provoke a fight," Mercer said. "Long ago I made arrangements with my brothers. If anything ever happens to me, your gulch will be covered with miners in three hours."

"You lie, Mercer. You haven't even told Ed and Harvey what you found there."

"Told them, no. I said I had made arrangements. Find out the hard way, Meade, if you want to throw away your gulch."

Once more it was gold that outweighed all else. Meade raised his hand to strike Mercer again, and then he let it down slowly. Most galling of all was the thought that Mercer had judged him so accurately.

Ben Mercer smiled. "Call the hand."

Meade knew that he could not do so, and he was filled with the terrible frustration of a man who is not sure of whether he is being bluffed or not, but who knows he cannot take the long chance and find out.

Mercer brushed the sleeves of his coat where they had rested in the gravel. He turned his back and walked away.

VII

At noon there was a meeting near Blaisdell's hut. Meade looked down from his tent on the hill, wondering what was going on. Ben Mercer appeared to be directing things. After a while, unable to make head or tail of the meeting, Meade went in to cook his dinner.

Shortly afterward Billy Bland came up the hill.

"Ben is throwing his extra ground into a lottery down there, Meade. He claims you refused to have anything to do with the idea. Did he ask about it this morning?"

"No, he just made enough noise so people would think he was asking."

"It wouldn't be a bad idea if you fooled him, and did give the claims away. Ben figures you won't. It's a deal to cause trouble, Meade."

"Let Mercer give his ground away. I'll keep mine."

"You really don't want the extra ground."

"I'll have to judge that myself, Billy. What's your interest in the thing?"

"Let's say I'd like to see you live long enough to give me that claim we talked about. That puts it on a basis you can understand, Meade." Bland's voice was mild enough, but the meaning of his words cut sharply into Meade.

A stubbornness that was more anger than will made Meade say: "You'll get your claim, Billy, if I ever find anything. In the meantime, let me run my own business."

"Run it." Bland walked out unhurriedly.

Luke Reardon and Oatis Peek asked to come in.

"He's giving his extra claims away . . . that Ben," Reardon said. "Folks are gonna think we ought to do the same, Mister Meade. Trouble coming from that. Mister Mercer figures to see some trouble from that."

"So you want advice again?"

Reardon stiffened at the tone of Meade's voice. Peek said placatingly: "Them claims always made bad feeling, Mister Meade. We just wondering what you plan about yours."

"So, if I give mine into a lottery, you fellows will, too?"

"Yeah," Reardon said. "We wouldn't want to put ourselves against the whole camp, rights or no rights."

"I'm keeping my claims," Meade said.

Reardon frowned. "You sure that's the thing to do?"

"You asked me what I was going to do, and that's the answer," Meade said angrily.

"Come on, Oatis." Reardon took his companion away.

Ben Mercer was announcing the results of the drawing when Meade went toward the creek. There were happy shouts from the winners, good-natured complaints from those who still held poor claims in a gulch that was petering out.

"I regret that I was unable to interest certain others who hold several claims," Mercer said, "our friend, Jay Meade, and Reardon's bunch."

All at once there was no good nature left in the miners. They glared across the creek where the Negroes were at work.

"You'll find hogs everywhere!" Unruh shouted, looking at Meade.

Either by design or chance, only two Southerners had won claims to replace their worked-out grounds. Meade chose to think it was by Ben Mercer's will; the man was stirring trouble with a big paddle. He had aimed with a purpose to bring about what Meade had thought to let attrition do—break up the camp. Meade thought he knew Mercer thoroughly now, even if there were fools in Poverty who still looked up to him.

Meade worked without interest, glancing now and then toward Old Bugle. Ed Mercer was not with his half-brother today, but Ben was at the sluice. Where was Ed? The thought kept worrying Meade, and the only answer he could think of was Kansas Gulch. He forced himself to stay where he was.

Johnny Creston was going from sluice to sluice, gesturing, talking earnestly to Northerners and Southerners alike in a low voice. After an hour of that there was less and less work.

Then Creston yelled: "All right, let's go!"

About one half the miners dropped their tools and followed Creston across the creek toward the sluice where Reardon's group was working. Luke Reardon saw them coming and walked toward them, waving his companions back. He drew a pistol and waited, a stocky, defiant figure standing there, with his shoulders bursting from his torn shirt.

"We're taking over your extra ground," Creston said.

Reardon shook his head. "You ain't taking nothing that belongs to us."

His quiet assurance and the pistol stopped them for a moment. Meade knew that if he or anyone else threw themselves strongly into that instant of hesitation, taking the Negroes' side, the quarrel could be turned into an argument that would end in compromise.

Habit kept Meade from acting. Creston was unarmed. He was in the forefront of the miners, and now he went on forward. "No use to try to make trouble, Reardon. You're the only one that'll get hurt."

"You ain't taking nothing," Reardon said.

Oatis Peek yelled: "Let 'em have the old ground, Luke. It ain't worth. . . ."

Someone shoved Creston. He stumbled ahead. The miners came in with a rush. Meade saw Reardon fire two shots, both over the heads of the mob. He brought the pistol down to shoot directly into the miners, but by then they were upon him. He went down in the rush that carried over him and on to Peek and the other Negroes. Shouts and *thuds* and the grunting of enraged men. There were two more pistol shots.

The mob was trampling and kicking the Negroes when Ben Mercer came running. "Stop it before somebody gets killed!"

It did not stop until Reardon and his men were kicked insensible. Someone yelled: "That nigger killed Creston! Let's finish 'em off right now!"

For once Ben Mercer's voice was lost in a tumult of enraged shouts. Driven then by things he thought he had renounced, Meade started running toward the mob. Ora Sammons and his Free State men were ahead of him. They had taken no part in the action, but now they came in a wedge, brandishing picks and pick handles.

Sammons's hat flew off as he leaped a sluice. He was roaring like a buffalo. The Free State men smashed into the mob, and without regard for politics they swung their weapons. Unruh, who always seemed to be in Sammons's way, went flying over a sluice section with his front teeth smeared through his lips.

The mêlée was over before Sammons spoke coherently. "You ain't stomping 'em to death!" he bellowed. "I seen where Reardon shot, clean over everybody's heads!"

Meade stopped where Creston lay. No one had paid any more attention to the prostrate man than to observe that he was down. Creston was shot in the back but he was not dead. Mercer came over and stayed long enough to see the facts, and then he shouted: "Creston is shot in the back! It couldn't have been Reardon!"

As usual Ben Mercer was emerging from trouble as a peacemaker, Meade thought.

Someone yelled: "The damned Yankees still didn't have no business mixing in!"

Staggering from a blow that had bloodied his nose, Hardin Clements came from his dazed condition enough to respond to the war cry. He started to draw his pistol. One of Sammons's men clubbed him with a pick handle.

Kneeling by Creston, Meade saw that one blow changed the whole meaning of the action. The original purpose of the mob was a thing apart from now. Sammons and his Kansas followers had restored the issue of politics in one skull-thumping charge. The Southerners drew apart resentfully, and even the Northerners who had been bruised by the Free State men now sided with their kind, suddenly finding reasons to believe their hurts had been caused by the pro-slavery group, at least by indirection.

Meade knew it was no great mental feat for them to make the change, with politics ever smoldering in a coal bed of emotions. He lifted Creston and started across the creek.

Ellen met him as he walked around a sluice. She looked at him sharply for an instant, as if accusing Meade of the trouble.

113

"Bring him to my tent," she said.

Behind Meade, Mercer said: "You've had enough grief, Ellen. We'll take him up to my place."

"My tent is closer, Ben."

Meade put the wounded man on Ban Phillips's cot. Creston opened his eyes. "How bad is it, Meade?"

"We'll see. Who was right behind you, Creston?"

"Everybody," Creston whispered.

Ben Mercer said: "Some fool trying to shoot Reardon stumbled or was jostled."

"This is a bad time to die," Creston said. "I don't want to die just now."

Billy Bland came in. He knew more of gunshot wounds than any man in camp. Mrs. Pingree was right behind him. She said: "Come up to my tent, Ellen."

"In a minute." Ellen glanced at Meade.

"I'll take Ripley with me now." Mrs. Pingree shook her head. "A slaughter pen, that's what this camp is." She went out and called to Ripley.

Bland was turning Creston over. The wounded man stared at Meade. "I didn't want you to hang, Meade. I. . . ."

"Take it easy, Creston," Mercer said. "Bland can patch you up as good as new."

Meade took Ellen's arm and guided her outside. Sammons and a group of Northern men were bringing the Negroes across the creek. Reardon was the only one who could walk unaided, and one man was being carried.

"I haven't had a chance to talk to you, Ellen. . . ."

"There's not much you can say. Today just about settles my mind about you, Jay. This could have been avoided if you had listened to Ben when he asked you to put your claims into the drawing. Then Reardon would have done the same."

"He lies if he says he ever asked me."

Ellen shook her head. "Ben Mercer doesn't lie."

"Oh, hell."

"He's the only man in this camp who has tried honestly to prevent trouble. At first, I thought you didn't care one way or another, but now I'm beginning to believe you're the one who's stirring the Northern men to make trouble."

"Me?"

"My father thought so, too."

"Mercer pumped him full of lies, and he's told you the same lies. I'll drag him out here and choke the truth out of him."

Meade turned back toward the tent. He was at the fly before he remembered what might happen to Kansas Gulch if he laid hands on Ben Mercer.

"What's the matter?" Ellen asked. "It isn't lack of physical courage entirely, is it? You've already attacked him once. He faced you down with moral courage and honesty. Ask him out, Jay. You won't have to choke him to find out the truth. He's already told it."

Trembling, Meade walked away from the tent. To lose Kansas Gulch was to lose everything. He had held the thought so long that he could not now deny it. He went back to Ellen.

She was frowning, and her expression had changed from calm contempt to wonder. She gave Meade a chance. "Is there some trouble between you and Ben that I don't understand?"

Bland had asked the same question. It was a pattern, a threat to Kansas Gulch. Meade said: "Ask Ben. He doesn't lie."

She let her silence tell him how weak an answer he had made. In the tent, Creston cried out in pain.

"Is there anything wrong in wanting to keep what's mine?" Meade demanded.

The Northerners were clustered in front of the Negroes' bough huts now. Ellen looked in that direction as she answered. "Ben asked you to release your ground to avoid ill feeling and possible trouble, and then he sent Reardon and Peek to ask you." She shook her head. "You're right, what's yours is yours, no matter what. I guess I was mistaken in thinking you ever have been any different."

"Mercer lies. He never asked me. He engineered everything to cause trouble."

"I don't see how you can say that." Ellen gave Meade a long look that carried regret, the sad expression of lost confidence.

Ben Mercer came out of the tent and called her name. She hesitated, looking at Meade. She gave him a small, dismal smile, and went down the hill to Mercer.

Meade walked away then, not to his tent, but into the trees on the hill. He kept walking, using physical exertion as a means of clearing his mind. Ellen had gone with Ben Mercer. She would stay with him. Meade had seen as much in the last look she gave him. The events of the last few days had upset her, left her vulnerable to Mercer's smooth talk and politeness.

Without throwing Kansas Gulch on the board, Meade had no way to combat Mercer's lies. Shaken with anger, remembering the faint regret in Ellen's eyes when she walked away from him, Meade kept plunging up the hill. It was after dark when he went home.

The first thing he noticed when he came from the trees was the absence of lantern light in the Mercer tent.

When Meade struck a match in his own tent, the light fell on Bland's broad face. He was lying on Meade's cot.

"Make yourself at home, Billy. Who's running your business?"

"Ledbetter. There's trouble stewing up tonight, but I can't put my finger on it. Fix yourself a bite to eat, Meade. You and me may be up all night. Creston is a little tougher than I thought."

"What's he got to do with anything?"

"I'll have a bite myself." Bland sat up. "Go on, cook something. I kept the fire up for you."

Meade knew he should resent Bland's intrusion; no one had shared Meade's life for a long time. But there was assurance and strength and common sense in Billy Bland, and Meade now recognized his own need for all three qualities.

"What's Creston got to do with things?" Meade asked.

"I'll tell you when we're eating."

Meade went to work. Suddenly he said: "You're right, Billy. I found a pile of gold, and now I'm hoping I live to use it."

"And Ben Mercer is sure of it?"

"Good and sure. He knows where it is."

Bland was silent for a while. "You could beat him any time by throwing the whole works open to everyone."

"Am I a damned fool?"

"Maybe, under the circumstances. Everybody in camp is beginning to suspect you've got something. Suppose a third man finds it?"

"He'll be just like me and Ben," Meade said. "He'll keep his mouth shut and wonder how to get rid of me and Mercer."

"And that's what you're wondering now?"

"I may be."

"Put more salt in the beans." Bland pointed. "Well,

you had your chance. What happened?"

"He wouldn't fight."

"I saw that. What else, though?"

"He said he'd tell the world about my find if I touched him again."

"Bluffing?"

Meade cursed. "Would I have let him go if I could have told that?"

They said no more until the food was ready.

Then Bland opened: "Two of Reardon's boys are so stove up, busted ribs and things, that they can't move."

"Why don't you say it's my fault?" In a way it was Meade's fault; he knew it and that was why he spoke defensively.

"Mercer rigged it, up to a point, and then it went all in his favor by accident. The luck is always with the devil, Meade. For an Abolitionist, Creston talked too many times to Ben in the last few weeks."

"So I noticed. How do you figure Ben used Creston?"

Bland took a bite of salt side. "When I get rich off that claim you're going to get me, I'm going to buy a thousand dollars' worth of carrots and string beans and eat them at one sitting. Sure, Ben used Johnny Creston. Just how is something we may find out before morning."

They finished eating and rose.

"Be sure you got your pistol," said Bland. "We're going down the hill."

There was still no light in the Mercer tent.

Bland stopped just a moment to glance into the saloon. It was not crowded. A bad sign, Meade thought, for the few men at the plank bar were miners with no strong political sentiments.

Burris Pingree met Meade and Bland as they turned

away from the saloon. Meade had to ask it. "Is Ellen up at your place, Pingree?"

"Why . . . ?" Pingree hesitated. "Yeah, I think she is, Jay. I haven't been there for about a half hour."

She was not there, Meade knew; Pingree was a poor liar.

Johnny Creston was propped up with blankets. There was bright blood at the corners of his mouth and the pinch of death was on his features. On a cot across from him Ed and Harvey Mercer sat like black vultures, waiting.

"How many of his friends did you run away?" Bland asked.

Harvey shook his head. "Nobody but Stella Kinnison came since you left. He never did have any real friends. It's sure that Meade ain't one. You can leave, Meade."

"I'll stay."

"No," Harvey said, "you're going to leave."

Meade drew his pistol and put it on the brothers.

"That's right," Bland said. "Keep the boys quiet."

"What the hell is this?" Ed started to rise.

Meade knocked him over the cot and leaped around the end of it. He kicked Ed in the elbow when the man reached for a pistol in his belt. "Pull it out with two fingers, Ed, and toss it over here."

Bland was covering Harvey with a pistol. "The same goes for you," Bland said. "It's bad enough that a man should die, without two buzzards sitting beside him to see that he don't unburden his soul."

"Ben," Creston said in a bubbly voice. "Ben, you promised. . . ." He coughed up blood and nearly choked.

Bland grabbed a towel and leaned over him.

When Creston could speak again, he said: "I don't feel so bad, Billy, just tight in the chest. I'll be all right, won't I?"

"We'll do what we can," Bland said.

"What did Ben promise you, Creston?" Meade asked.

"Nothing. I'll be all right."

The Mercers looked at each other.

"Don't let anyone force any lies out of you, Creston," Harvey said.

It was a dismal wait that lay heavily on Meade. Perhaps Creston had played the game as Meade had played it, with no regard for anyone else. Now he was dying and no one came near the tent, and those who waited beside him were not his friends.

The coughing grew worse. The well of life was draining inside Johnny Creston, and now he realized it. His eyes were wild as he looked around the tent, where the shadows of four men looked like great blots on the canvas. He fixed on Meade.

"I didn't want to hang you, Meade. It was the gold I was thinking of."

Ed Mercer said: "You're crazy, Creston. You're seeing ha'nts. You're dying and. . . ."

"Shut up!" Harvey said. "He ain't dying. He's going to be all right, ain't you, Creston?"

"No," Creston said. "I. . . ." He choked again and for a few moments Meade thought he was going, but his voice came again weakly. "I killed him. I didn't want to see Meade hang, but Ben said it was the only way."

"You killed Phillips?" Meade asked.

"Yes. You and him had a rich strike. Ben said it was a way to get rid of you both. I shot him."

"You swear before God you're telling the truth?" Bland asked.

"Before God, I do."

"Ben put you up to starting the trouble over the claims,

too, didn't he?" Bland asked.

Creston did not hear. He had the vague look of a man trying to remember where he had lost something long ago. And then he began to speak about the rights of Negroes, and it was not long afterward that the life frothed out of him and left him neither Abolitionist nor pro-slaver.

Ed Mercer laughed. "What good do you think you've done? We never heard him say a thing, me and Harv."

"Two against two," Harvey said.

Meade stepped aside. He motioned with the pistol. "Get out. Run to Ben and tell him he'll have to figure up another sneaky plan."

"You're handy with that pistol," Harvey said. "One day I'll catch you when you don't have it."

Meade put the pistol in his belt.

"Pick your gun up, Harvey. Both of you pick up your guns if you want to."

Harvey licked moisture from the corner of his mouth. "Oh, no, mister. Don't touch it, Ed. There'll be another day."

The Mercers went out.

Bland said: "For a man that thought he was living as he damned pleased, you've managed to get mixed up with the camp pretty well, after all. This is just a start."

"So we know who killed Ban Phillips, and we know who sent him to do the job. Now we. . . ."

"Harvey was right when he said two against two." Bland shook his head slowly. "Notice how quiet it is out there? At the moment nobody much gives a damn who killed old Ban, even if we could make them believe."

"You think they're getting ready for more trouble?" Meade asked.

"For something that almost started when that crazy

Barto was here. I'll bet you money that Ben Mercer sent for him. If I had been two days late coming back from that trip, I would have walked smack into a war in this gulch."

Meade nodded. "So maybe we've got it now."

"It's what you want, ain't it?"

Meade shook his head. "Why would it be?"

"You were holding out your strike until the camp was gone. This will help it go."

"But I wasn't trying to start trouble."

Bland was looking sideways at Meade. "No, you didn't try to start trouble."

"But I didn't care if it came . . . is that what you're getting at, Billy?"

"Yeah," Bland said curtly. "You and Ben Mercer played the same game, only in different ways."

"Why, damn you, Billy. . . ."

"Damn me all you want," Bland said wearily. "Get a couple of buckets of water and let's wash these blankets for the girl."

The saloon was dark when Meade went to the creek. Reardon was tending a fire near the Negroes' huts. Inside one of the bough shelters an injured man spoke plaintively.

Up the hill, at the Mercer tent, Harvey called urgently: "Ben! Ben!" And then there was a mutter of low voices, as if Ben had stepped out and rebuked his half-brother for being loud.

After that there was an uneasy silence in the gulch. It was late night and there should be quiet, but it seemed to Meade, standing at the creek with his buckets, that the place was deserted.

He was washing blankets with Bland when the saloon man said casually: "Where did Ed and Harvey go to sleep?"

Meade stared at him wickedly.

VIII

In the bleak, chill hours before dawn Ellen came out of Ben
Mercer's tent. It had been a mistake, more hers than his, for
she knew what a man was. She stood on the cold hillside,
thinking of all the arguments she could summon to justify
her act—she had been sick and tired of the brutality of Poverty, and Ben Mercer had been the only gentleman in camp,
so she had turned to him when it was apparent that Jay
Meade was so steeped in selfishness that she would never
want him on any terms. She had been vulnerable. The cold
and the silence jeered at her. No matter what arguments she
gathered, one thought overshadowed all the rest; she had
gone of her free will to Ben Mercer's tent. It had not been
what she wanted, and now she knew it.

Let the truth revile her later; she was chilled now and
low in spirits. She saw a dim light in her tent. Creston was
still struggling for his life, she thought. She did not want to
go home, but she could not go to Pingree's now, sneaking
in like a bedraggled trollop.

Death had drained the bitterness from Creston's face,
but he was not a pleasant sight when Ellen pushed through
the flaps. She recoiled with a start.

"I'm sorry. Just a minute, Missus Greenaway." Billy
Bland was keeping vigil. He removed his coat and spread it
over the dead man's chest and face. "He died a few hours

ago," he added unnecessarily.

She should have known it, Ellen thought. Harvey
Mercer, when he called Ben out, had said—"That damned
Creston spilled everything before he. . . ."—and then Ben
had cut him off. Spilled what? She wondered vaguely for a
moment, but whatever it was it could not be important to
her.

"I can take him outside," Bland said. "You. . . ."

"No, leave him. I don't feel like sleeping, anyway."

"Meade was here until a while ago," Bland said. It
seemed irrelevant, but Ellen knew that it was not. "Was
he?"

"Yeah." Bland looked at her sideways. "You don't blame
him for all the grief in camp, do you? You've sort of acted
that way for some time."

"I blame a group of greedy men," she said. "And of
them, Jay Meade is by far the worst."

"You're sure of that, Missus Greenaway?" There was
something penetrating in the question that shocked her into
realizing the truth—she had not completely doubted Meade
no matter how she tried. Perhaps she should have tried to
help him become the man she wanted him to be, instead of
criticizing his one-way attitude. But all that was done now.
If anger against Jay Meade, more than anything else, had
sent her to Mercer, all that was also beyond changing.

She said: "Good night, Mister Bland."

"You've got a lot of guts to stay here alone," Bland said.
"I know men who wouldn't do it. It's a shame you haven't
the guts to . . . to. . . ." He started out.

"To do what?" she asked.

"To stand by a man, no matter what." Bland went out.

The rebuke went through all her defenses because it was
akin to her own thoughts. She stood alone in the tent, with

the lantern burning low, and the dead man a lump that could not be forgotten because it bore human form. She turned her back on Creston. She wanted to run from the tent, but there was no place to go.

She herself had closed the door at Pingree's. She could never go back to Ben Mercer, and she had put a solid wall between herself and Meade. Slowly she sat down on a cot, holding her forehead with spread, tense fingers.

Billy Bland paused at the door of his saloon, looking up at Meade's tent. People who tried to walk alone got themselves into hellish fixes sooner or later, and that was just what Meade had done. That woman alone in her tent was worth more to a man than any gold he would ever find in the mountains. But you had to have had gold and lost it—and lost other things, too—before you knew. Bland had lost them all at times. He knew. He had given words to Meade and Ellen; he could not give them his experience, or even an understanding of it.

With an irritability uncommon to him, he jerked open the careful ties Ledbetter had made in the tent flaps when he closed the saloon. Bland strode inside and lit a lantern. By lifting the two kegs on the bar, he made a rough check into the evening's business. There had not been much business. His mind was not fully on the saloon until he noticed that the four full kegs of whiskey that should have been near his cot were not there. After a while he discovered, also, that his five gallon tin of coal oil was gone.

John Ledbetter was painfully honest. Someone had raided the tent after he closed up. Bland stepped outside, listening, almost sniffing for the trouble four kegs of whiskey could cause. Although he could not say exactly why, it seemed to him that few men were in camp tonight.

The quiet bore a heavy waiting quality that Bland did not like.

He walked down the street to Ora Sammons's hut. Sammons usually grunted in his sleep and snored like a rheumatic bear, but now the dark pile of brush and boughs was still.

"Sammons!" Bland called. There was no answer. He lit a match, cupping it in his hands to direct the light. The hut was empty.

Bland went on to the lean-to where Hardin Clements and three other Southerners lived. They were not there.

Bland then went back up the street and climbed swiftly to Meade's tent.

"Meade?"

"Come in!" Meade said at once, and Bland knew he had been lying awake inside.

"The camp seems to be deserted."

"That's good," Meade said. "I hope they're all halfway to Denver by now."

"You know what's up . . . the scrap today has brought all the bad feeling to a head. Someone stole four kegs of whiskey from my place tonight."

"You can stand it," Meade said.

"I'll keep trying," Bland said patiently, "although I'm beginning to doubt that you're worth it. They're split into two camps, somewhere out in the timber, I'd say. They're getting fixed to fight over this damned gulch."

"That's fine," Meade said. "Let them do their best."

"If I thought you meant that. . . ."

"You'll get your claim all the quicker, Billy, if they kill each other off. I hope only that Ben Mercer isn't overlooked when the firing starts."

There was a savagery in Meade's tone that gave Bland

the clue to Meade's thoughts. For a while it was silent in the tent, and then Bland said matter-of-factly: "It's your fault about Ellen, Jay. You drove her to Ben."

Meade said nothing for a while, and then his anger gushed from him. "You're just like her, Billy, You think a man should spend his time doing things for a bunch of fools and hotheads who can't take care of themselves. You want them nursed along and coddled and kept from cracking each other's skulls. You expect a man to forget his own problems to help someone else."

"Yes. Sometimes that isn't such a bad way of operating, Jay."

"It is for me. Let Ben Mercer stop their fighting. He'll get the credit for it, anyway."

"Who gets the credit for something is not always the most important thing," Bland said.

"I haven't noticed you busting yourself to be a peace-maker, Billy."

"No, you haven't."

"Then what do you want me to do, hunt up these imaginary camps and get the boys to shake hands with each other?"

"Some things are right, and some ain't right," Bland said evenly. "I never did consider a senseless fight as being helpful to anyone. As for the claim you mentioned . . . you keep it, Meade. My saloon . . . I've had saloons and other businesses in a dozen places, some good, some bad. You lay here in the dark, Meade, trying to tell yourself you don't care about losing Ellen, thinking that gold will fill any need you'll ever feel."

Bland started out.

"They may not be split up, getting ready to fight," Meade said. "Maybe someone besides Creston was tipped off to Kansas Gulch. Maybe they've all stampeded over there."

"I hope so," Bland said. "I hope so."

When dawn was a bare promise and life was at its lowest point, they came down the hill and went toward the huts of the Negroes. They were viciously drunk, but they walked carefully in the dark. One was carrying a five-gallon tin. The contents kept sloshing up against an axe slash in the top of the can.

That one was George Unruh. With him walked Loy Blaisdell and two others. It was Unruh's plan. Hardin Clements, who had led the Southerners away from Poverty to a camp deep in the timber above Stella Kinnison's place, had cursed the idea. Clements was for war, but not for a sneaky, vicious sort of war. But now Clements was in a drunken slumber and Unruh was leading men to strike a blow.

Beside a dying fire, Luke Reardon lay curled on the ground, trembling a little from cold even as he slept. He did not waken when Unruh and the others came up behind the huts. Unruh swung the can, making shoveling movements. Through the rent in the top coal oil spewed out on the spruce boughs of the first hut.

"Soak it good," Blaisdell muttered. "Whoever heard before of niggers wanting to own the whole world? Soak it good."

"Shut up," Unruh whispered hoarsely. He moved to the second hut and swung the can.

One of the injured men inside cried out: "Someone's throwing water on us, Luke!"

Reardon roused on his elbow, staring blankly at the embers of the watch fire. "Luke! They's somebody fooling around!" Oatis Peek said. Reardon smelled the heavy fumes of the coal oil then. He leaped up, dragging at the pistol in his belt.

Someone shot. Reardon fell across the fire. Grunting in pain, he rolled clear and got on his knees. He emptied his pistol blindly at the sound of men behind the shelters. An instant later a match flared in the hands of a man crouching in the darkness. One hut was ablaze in seconds, and then the other. One of the attackers gave a drunken, triumphant whoop and fired into the burning mass of black-edged smoke and crackling boughs, and then the Southerners ran up the hill.

"Oh, God!" Reardon cried. He began to crawl toward his screaming comrades. Peek alone came out, scrabbling on his hands and knees, the front of his clothing in flames.

"Roll on the ground!" Reardon cried. "Roll, Oatis, roll!"

Luke Reardon crawled into the first hut and got his powerful hands around a man, but the man was struggling, burning, and Luke, too, was aflame by then. He could not pull the man out before the smoke and heat choked off his strength.

Ellen Greenaway came running with one of the wet blankets Meade and Bland had washed that night. She used it first as a shield to get close enough to grab Reardon by the ankles. She dragged him toward the creek, and then she used the blanket to smother his burning clothing.

The huts were crackling, fiery pyres then and the screams had ended. Peek's clothes were still smoking. He began to throw dirt with his hands. He ran toward a sluice to get a shovel, falling into the creek when he slipped. He came back with a shovel and threw dirt on the huts.

He was still throwing dirt, with tears running down his cheeks, when Billy Bland took the shovel away from him gently, and said: "Let's see what we can do for Luke, Oatis."

Meade arrived a moment later, and then the Mercers.

The heavy stems of branches were still burning, throwing an orange glow on the scene. Meade got a clear picture of Ben Mercer's expression. Ben's face was pale, his lips slack, and sheer horror had shattered his poise.

This was not on Mercer's order then, Meade thought; it must be the work of drunken maniacs. As he watched Ben, it came to Meade that the shock on the man's face was caused by the physical moment and not by any moral revulsion.

"Mother of God," Mercer muttered. "Who . . . ?"

"Take Luke to my tent," Ellen said to Bland.

"Creston is already there." Bland chewed his lip. "What a camp," he murmured.

Ben Mercer recovered. He said to Ed and Harvey: "Get over there and move Creston. Quick!"

Reardon was conscious as they put him in a blanket litter. His eyes kept rolling toward the flames. "Get Plym and Mack and Douglas out of there. Where's Oatis? Is you all right, Oatis? Get the boys out of there, please." When they were carrying him toward Ellen's tent, he said: "I'm cold . . . I'm so awful cold."

Meade was on one corner of the litter. He saw Ben take Ellen's arm and motion with his head. "You've had plenty, Ellen. It won't be any place for you."

She pushed his arm away, not looking at him, and walked beside the litter. The Mercer brothers came out with Creston's body. They dumped it in the street and stood there, rubbing their hands on their pants, looking to Ben for further orders.

"Put something over him," Ben said.

Harvey shrugged. "There ain't nothing."

"Get something, then, you idiots!"

Ben was in a fine mood, Meade thought, starting with that rebuff of a minute before. He watched Ben and Ellen. Once more, at the doorway of the tent, Mercer tried to dissuade Ellen from going in. Again she pushed his hand away, not looking at him.

Ben Mercer looked at Meade then. Meade gave him a thin, one-sided smile and a wicked nod, and then he helped carry Reardon inside.

"Grease," Bland said. "Round up all the grease you can, Ellen."

She gave him what she had, and then she darted out to go to the other tents. Meade heard Ben say something to her in a protesting tone. She did not answer. Then Mercer said to his half-brothers: "Start digging some graves." He spoke loudly. "You may as well dig one for Reardon while you're at it."

Reardon smiled vaguely. "Old Ben . . . he cain't scare me now. I know. I'm cold, Mister Bland. I been shot, too. He cain't scare me none now."

"You got one of them," Bland said. "You got Unruh right there at the edge of the huts. He burned a little, too."

"That don't make me feel no better," Reardon said. "Do you suppose if we'd give up our claims, like they wanted . . . ?"

"It wouldn't have made any difference, Luke," Bland said. "See if you can get that other shoe off, Meade."

Luke Reardon might have died from the bullet wound in his side alone; the burns were terrible. He lived until afternoon, and they could not put enough blankets on him to keep him warm.

He looked at Meade and said: "You remember, Mister

131

Meade, what I tell you once about that Old Bugle up there on the rocks?"

"I remember."

"That was right. Someday she gonna blow long and loud against some things, Mister Meade." He died with a smile on his blistered lips.

Ellen, who had been away since noon, came back into the tent.

"He's gone?"

"Yeah." Bland still watched Meade.

"We'll have to hang somebody for this," Meade said. "It didn't come from politics. It's a crime against all of us."

"You're progressing." Bland covered Reardon's face. "Where's Ben, do you know, Ellen?"

She gave Bland a quick look, as if searching for the meaning behind the question. "He and his brothers went into the timber where all the other Southerners are."

"And Sammons took his crowd into the timber on the other side of the gulch," Bland said. "I don't think you're going to get anybody together for a hanging, Jay."

"It wouldn't help matters if he could," Ellen said.

"What will?" Meade asked.

Ellen shook her head wearily. "I don't know. I do know that I'm taking Rip and leaving here as soon as I can get away."

Bland nodded. "In a few days I can let you have my mules. I'm about ready to go myself. You, Meade?"

Meade thought of Kansas Gulch.

"No!" He looked at Ellen. "If they fight across this gulch, and they will, you'd better stay at my tent, you and the boy. I won't be there."

Ellen gave him a long, even look. There was a bleak, bone-tired expression on her face. "All right."

Bland got up heavily. "The Ledbetters and the Pingrees had best move their tents. I guess Stella is far enough out of the way to be in the clear." He shook his head. "Well, the camp was about played out, anyway. I want no part of what's coming. They're fools, but it's been breeding ever since that crazy Barto was here."

"You what?" Meade asked. "That's not the way you've been talking."

"Well, now I've changed my mind." Bland shrugged. He went out.

"I could have given up those claims," Meade said. "It might have prevented this."

Ellen eyed him steadily. "It might have." There was no bite to her words.

"I liked the Negroes."

"I liked my father, too."

For a moment Meade was of a mind to tell her about Creston's confession, but then he thought that Ben Mercer would deny it, and his half-brothers would sustain him. Even if she believed Meade, knowing who had killed old Ban would not make her feel any better.

The exhausted look of her hurt him. He reached out gently and took her in his arms. She came to him without protest, but then she was inert, merely resting her head against his shoulder for a moment with a tired sigh, and then she stepped away from him.

"You'll have to get some rest, Ellen. Show me what you want to move up to my tent."

"I can do it."

Meade started out. "I'll get some help for Reardon."

Bland had already done that. He and Peek were standing in the street, waiting for John Ledbetter, who was coming down the hill.

"Everything is ready," Peek said. There was a gray and lonely look about him. He kept raising his eyes toward the sky.

Meade looked at Old Bugle. It was not a protest of sound, no matter how loud, that was needed, but fire and the sword, the straightforward vengeance of Osawatomie Brown.

We are responsible only to the Lord. Strike them down! I will not be judged by men. The words fell distantly now on Meade's senses. Old Brown was partly right and greatly wrong, but still a man to act upon his convictions.

"Look there," Bland said, nodding his head toward the hill above Ledbetter.

Hardin Clements had come from the trees. He was carrying a rifle. He raised it high in both hands, and then he laid it on the ground and started down the hill.

From the crest of the steep rise across the creek a rifle boomed. Dirt flew off to the side of Clements. He stopped. "Sammons! I'm coming down peacefully! Sammons . . . !"

Sammons's answer came heavily. "What are you after, more coal oil, you pro-slave bastard?"

There was no more shooting. Clements came down to where the little group waited in the street. His eyes were bloodshot, his mouth thin and tight. "I didn't want anything like that burning to happen. Unruh sneaked away after we went to sleep."

"There were others with him," Meade said. "Where are they now?"

Clements ignored him. "I didn't want it to happen, Oatis."

"I know you didn't, Mister Clements," Peek said. "I know you didn't."

"We can stop this thing before it starts," Meade said. He

knew the gulch claims were not the entire point of trouble now, but he used them as a feeler. "Is it the extra ground you fellows want?"

"Whatever we want, we'll take," Clements said. "We've made up our minds that there's too little gold here and too many Yankees, and you're one of them, Meade."

"If what happened last night meets the approval of your bunch, then I am a Yankee again," Meade said.

"He didn't want it to happen," Peek said.

Meade held his temper under the hot, insulting look Clements gave him. "If I can get Sammons down here to talk it over with you, Clements. . . ."

"Never mind." Clements shook his head. "I don't know who the hell you think you are, Meade. You've stuck you nose in the air ever since this camp was made, and now, when it's starting to blow up in your face, the yellow streak starts running in you and you whine for peace."

Meade stepped forward, but all at once Bland was blocking the way to Clements. The saloon man was bulky and his body was hard. He shoved Meade back with his hip almost casually. "What did you come for, Clements?" Bland asked.

"No more than to tell Oatis I'm sorry for what happened."

"If you're so damned sorry, then turn in the men that did it," Meade said.

"Turn them in to whom?" Clements looked at the ridge where the Northern men were waiting. "To them?"

"Bring your bunch down, too," Meade said. "We'll have a trial. There's several things that I'd like to bring up."

"You've waited too long to become a citizen of this camp," Clements said. "When my bunch comes down here, they'll be coming to stay, and there won't be any Yankees here."

"Your bunch . . . or Ben Mercer's?" Bland asked mildly.

"They're Southerners, that's enough." Clements put his hand on Peek's shoulder. "I'm sorry, Oatis."

"Luke was the last," Peek said. "He went just a while ago. He was the last one. The others, they went real quick. It'd be nice if you could stay for the burying, Mister Clements."

"I'll stay, Oatis. Luke was a good boy."

Meade was baffled; he had seen the same understanding before between Southerners and Negroes, a sensing of things that no true Northerner could fully grasp.

John Ledbetter was nervous. "Well, we'd better be about it. I've got to move my tent right away."

"A good idea," Clements said. "Where you from, Ledbetter?"

"From South Carolina, Clements, but I came from the hills. Your politics are not mine, remember that, and neither are they Abolitionist."

"Our side will leave you alone," Clements said. "I can't speak for the Yankees."

"My God, Clements!" Meade cried. "Do you understand what you're trying to start here?"

"I'm trying to start it? It was one of your fine Abolitionists, Johnny Creston, that opened the ball yesterday. He was all for the rights of niggers until they got one more claim than he owned," Clements said. "Why do you think we pulled out to the hills? You stinking Yankees took a sneak in the night, and we caught on. You would have liked to caught us in the gulch here, with you up on the hill, wouldn't you?"

"Let's bury Luke," Bland said. "We can agree on that, at least."

When Ora Sammons saw what was going on, he shouted

that he was coming down unarmed.

Only Peek was not nervous when they put Reardon into the ground and covered him up. The others kept looking at the hills on both sides of the gulch.

Could I have stopped this? Meade asked himself, and knew it was a question that never could be answered.

Sammons and Clements eyed each other coldly across the grave before they turned away. Ellen was going toward Meade's tent with a bundle on her shoulder, holding her son's hand. Stella Kinnison and her girls had already helped the married women take down their tents. The bough huts along the creek were silent clumps, tools leaned against sluices that might never work again, and there was an air of deadness about the whole camp that was oppressive.

And this, Meade thought, *was what I wanted to happen, though not the way it has come about. Or did I care how it came about?*

When Sammons was about to the rocks on his side of the gulch, a rifle bullet from the Southern side snarled close to him. He turned and shook his fist, roaring, and then he ducked behind a rock and scrambled on to safety. At once there was a roar of guns replying to the single shot.

From the Southern side of the gulch a long quavering yell of defiance came.

"Well, there you are." Bland shrugged. He and Meade were alone in the street.

An instant later a bullet plucked the skin on the side of Meade's neck. He and Bland ran toward the saloon, throwing themselves flat behind the tent. Someone yelled an insult from the Southern side. A half dozen slugs ripped through the canvas, and then the main fire of the Southerners was directed across the gulch.

But two cold-minded riflemen kept feeling out the tent,

raking bullets through it low. *The Mercers*, Meade thought. The day he had let Ben step away from a fight, bluff or not, had been a day when Meade made one of the worst mistakes of his life.

"My rifle is in there," Bland said coolly. "I think I'll get it." He crawled under the tent and came back soon with his rifle in one hand and a whiskey keg in the other. He grinned, lying on the ground with his face dust-smeared. "Ordinarily I'm not a drinking man, but I may begin any time. Which way . . . the creek and then up it to the first trees?"

For a beefy man, Bland was fast. The whiskey sloshed high in the keg as he ran. They made the creek and lay behind a waste pile near a sluice to catch their breaths.

"Blessed are the peacemakers," Bland grunted. A bullet made a soft tearing sound near the top of the keg. He pulled the oaken container below the crest of the gravel.

When the next two shots splashed small rocks from the waste pile, Meade and Bland got up and ran again. They reached the safety of the trees at the upper end of camp. Bland lifted the keg and drank from the spigot. He coughed and spat. "No wonder they're fighting each other."

It was all sound and enthusiasm there across the gulch. Both sides were under good cover and the range was long. But someone would get hurt or killed, and then the fight might go to any length, Meade thought.

"Where do we fight now?" he asked.

"I don't know."

They stood up and looked back at the camp. Oatis Peek was sitting near the graves of his companions, carving on a pine slab. The bullets went above him and they might not have been there. He sat with his head and shoulders bent, making strokes with his knife.

"Let's go back to the little pasture where I keep the mules," Bland said. "I think they got more sense than men ever will have. What are you going to do with all your gold, Meade?"

IX

In the Southern camp Ben Mercer sat on a log and tried to think of means of speeding up the action. If he were a leader in a military sense, it would be simple: he would get an attack started on the Yankee position and have it pressed until men on both sides were killed and wounded, and then the fight would carry itself. The faint-hearts would leave the area for good, as some had done already, and the idiots would wear each other down until there was nothing left worth fighting over.

As it was, the gold of Poverty Creek was not worth this fight, but because of political factors it was a bone of contention. The main thing was to keep trouble going until blood had sealed all chance of settlement. Unruh's death was nothing. Even the Southerners had disliked him, and what little good had come from his death had been greatly overshadowed by revulsion against what he had done. Creston was a Northern loss, but he had alienated himself with the Free State group by turning against the Negroes.

Not greatly emotionally involved himself in the scrap, even though he hated Yankees, Ben Mercer could gauge the temper of conditions better than any man around him. The enmity was just not deadly enough yet. They would shoot and whoop and have a time, but unless the thing came to close quarters, hunger and inconvenience and sheer lack of powder would slow things down to where some meddling fool like Bland might bring about a truce. In time things could be made to boil high again, but Mercer did not have all the time in the world. The summer was wearing on. When the ground froze, working the secret gulch would be a chore. Speed the fight up, then, until it was apparent to both sides that neither could have Poverty Gulch. If a few die-hards stayed on after that, it would be no great trick to have another man like Barto come into the camp with news of a strike somewhere far away.

Ben called his half-brothers to him.

"That was poor shooting when you missed Meade," he said.

"It was a long way to shoot," Harvey said. "You changed your mind at a bad time. We could have had him a month ago but you wouldn't let us do it."

That was before other means failed, that was before something went wrong with Ben's ideas about Ellen. She had gone to Meade's tent now, and to Ben Mercer that meant only one thing.

"So I changed my mind," Ben said. "I had to. In the gulches somewhere behind where the Yankees are now is a new strike. You two followed Sammons and some others almost there. You heard them talking about it, understand? That's why the Yankees picked that side of the creek last night. They want to keep that strike for themselves. Is that clear?"

Harvey and Ed looked at each other, slowly considering this new lie. "About as clear as most of the around-the-bush things you plan," Ed grumbled.

"Never mind that. Just back up what I'm going to say."

It irritated Ben that it was always necessary to instruct Ed and Harvey beforehand, but otherwise, if their thinking in any way matched his, he would have had trouble with them long ago. Ben got up, and sauntered through the trees to where Clements was looking out at the Yankee position across the gulch. The firing on both sides had dwindled down to an occasional rifle shot when men on one side thought they saw movement on the other side.

"You know why they picked that side, don't you?" Ben asked.

"It was closer, that was all. We'll never get them out of there and they're not going to do any good with us, either, so what have we got?"

"They've got one thing we haven't," Ben said. "They've got a rich gold strike. That's why they're on that side of the gulch. The whole bunch swore they'd keep it quiet and never let a Southern man in on it."

Clements was skeptical. "How do you know?"

"Ed and Harvey trailed Sammons and some others one day. They heard them talking on the way back."

Blaisdell and two other Missourians got up from where they were lying behind logs and came over. "What's this about gold?" Blaisdell asked.

Mercer repeated the story. It ran as fast as any acceptable lie can run, and this one was veined with gold. More men began to crowd around Mercer and Clements.

"I knew it," Blaisdell said. "Sure, that's why they started this whole thing."

Someone ran to Ed and Harvey. "Where is it, where is the strike you trailed them to?"

"We didn't trail them all the way," Harvey said. "We just got the general direction." He pointed across the gulch. "About four or five miles that way."

"Let's blast them off that hill and go take it!" Blaisdell yelled.

"Shut up a minute!" Clements said. "I don't quite get this, Mercer. Your brothers knew the Yankees had a strike, but this is the first we hear about it."

"I wanted to know where it was first, so the whole camp could share it."

"The whole camp, hell!" someone cried. "We'll take it ourselves. That's what they figured to do, wasn't it?"

"We can flank that hill and shoot the hell out of them," Blaisdell said.

Clements looked at him disgustedly. "That wouldn't be like throwing coal oil on sleeping niggers, Blaisdell. There's a tough bunch over there." He glanced at Ben Mercer. "I'm not so sure, Ben, just what you've got in mind."

Mercer shrugged. "I told you why they're on that side of the gulch, that's all. If all this hadn't come up, I would have waited to avoid trouble, until I knew where the strike was, and then I would have told everybody."

"I'm not sure about that," Clements said.

I've underestimated him, Mercer thought. *He's dangerous because he doesn't want to go on with this fight.*

"Let's cut in behind them, then," Blaisdell said, "and find their damned gold strike." There were shouts of approval.

"You're still drunk, Blaisdell," Clements said. "If we go blundering off into the hills, not knowing where we're going or what we're doing, we're going to lose everything." He walked away.

Clements had gone sour, Ben Mercer thought, but the hook was in the others, a golden hook that never failed. They began to talk excitedly, finding more and more reasons why the story must be so. They questioned Ed and Harvey repeatedly, and Ben was glad that his half-brothers lacked the vanity to try to enlarge upon the story; they stuck to the bare details he had provided, which made their tale more credible to those who wanted to believe, anyway.

Blaisdell broke out another keg of the whiskey he and Unruh had stolen the night before. Clements ordered them to leave it alone.

"Look who's talking," Blaisdell said. "Who was so drunk last night he almost fell into the fire?"

"I'll have a drink myself," Ben Mercer said. He watched Clements turn away, frowning. The Virginian was the natural leader of the Southerners now, but he was powerless against the spell of gold. It was going well enough; a few words here and there, a gesture, the whiskey—it would all combine to lead the Southerners into some suicidal action that would close forever the possibility of stopping the fight.

Mercer now had time to give to the fringe details that were troubling him. One was Billy Bland. The way Meade and Bland had been sticking together lately it was likely that Meade had told him about the strike, with the two of them planning to share it. All right, then, Bland would have to be handled the same as Meade. For a few moments Ben was bothered by the realization that things had come to a point where he could calmly consider violence, with himself participating. There was something wrong in that because a truly clever man should manipulate only and never be drawn into the conflict itself. Perhaps he would not become actively involved if he continued to handle things well.

A bullet came high through the trees. The Southerners had grown careless. They realized it now only enough to seek better protection and to go right on with their drinking and heady talk.

Ellen was the next problem that troubled Ben. What the devil had happened to her since last night? Women generally did not strike Ben Mercer's hands away or refuse to look at him after they had been with him. Meade had told her about Creston's confession, that was it. It did not occur to Ben that Meade might not have done so; the confession was a weapon, and Ben would have used it instantly if he were in Meade's place. She could be talked out of believing, Ben decided. When Meade and Bland were dead, there would be only Ed and Harvey who had heard Creston's words—and they knew what to say.

Clements was standing apart from the others, looking gloomily across the gulch. He had a hellish hangover, Ben thought, and he was beginning to realize how foolish this whole affair was. If there was any way he could save his pride, he would probably be willing to settle for peace; therefore, he was dangerous to Ben Mercer's plans. But Mercer needed him to lead the rush against the Free State men. It was altogether likely that he would be killed. Luck had favored Mercer in such matters so far.

I'm an unusual man, Ben told himself. *Here I am on a miserable hill, all grimed with smoke and soot, existing like an animal, but I'm planning far ahead while the fools around me babble over a lie and swill whiskey and work themselves up to getting killed. Any fool can be brave in battle, but how many men can sit back calmly and plan as I do?*

"I never knew that Sammons to leave camp very often," someone said.

"You bet! He was cagey that way. He knows where there's gold, don't worry. Most likely those niggers put him on to it, him being Free State and all. What use have niggers got for gold?"

"There's some down there in the gulch that sure ain't got no use for it."

For once Loy Blaisdell was silent.

145

Meade kept getting closer to the Southern position. He heard the run of excited talk, with the word gold repeated over and over. He went a little closer, still not encountering the pickets he expected to find, and then he began to catch whole fragments of the talk about a gold strike. He hesitated behind a tree, hot with rage and a sense of failure. Ben Mercer had spilled the truth about Kansas Gulch; he had worked out some kind of deal to have the Southerners take it over. Meade almost went back then, but after a few moments hard common sense stayed him. Ben Mercer would not share anything if he could help it.

Meade hailed the camp. "I'm alone. I want to come in."

Someone yelled: "The dirty Yankees are sneaking up on us!"

"Clements!" Meade shouted. "I'm alone. I want to talk to you."

There was a scrambling in the trees. A rifle barrel bumped against a tree. A ramrod clashed on steel.

Hardin Clements said: "Come back here, Harvey. And you, Ed. We're not a bunch of savages yet." A little later he called: "Come on, Meade!"

It was a sullen, deadly group that Meade walked into. He sensed that Clements's leadership was hanging by a thread. The Virginian's eyes were holding the Mercer brothers in a narrow grip. Meade's sudden appearance and natural curiosity were serving for a time, but this might have been a bad mistake.

"If it's gold you fellows want, it can be arranged," Meade said. He saw Ben Mercer stiffen as all his gambler's poise deserted him for an instant. "We can work out something to split the gulch up fairly."

Mercer relaxed.

Blaisdell said: "See? He'd throw us an old bone while the Yankees sneak away to work their strike."

"What strike?" Meade asked.

"He doesn't know about it!" Blaisdell laughed. "Don't lie, Meade, we know why you fellows took the other side of the gulch, but there won't be enough left of you to work the strike after we get through."

"What's the other side of the gulch got to do with it?" Meade watched Ben Mercer's face.

Blaisdell pointed. "We know about your strike over there, don't we, boys? We'll be in on it."

"Shut up, Blaisdell!" Clements said. "Is that all you came here to say, Meade? If it is, you told me that much in the gulch a while ago, and you had my answer then."

"I'll say you're all a bunch of fools, both sides. There's no strike over there. It sounds to me like one of Ben Mercer's lies to get a pile of you killed."

"We'll take that chance," someone said.

Ben Mercer smiled.

"Bland is over there talking to Sammons's crowd now," Meade said. "If he can talk them into having three men meet with three of you to talk over your differences, you'll be fools not to take it up. What are you going to gain by shooting across the gulch? You're going to run out of food, you're going to run out of powder. Do you think you can fight here all the summer? What's going to happen when you're sick of the whole thing and somebody has been killed? There won't be a chance then that you can go back and work the gulch again. You'll have to sneak away, both sides, with nobody the winner."

"Sammons would like it if we sneaked away now," Ben Mercer said. "Then all you Yankees would have that gold strike to yourselves."

Meade used the same defense Mercer had used against him. "If there is a strike anywhere, and I find out about it, I'll see that every man in this camp gets in on it."

Blaisdell laughed. "I'll bet."

Ben Mercer understood. His own bluff, if it was bluff, was being thrown into him. He studied Meade's face.

"I could do one other thing, if there was a strike. I could lead just the Northerners to it," Meade said. "That wouldn't be good for anybody, would it, Ben?"

Some of the Southerners were confused by the by-play between Meade and Ben Mercer. Clements kept eyeing them both sharply.

"You talk in riddles, Meade," he said.

Meade told himself that his whole play was bluff. He wanted peace because Ellen and Bland had made him feel in some degree responsible for what had happened already, but he did not want peace at the price of giving up Kansas Gulch. Now he saw that Mercer could not afford to call the bluff, and he could not let Meade leave if there was a way to stop him.

"You puzzle me, Meade," Ben said coolly, "but only because you lie so fast. You and Bland drew pistols on my brothers when they were doing an act of decency."

"When they were sitting at Johnny Creston's bedside to prevent anyone from hearing him say that you sent him to kill Ban Phillips."

"What was that?" Clements asked.

"Creston, before he died, admitted that he killed Phillips because of a lie Ben Mercer told about a gold strike."

"That Meade lies faster than a dog can trot." Loy Blaisdell drank whiskey from a tin cup. "We started to hang him once. It's not too late yet."

"Do I lie about Creston, Ed, Harvey?" Meade asked.

The Mercer brothers looked at each other, and then they looked at Ben. Clements observed their odd hesitancy.

"Sure, you lie," Harvey said. "We said we'd catch you someday without a pistol." He came forward. "Now we have."

"He won't fight," Blaisdell said. "He's a Jayhawker swamp rabbit. We got to hang him."

Clements watched Meade as Harvey Mercer neared him. "He'll fight." Clements drew his pistol, looking at Ed. "Let's keep it one at a time, Ed."

Harvey licked his lips. Squat and powerful, he groped toward Meade, half crouched. Meade knocked him flat with a sweeping blow. He saw Harvey fall, saw the look of surprise on the dark face, and no great pain at all. Harvey rose and came in with a rush then, trying to get Meade around the waist.

Meade tried to knee him in the face. He caught Harvey in the chest instead, and the man bore him backward into a tree. Limb snags gouged cruelly into Meade's back. He beat both fists against the back of Harvey's neck, and then he slammed his elbows down. Harvey bunched his shoulders, clawing at the tree to get his hands around Meade's back.

The elbow in the back of his neck was brutal punishment. Harvey straightened suddenly, exploding upward in an effort to butt Meade's face with his head. Only Meade's flailing arms saved him. He jammed his hand into Harvey's face and used the leverage to push clear, sliding away from the tree.

Harvey dived against his knees and knocked him down. They rolled apart, and it was then that Ed Mercer kicked viciously at Meade's temple. His heavy boot skidded along the top of Meade's head, half stunning him.

Hardin Clements yelled something.

149

Meade heard Ben Mercer say calmly: "Under the ear the next time, Ed."

When Ed lashed out again, Meade caught the foot in both hands and, sitting on the ground, twisted as if to tear the leg off. Ed went off balance, staggering back into Blaisdell. He knocked the tin cup from Blaisdell's hand as he fell.

"Damn you!" Blaisdell roared.

On his hands and knees Harvey Mercer had been trying to pull a rock from the forest mat, but the stone was too deeply embedded. When he saw his brother fall, Harvey let the rock go and dived at Meade's stomach with his knees doubled up. Meade caught him with one foot and turned him so that he fell sideways. Then Meade was up, his buckskin shirt plastered with dead needles, blood running down the side of his face from Ed's kick.

With all his power he tried to put his boot against Harvey's jaw. Harvey took the jolt on his arms. And then Meade used the other foot. He kicked Harvey in the groin. Harvey gasped and doubled up.

From behind, Ed struck Meade like a rock, bearing him down across Harvey. Blunt fingers came around Meade's face, feeling for his eyes. He could hear Ed breathing through clenched teeth. With his left hand Meade broke one of the groping fingers. He strained the other hand down far enough to grind the thumb between his teeth.

Ed roared with pain. He bounced his heavy body up and down on Meade's back, and broke free, trying to break Meade's ankle with a stamp of his boot as he stepped back. Meade kicked him in the knees and knocked him back, and got on his feet.

With lowered head the squat man came driving in to butt Meade in the stomach. Meade side-stepped him twice, striking him in the side of the neck with no effect. Ed was all brawn and fight, all savagery. If he ever got his short, powerful arms around Meade, Meade doubted that he would be able to break the hold.

He kneed Ed in the face and straightened him out on the next rush. He slammed him in the face and drove him backward. Ed rocked on his heels, and then came driving in once more, clutching at Meade's lashing fists.

"Break his back," Ben Mercer said.

Meade side-stepped again and turned to follow the rush that carried Ed Mercer crashing over a log and into a serviceberry holly bush. Meade would have leaped upon him then but someone tripped him.

Clements roared a protest too late.

When Meade scrambled up, Ed was out of the bush and surging in once more. There was something elemental and determined in the man that awed Meade and touched him with fear. Suddenly Meade remembered his side. He wanted to drop his elbow to cover it, to use the shoulder on the other side to take Ed's charge. Instead, he dropped both hands, interlacing the fingers. He swept the hands up into Ed's lowered face when the man came in. Meade thought the jolt might have broken both his thumbs, but he struck two savage blows when Ed straightened up. They made solid, sodden impacts against the blood-smeared blue-black whiskers on Ed's face. Ed Mercer shook his head, his eyes foggy, and an instant later he was coming in again.

The Southerners shouted a savage plaudit. Meade's arms were growing numb from the impacts that could not stop the other man, and his breath was a fiery blast against the side where his ribs were shot away.

"Break his back, Ed," Ben Mercer said calmly.

Meade began to back up. Someone tried to shove him

ahead into Ed, but he lashed out with his elbows and kept backing toward the log Ed had fallen over. Ed Mercer came on with one idea fixed in his mind—to drive low and get his arms around Meade's back.

Meade took part of the jolt on his hip. He locked his arms around Ed's neck and swung him, using the impetus of the man's rush as leverage. Ed twisted and fell with his back across the log, and then Meade got his arms across the man's throat and threw all his weight down. Ed Mercer's neck kept bending back. Another moment, another pound of effort. . . .

Meade's right arm went limp suddenly. Legs bumped against him. Clements cursed and shoved away the man who had swung a pistol butt at Meade's head. The blow had been deflected enough to come down on the shoulder muscle at the base of Meade's neck instead of against his skull.

Clements grabbed his arm. "That's enough!"

Meade got up slowly. Sweat in his eyes and near exhaustion made his vision hazy, but he saw well enough to note the hatred in the faces of the men around him.

Blaisdell said: "Let's hang him."

Clements still had the pistol in his hand, and his leadership was now a little stronger by virtue of his attitude during the fight, but there was no compromise in his expression when he said: "Get out, Meade."

Meade staggered away through the trees. He had accomplished nothing, but increased the hatred, he thought. Before he was aware of it, he went into the open. Someone on the Northern side of the gulch sent a bullet into a tree beside him. He jumped back to cover, staying in the trees while he went to the meeting place to see how Bland had done. But he knew already; the bullet had told him.

The saloon man was waiting. He took one look at Meade. "Whew! Did you leave anybody alive?"

"It's worse than before. I got into it with the Mercers."

"Sure. I knew you would. What's the matter with your side . . . knife?"

Meade took his elbow away from his side. "Nothing."

"Go over to the spring and wash," Bland said. "And then we'll try to figure something out."

"I thought you were leaving."

Bland said nothing.

The icy water made Meade feel a little better. He lay down near the rough fence in the aspens where Bland kept his mules. "What did Sammons say?"

"About the same thing Clements did, I imagine."

"We're damned fools. Let them fight."

"I guess we'll have to," Bland said.

After a while, Meade said: "No. There should be some way to stop it."

"Make up your mind."

"Are you pulling out or not?"

"I've thought of it. Maybe I won't. Ellen says she's leaving. How you going to stop that, Meade?"

"I can't."

"You could go with her."

"I don't think she wants me around."

"Probably not."

Bland's casualness annoyed Meade.

"What about your gulch?" the saloon man asked.

"I won't give it up to the Mercers."

"And Ben won't give it up to you. You should have killed him, Jay, that day when you let him crawl out of it."

"Just because of the gulch?"

"For a lot of reasons," Bland said. "He's made all this trouble. He'll keep it going. I don't think you can beat him."

"The hell I can't."

Bland shrugged.

"He's told another lie," Meade said. He told Bland what Mercer had said about a strike the Northern men were trying to keep for themselves.

"And they got all heated up over it?" Bland asked.

"Of course. Sammons's bunch would do the same if we told them the Southerners had a strike. Clements didn't fall. I think he's catching on to Ben Mercer. Hardin Clements is a better man than I've given him credit for."

Bland grunted. "There may be a lot of men around here like that."

"What do you mean by that?"

"Just what I said. There's no difference between the men on one side of the gulch and those on the other side. There's people that think the North and South will have to have a war someday. That's wrong. We won't have to have it unless the politicians promote it, and then, by God, we'll have a dirty one. But it doesn't have to be, Meade. Give men something to change their minds away from slavery, and we'll never have a war. Give these men right here in the mountains something to shift them away from their ideas and they won't be fighting."

"I'd like to know what that something would be. You're not going to do it with a barbecue and a free picnic, Bland."

"I don't know how you're going to do it, but I know this. Sammons and some of the others see what a silly position they're in, and from what you say, Clements, at least, knows the same thing. If there was something that would give both sides a chance to back out, without it appearing that either side was afraid, then we could settle things."

"We tried to get them together, didn't we?"

Bland said: "We didn't have enough to offer. Now if the Utes started attacking the camp, that would do it. That would be substituting one big excitement for another. You'd see Clements's crowd and Sammons's crowd shoulder to shoulder then, and, when it was over, a lot of the meanness between them would be forgotten . . . for a while, at least."

"Indians," Meade said gloomily. "I'd welcome about a hundred of them right now, all on the warpath." From down the gulch there came the sound of three shots. The war was still on, and no Indians or any other outsiders were going to blunder along at the right moment to stop it, Meade thought sourly. He said: "I've got a notion to go over with the other Northerners and fight the thing out, and to hell with what happens."

"Sure," Bland said. "That's easy. That's just what Ben Mercer would like us both to do."

"Why should we be the two to try to stop it?" It was all at once incredible to Meade that he had tried.

"I know my reasons," Bland said. "What are yours?"

"Selfishness. I want Ellen. She wouldn't have me the way I was, so now I'm trying to prove I'm a great lover of my fellow men. And another thing . . . if it isn't stopped, Ben may get desperate enough to take the Southerners over to Kansas Gulch."

"No. If he did that, he'd know you would run the other side at him. Wouldn't you?"

"Why, sure. Do you think I'd let him get away with everything?"

There were two more shots. Someone on one side or the other yelled defiance.

"They're fighting over your blessed Kansas Gulch now," Bland said. "Only they don't know it."

And Ben Mercer was plotting, planning, taking no part in the action himself, but still almost everything that had happened could be laid to him. Meade remembered that Bland had said long ago that Mercer could out-fox both of them. Meade knew at last how much he hated Mercer, and how much he feared him, for the man himself was strangely devoid of personal violence, and therefore utterly ruthless.

Someone came tramping through the trees. Meade rolled over and grabbed his rifle, and the motion made him realize how many aches and bruises the Mercers had given him.

Oatis Peek came toward them. He was unarmed. He was carrying a meager pack of something slung in canvas.

"I thought you'd maybe be around the mules, you two," he said. Peek rested one foot on a log, peering at the trees ahead. "Sure nice and quiet here," he said somberly.

"Where to, Oatis?" Bland asked.

"Just going somewhere away from here. There ain't much left here for me now. Missus Greenaway, she give me a little eatables and stuff. Just going away from here. You boys been kind. I wanted to thank you."

"You've got gold, haven't you?" Bland asked.

"I got gold heavy around me so it nearly chokes," Peek said. "I got all our gold that Luke took care of. It's powerful heavy on me, Mister Bland. Maybe I can go somewhere and be a big man with it. I don't know. It didn't do Luke and the boys no good. I got it, though, right here around my belly, and the belt is all scorched. Whenever I use any of it to buy something, I got to look at the burns on that old belt and think that all the gold can't buy Luke and the boys nothing at all. How come they got burned up, Mister Bland?"

Meade and Bland looked at each other, and in the silence another rifle shot sent echoes rocking toward the mountains.

"Why don't you go over with Sammons and the Free State men, Oatis?" Meade asked.

"They all right, I guess. Clements, he's all right, too, if you know how he has to feel about Negroes. Little Johnny Creston talked big for us for a long time, and then he got all sore about us having all that ground. No, I guess I don't belong to go with nobody, Mister Meade. They tell me I'm a free man when I got the paper a year ago. I just ain't free the way I thought."

Peek started away.

"Wait a minute," Meade said. "You don't know where you're going?"

Peek shook his head.

"Then stay here a while. Maybe you can help me and Bland stop the fight down there."

"They ain't fighting over us now," Peek said. "They just shooting. They don't know why. I can't help no way."

"Yes, you can," Meade said. "You can help us. They don't hate you, Oatis, like they do me and Bland, the Southerners, that is."

"They don't hate us. They just throw coal oil on us and burn us," Peek said tonelessly.

"Stick around," Meade said. "You can help."

Peek stared at him solemnly, and then he swung his canvas pack down. "All right, if you say so, I ain't got nothing to do, anyway."

Ben Mercer watched whiskey and talk of gold run fevers high in the Southern camp. Things reached a pitch where the Southerners were ready to storm the other side of the gulch, sweep over it and go driving on to find the strike the Northerners were protecting. There was one bad flaw. Clements stayed cold and hostile. He would not drink and he kept slicing sharp remarks of doubt through the heady cloud of talk about gold.

Ben Mercer could not lead a charge, and his half-brothers were too badly beaten to do it, even if they had the fire of leadership. Ben watched Loy Blaisdell keenly. The man was wickedly drunk, and he kept throwing more whiskey through the gap where Sammons had knocked out front teeth.

"All we got to do is save one of 'em alive," Blaisdell said. "Sammons would be the best. There's ways I know of making him talk. We'll find out where their strike is."

"If they have one," Clements said. "If any of you think you can get far enough up that hill to get close to a live Yankee. Could they cross the gulch and come up the hill against us?"

Someone said: "I wish they'd try it!"

"We can do it, too!" Blaisdell lurched to his feet. "Lead away, Clements. We'll show you what we can do."

Clements shook his head. He glanced at Ben Mercer.

"By God, I'll take the boys over there, then!" Blaisdell made two attempts to pick up his rifle before he succeeded. He let out a roar and staggered away through the trees. A dozen men began to follow him.

"Better load that rifle first, Blaisdell," Clements said.

Blaisdell was weaving when he pulled his ramrod free. He spilled powder when he tried to load, and then he sat down on a log to steady himself. He slipped backward and the ramrod went over his head into the bushes. He shouted for someone to recover the ramrod and help him up. Several men laughed. Sanity came threading through the whiskey fumes and the whole project dissolved.

Ben Mercer said: "Why won't you drive the Yankees off that hill, Clements?"

"Because there's another hill behind it, and then another." Clements stared at Mercer. "And because I don't think they've got any more of a gold strike than we have."

"Is that all that's stopping you?"

Clements's hot temper flared instantly. "Say what you mean, Mercer, and then I'll answer you as you deserve to be answered."

"I mean nothing," Mercer said quickly, "except that you are entitled to a reasonable doubt about the strike. My brothers could have been mistaken. Suppose I find the Yankees' strike and bring back evidence. Then wouldn't you agree that it's time to act?"

"I might," Clements said.

Ben smiled. "You don't trust me, Clements."

"No."

That often happened, Mercer thought, not because he made serious mistakes, but because of some filtering process of other men's minds that he could not quite understand. "I'll have a look for that gold, and I'll try to get back here right away, if the Yankees don't get me first."

It went over well with those who believed that Sammons really did have a hidden strike, but Clements was still unimpressed. He said: "You're carrying gold around your belly now, Mercer, a lot of it."

"Gold varies," Mercer said. "You know that. It darkens a little after it's been washed and carried around. And then some gold is coarser than other. You know what comes out of the gulch . . . fine as flour. If I'm lucky enough to find the Yankees' strike, you'll be sure it's new gold after you get one look at it."

He began to rustle equipment, a pan, a shovel; he did not need them because he had left tools on Old Bugle, but he must make his expedition look real. A half dozen men wanted to go with him. Ben shook his head. "Too risky."

"They'll have their strike guarded, won't they?"

"Possibly. I'll have to take that chance." It amused Ben to speak casually of something that most men would consider heroic. Long ago, when the Kentucky flatboat men had taken his pistol away and tossed him all over the street, he had learned that heroics were for stupid men without wits to do anything except in a violent way.

He saddled his horse and rode away. After he was a quarter of a mile from the camp, he hid the tools in the bushes, and then he rode directly toward Kansas Gulch.

New gold, pale and shining, would do the trick. It was stronger than politics, stronger than Clements's cold doubt. Under the goad of it the Southerners would go wild to shoot down Yankees. Neither side could win.

There would be complications afterward, and demands, if enough Southerners survived, for Ben to reveal the Yankee strike. He was running a little ahead of himself now, he realized, but time was important. In a day or two both sides would find the will to maintain the fight greatly diminished by natural factors.

Soon after dark Meade and Bland crept into Poverty and fired all the bough huts in the gulch. There were a few angry shots out of the darkness on both sides of the gulch. Panting, the two men raced up the hill and stopped near Meade's tent.

Ellen was standing outside with Rip, watching the burning shelters.

"Why did you do that?" she asked.

"They took everything out of them when they left," Meade said. "The huts themselves didn't amount to anything. But tomorrow morning both sides will look down there and realize they haven't even got a place to creep into now. It will help them realize that they're out here in the mountains, all shut off from the things they're trying to fight over. It will make them feel sort of homesick and worried, instead of savage."

"I hope," Bland said. "I hope you're right."

"You've changed, Jay," Ellen said.

"No," Bland said. "He's just beginning to admit that the things a few men do don't necessarily destroy an entire principle. You still leaving, Ellen?"

"As soon as you can let me borrow a mule. One would be enough, Billy, just for Rip and the few things we have to take. I can walk."

"I'd like it better if you waited until Meade and I left. We'd feel better about you getting back."

"I'll wait. The Pingrees and the Ledbetters are leaving in the morning."

Meade and Bland went on toward their camp. "Now

what's your plan?" Bland asked.

"I'll see in the morning. Sometime tonight I'm going back to talk to Ledbetter, and see if I can get him to stay."

Peek was cooking grouse when they reached their camp. "I see the flames on the sky," he said. "It didn't look good."

They had eaten and were sitting in the darkness without a fire when John Ledbetter hailed them from the trees. He came in, softly cursing a branch that had jabbed him in the eye.

"We're leaving," he said. "Me and Pingree. I'd like to buy a couple of your mules, Bland."

"Would you wait a day or two?" Meade asked. "We need your help."

"I can't see how."

"I'll tell you tomorrow."

Ledbetter was silent for a time. "The women are dead set on getting away tomorrow morning. There'll be trouble if I tell my wife we're staying a minute after that."

"There'll be worse trouble afterward if you let her run you away from getting rich," Meade said.

"What's that?"

"I'll tell you in the morning, if you're here," Meade said. "If things don't work out, you can still leave tomorrow afternoon."

"What was that about getting rich?"

"Come back in the morning," Meade said.

After a long silence Ledbetter said: "Well, I'll see."

When he was gone, Bland said: "I hope it works."

"You've guessed what I've got in mind?"

"I think so."

"If I only knew what Ben Mercer was doing. I'm afraid of him, Bland."

When Peek heard what Meade explained to him the next

morning, the Negro said: "No, I ain't afraid to go up there, Mister Meade. I'll try, but there ain't nothing going to come of it."

"Just try, Oatis. That's all any of us can do."

Peek went away, headed for the Southern camp. Ledbetter and Pingree arrived a few minutes later. Ledbetter was not happy. "I had a hell of a time with my wife, Meade, and so did Pingree. I hope you knew what you were talking about last night."

Pingree looked toward the gulch. "I don't see how anybody's going to get rich down there," he said gloomily.

"We're going to bring three men from each side into the gulch for a parley," Meade said. "The Southerners don't trust Bland and me, and for all we know maybe the Northerners don't, either, but I think both sides will trust you two."

"What do you want us to do?" Ledbetter asked.

"Just go down into the gulch and wait there in plain sight, about where Unruh's hut used to be."

"Oh, hell," Pingree said. "Both sides will start shooting as soon as we come out of the trees."

"Not if you go down from your tents, they won't. Take something white with you."

"Something white," Pingree muttered. "That'll cause another big argument with my wife. You mentioned something to Ledbetter about getting rich. What . . . ?"

"We'll see," Meade said.

"Come on, Pingree," Ledbetter said. "We'll try."

While Meade and Bland were working around to the Yankee camp, they paused on the hill to watch Ledbetter and Pingree leave their tents and start into the gulch. Pingree was carrying a long aspen pole with a white garment on it. His wife and Mrs. Ledbetter were watching.

Meade was again moving toward Sammons's camp when he saw Ellen go down the hill. A moment later the two married women started toward her. Mrs. Pingree's voice came clearly. "Whatever it is, Amelia, we'd just as well be in on it."

A picket lying behind a rock saw Meade and Bland coming. "It's about time you two got up here where you belong," he growled.

The Yankee camp was in rocks and timber on the crest of the hill, without water. The men who held it were dirty and hungry-looking, and they showed the strain of their senseless waiting here.

Sammons asked: "Was it you two that burned everything down there?"

Meade nodded. "You won't be needing anything in the gulch."

"We'll hold the gulch as long as the slavers do."

"They don't want it," Meade said. "They want the rich strike you fellows made out north." He pointed.

"What the hell are you talking about?" Sammons scowled. "Who said there was a strike anywhere?"

"Ben Mercer."

"We ain't got no gold strike." Sammons's eyes narrowed. "Have they?"

"No," Meade said. "But we all have."

"Down there?" Sammons cursed. "You can't make fifty cents a day there now."

"Peek is over talking to Clements," Meade said. He had a long bad moment thinking of what Ben Mercer might do to Peek's proposal. "You've seen Ledbetter and Pingree in the gulch. You know you can trust them. What we want is for you to go down with Bland and me to meet Clements and two men from his side."

"To hell with that!" Sammons shook his head. "What good would that be?"

"I'll guarantee just one thing. If you go down with us and Clements shows up, I'll tell you where the richest strike in these whole mountains is."

"Yeah?" Sammons scowled. He looked at his followers crowded around him to listen. "Just us, huh?"

"No. I'll tell everybody."

"Those slavers, too?"

"Yes. We're not in Kansas now, Sammons."

"No," Sammons said. "I don't like that. If you know where there's a strike, let's go. We can hold it against all the damned slavers that care to show up."

Meade shook his head. "It goes to everybody, or nobody gets it."

"You're bluffing."

"Suit yourself." Meade turned to walk away.

"Wait a minute," one of the Free Staters said. "It won't hurt none to hear about it, Sammons. We can get our share and more. . . ."

"That's the wrong idea." Meade kept on walking with Bland beside him

"Hold up," Sammons growled. "You don't have to get touchy." He looked at Bland. "Do you know about this here strike he's talking about?"

Bland nodded. "It's there. I've seen it. There's plenty for everybody and then some. There's water to work it, practically no boulders to fight. . . ."

"Where is it?" someone asked. "Let's beat the Southerners there."

"You're a fool," Meade said. "You've got a war on your hands right now and you don't know what to do. If you tangle with Clements and his bunch over gold, you'll really have something you can't handle. Nobody can fight and wash gold at the same time."

"If there is any gold. If this ain't some dirty, sneaking trick to get us. . . ."

"Stay here and starve then." Meade started away again.

"Now wait." Sammons rose. "I'll go down and listen, but I ain't promising nothing to you or Clements or nobody else."

Sammons walked toward the group in the gulch with Meade and Bland. On the Southern side no one appeared. If Peek had failed. . . . The whole thing was a tricky affair that might make everything worse. Meade began to sweat.

He reached Ledbetter and the others. There was still no sign of any Southern emissaries.

"What's the story?" Pingree asked. He was careful to hold the white flag high.

"They'll be along," Bland said calmly. "We've got nothing else to do anyway, have we?"

Meade looked at the burned huts, at the graves on the hill. This had been a costly affair, and it might cost more yet, and then he would be a fool who had tried something he should not have tried. He saw Ellen watching him. She gave him a brief nod that might have been hope and approval.

"If they think they're going to keep me standing here flat-footed, they got another guess coming," Sammons said. He turned as if to go.

"Shut up, Ora," Bland said. "You act like a kid."

They waited. There was silence on both sides of the gulch. Meade wiped his brow. Ellen touched his arm. "I'll go up and talk to Clements, Jay."

"I'll do it," Bland said. "Before Sammons goes flouncing home like a spanked brat." He started.

And then Oatis Peek came from the trees on the Southern side. He was alone. Meade's heart sank. Then Hardin Clements and two others came into the open and started down the hill.

One great worry over, Meade was at once assailed by another—how to make them believe and how to work out the details if they did believe. There was hope in the fact that none of the Mercers was with Clements, and then that, too, turned to worry.

Clements spoke pleasantly to the women. He ignored Sammons. To Meade he said pointedly: "I see you and Bland consider yourself Yankees."

"There had to be three on both sides, so we'll pass as Yankees, I guess," Meade said. "I'll try to make this as short as I can. Since the first month I've been here, I've had a strike, which up to now I figured to keep for myself. Ben Mercer found out about it. Since then he's tried to turn this camp against itself so everybody would give up and leave. Bland and I are sure he brought Barto here. We know he gave his claims away to start more dissatisfaction. He told Creston that Ban Phillips and I had a strike, and then he told some lies to Phillips . . . I don't know exactly what. Phillips was honest. He wanted to find out where the strike was and see that everyone shared it. Johnny Creston killed him. He told Bland and I so before he died, and the Mercer brothers heard him, too. Doesn't it seem odd to any of you that they were sitting with Creston? Did they ever have anything to do with him before? His friends weren't there but the Mercers were."

Meade looked at his listeners. He had their attention, but he did not know how much of their trust he had. Clements said: "Go on, Meade."

"Now Ben has lied again, telling the Southerners that

Sammons has a strike, figuring that will get both sides so used up they won't have any choice but to pull out of here after they get through mauling each other. Sammons has no strike, but I have, and I'll take both sides to it when they can agree to wash gold and quit trying to kill each other. That's all."

Meade still could not tell what effect his words were having on Clements. Sammons's face was easier to read; it showed that he was believing but having trouble including the Southerners in Meade's proposal.

"What makes you think Ben brought Barto in here?" Clements asked.

It was such a minor point that Meade took heart from it. He said: "This is an isolated place. He must have come directly to it, through much bigger camps, because he left Denver only a short time before Bland did. Why would he come directly here with news as big as that lie he told?"

Clements seemed to have forgotten his reasons for asking the question. He was watching Sammons. One of them had to make a move or a suggestion, and neither wanted to be first.

"How are you going to make a fair staking on this strike you have, Meade?" Ledbetter asked.

"One claim for every man, and also one for Missus Greenaway."

Clements eyed Meade speculatively. "The discoverer is entitled to two claims."

Meade nodded. "I'll take two claims." He turned to Sammons. "What do you think about the whole thing?"

Sammons shook his head, staring at Clements. "No, I don't like it."

"You'd better ask your men about that," Bland said.

"I'm the boss!" Sammons said.

"How long will you be the boss if the Southerners pull out and your men figure they've gone with Bland and me to Kansas Gulch?" Meade asked.

"Kansas Gulch?" Sammons muttered.

"It's just a name," Meade said. "You could scour the mountains for months and never find it." That was not so, but Meade relied upon the common belief that gold strikes are always in remote places.

Sammons kept shaking his head. "My men are not going to get along with any bunch that burned Negroes."

There was the jamming point and Meade had foreseen it without knowing how to get around it. Even gold could not drive some things from men's minds. Meade took a chance and put the matter squarely up to Clements.

"What about those men, Clements? You know who they are?"

After a while Clements said: "They were wrong, but we won't turn them over to Yankees."

"Let the whole camp . . . ," Bland began.

"No." Clements's Southern background was controlling him.

"That's what I thought," Sammons said savagely. "How are you going to get along with anybody like that, Meade, gold strike or no gold strike?"

"Will you punish the men yourselves then?" Bland asked Clements.

Clements hesitated. "You can't force us into anything, Bland. They should be punished, yes, but you can't force us into anything."

"That's what I thought!" Sammons roared. "They're all the same, every last pro-slave son. . . ."

"Banish them from this area," Ellen said. The voice of a woman sounded odd after the heavy male talking.

Clements considered the idea. "That could be done."

It was a way out for the Southerners, Meade knew, even though it meant the release of murderers. He balanced that against what would happen if the negotiations broke down, and was forced to accept a compromise. Now the whole matter hinged on Sammons.

"Banish them?" Sammons said. "Spank them with your hand, why don't you?"

"Let them live their punishment with themselves," Ellen said. "We'll spread the story and they'll be known everywhere for what they are and what they did. They won't be able to look a decent man in the eye as long as they live."

"Oh, hell," Sammons said. "They'll burn more Negroes tomorrow, if they get a chance, and be happy about it."

Sammons had more right on his side than Clements did, Meade thought, and Meade could not accept all of Ellen's argument, for it was a woman's way of thinking. But he knew that justice does not always fall in an even pattern, not in miners' courts or any other courts of law. To uphold Sammons would mean that others would die. If there was no uniting now, both sides would start a vicious scramble to find Kansas Gulch, and then the gold would be blood red.

"How many of them are there, Clements?" Bland asked.

"Three."

"Blaisdell, and . . . ?"

Clements was silent.

"They could be turned over to some territorial court, I suppose," Bland said.

"A fat chance of that," Sammons said. "If we don't handle them now, nothing will happen to them. Clements won't give them up, so I'll have nothing to do with his bunch."

"That suits me fine," Clements said.

"You two are trying to throw away the biggest strike you'll ever hear about," Meade said angrily. "That's all you'll ever know about it, too . . . just hearing, if you don't bring your men down here inside an hour and let them stack their arms."

"Let them stack their arms?" Clements raised his brows.

"Yes. Let them have a chance, every man, to wash out more gold than there was in this whole gulch. When both sides disarm, I'll take them to the strike. How about it, Sammons, Clements?" Meade studied their faces and wondered if he had overestimated the power of gold.

"What makes you such a humanitarian all at once?" Clements asked, and then he looked at Ellen. The shift of his eyes, rather than any expression on his face, showed that he knew the answer.

"Tell your men what the offer is, both of you," Meade said.

Clements shrugged. "I'll tell them. Sammons has bellowed loud enough for most of them to hear, anyway."

"Why, you pro-slave. . . ." Sammons stepped toward the Virginian.

"Go on." Meade gave Sammons a shove in the chest. "Go on and tell them, Sammons."

Sammons and Clements went back to their men, leaving behind a silent, uneasy group.

Mrs. Ledbetter said: "At least it's quiet for the time being. Do you really have this gold you told them of, Mister Meade?"

Meade gave her a surprised look.

Bland laughed. "He has it, and now he's trying to give it away. Does that make you feel happy, Jay?"

"No," Meade said. "I'd still rather have it all to myself."

171

Bland laughed again. "You see, we have an honest man in our midst."

Ellen gave Meade an odd, penetrating look. "I'll go make some coffee while we're waiting."

"There won't be time," Meade said.

"There's time to cook old beans when men start to talk," Mrs. Pingree said. "Come on up to my tent, Ellen. We'll make the coffee there." She looked at her husband. "If anything goes wrong, you hold that white flag high and light out of here. That's one of my best underskirts."

"If anything goes wrong," Pingree said, "I can't guarantee what might happen to your underskirt."

The women went up the hill together.

"Did you see Ben Mercer up there?" Meade asked Peek.

"I didn't see Mister Ben. His brothers was there, all stove up. Ed was hobbling around like he had a pain. The others was laughing at him, and he was feeling downright mean."

Bland asked: "How did Clements act, Oatis? Did he put up a lot of resistance against coming down here when you gave him the message?"

"He took a lot of time," Peek said. "He let 'em argue and argue. The Mercers say it was a trick. Clements don't say much at all, but I could see he was going to come right from the first."

Meade trusted Peek's understanding of Clements more than he did his own. He tried to take hope from the thought, but all the time he was worrying about Ben Mercer's absence from the Southern camp.

"You're sure Ben wasn't there, Oatis?" Meade asked.

"No, sir. He wasn't there."

The sun grew hotter while they waited. Now and then a voice, loud with argument, came from one of the contending sides. Bland was sweating. He sat down in the gravel, mopping his face. Peek went over to the graves of his companions and fussed with the border of rocks that outlined the mounds.

The women brought coffee down the hill. Ellen watched Meade as he drank, standing in the hot sun. "I'm trying, at least," he said. "You can't say I didn't try."

"You sound like you were losing hope," she said.

"I'm afraid Sammons will ruin it on his side and the Mercers will wreck things for the Southerners." Meade wished there was something to do but stand and wait.

The pistol shot in the Southern camp brought the stiffness of fear to the little group in the gulch. One shot, and then there was silence.

Ben Mercer, Meade thought. *He's come back and maybe . . . maybe he's killed Clements.*

XI

Ben Mercer was in a frenzy over time, for time could ruin him. He had turned just a little too far uphill on his way to Kansas Gulch last night, and as a result he had got so tangled up in down timber that he had been forced to spend the night sitting by the fire. Now he was here, but he could not find the tools he had hidden in the willows. For a while he plunged about wildly, searching everywhere. His heart was pounding, and he was filled with a terrible anger that was alien to him. But soon his cold mind took over, driving the hampering emotions from him.

He carried his saddlebags to the little stream, and with his hands he scooped sand and gravel from the bottom of the creek, clawing, dipping, with icy water running off his arms, until the saddlebags were full. When he was riding away, a thought jeered at him—suppose the gravel from the stream itself did not contain gold as did all the ground beside the creek? He flung the doubt away. Gold was everywhere in the gulch. But still the momentary worry had told him what a state of mind he was in. He was upset more than he could afford to be. Of course, there was good reason. This was not a gamble for a few thousand, but a game to make a man a king if he won. If he lost. . . . But he could not lose. As soon as one of the Southerners panned the gravel and saw how rich it was, there would be no stopping the Southerners. But what were Meade and that meddling Bland doing?

They waited for twenty minutes after the shot came from the south hill, and then Meade could hold out no longer. "I'll go see what happened."

"No." Bland caught his arm. "You may not have Clements to deal with now."

Meade pulled away.

"No," Bland said. He drew his pistol. "We've done everything we could. You're not going up there."

Peek said: "I'll go. They don't care about me."

It was then that Clements came out of the trees and shouted: "We'll come down! How about Sammons's bunch?"

Meade heard Ellen let out a long sigh.

"Sammons!" Meade yelled. "Clements will bring his gang in! What about you?"

"No!" Sammons answered. An angry shouting came close upon his refusal, and an instant later one of his followers stepped into sight. "We're coming! Sammons can stay if he wants to!"

Clements came down first. He gave his rifle and two pistols to Ledbetter. "Two of the men that were with Unruh and Blaisdell have left. Blaisdell tried to put up a fight about going. He's dead."

Bland shouted the news up to Sammons.

"I'll have to see that to believe it!" Sammons called, but a little later he came down.

One by one the warring elements came from their respective hills. They gave up their weapons reluctantly. They formed into two groups, watching each other carefully. *It would not take much to touch it off right here,* Meade thought.

"Get any tools left near the sluices," Meade said.

They broke up to do that, and there was an argument over ownership of a shovel, and, if Bland had not been at the creek to out-yell everybody, a deadly fight might have developed then.

When everyone was off the hills, Meade looked the miners over carefully. "Where's the Mercers, Clements?"

"I imagine Ben went to this find of yours," Clements said. "Ed and Harvey took off while we were arguing whether or not to come down."

"They're armed?"

"Of course," Clements said.

Sammons stepped toward the stack of weapons. "Then I'm taking my rifle back."

Both Meade and Bland shoved into him. "Nobody is! The Mercers can't stand against this whole bunch," Meade said. "Now everybody follow me. When we get there, we'll have a meeting to decide how to stake out claims and to settle any other details."

"Suppose you and Bland leave your pistols, too," a Southerner said.

Meade did not want to do so, but he could not refuse. "Somebody has to stay here to guard this pile of guns." Meade looked at Ledbetter and Pingree.

"Not me," Ledbetter said. "I'm not fixing to get left out."

"Me, either," Pingree said.

Meade looked at Peek. "I think I'd better go along," Peek said.

Ellen was standing with her son and the married women, and by now Stella Kinnison had brought her girls to the excitement.

"We'll watch the guns," Ellen said. "We may throw the

whole pile in the creek."

"Now, look here!" Sammons was instantly belligerent once more. "My rifle. . . ."

"Oh, shut up," Meade said. "Take your rifle and go back to Kansas with it, if you want to. The rest of you that want gold come with me,"

Sammons went along.

It would have been a wild rush from the first but no one except Meade knew where they were going. They pressed him to go faster, and, as their excitement grew upon them, their animosity toward each other faded until they were a disorderly mob straining toward a destination unknown to them.

In spite of himself, Meade began to hurry, as if he, too, were going to a strike he had never seen before.

He was sure about the Mercers now. Ed and Harvey had slipped away to tell Ben what was happening. All three of them would be together. Meade said so for all to hear.

"They can't stop us," Sammons said.

"To hell with them," a Southerner said. "They didn't get together on this thing, so they don't get any claims." And then he remembered that they were Southerners, too, so he added: "Unless there's some ground left over."

They did not meet the Mercers on the way.

Meade wanted to come into Kansas Gulch quietly because he was sure now that Ben and his half-brothers would be waiting there, and he wanted to give the Mercers no forewarning. But there was no possibility of quiet now. Men were crashing through the underbrush, banging tools on trees, shouting at each other. Oatis Peek came up close to Meade and stayed at his side, working Bland out of the way. They broke out of the trees and started down the slope into Kansas Gulch.

Someone yelled: "Is this the place, Meade?"

The Mercers were standing in a compact group in the middle of the gulch. Ben Mercer smiled and waved his hand.

"Welcome to Yankee Gulch," he called. "Of course, we can change the name."

Meade stared across the willows in helpless rage. He was afraid of Ben's clever mind, afraid of what it might have started already in the minds of the Southerners. Ben Mercer would say that this was the place the Yankees had been keeping secret, and, if he could not make that lie stick, he would have others to follow. As long as Mercer lived, there would be trouble, and here, because of the richness of the gulch, the trouble would be intensified beyond control.

"Is this the place, Meade?" someone yelled again.

"Of course, it is," Ben said. "This is the gulch the Yankees have been holding out. I finally discovered it. I was on my way back to tell you when my brothers met me."

"I'll just bet he was coming back to tell us," Clements said. "He said the strike was north of Poverty, as I remember."

Ben Mercer shouted: "You've been following the wrong man, boys! Clements has sold out to the Yankees. I intended to have this just for us."

"That Mister Ben. . . ." Peek shook his head. His voice was sad. "He just a big liar all the time." He pushed something against Meade's arm, nudging with it. Meade looked down and saw Luke Reardon's pistol. "Nobody bothered about me having a gun or not," Peek murmured. "You better shoot that Mister Ben before we have trouble all over again."

Meade put the pistol in his belt and began to walk toward the Mercers. Bland and Clements fell in at his sides.

"Stay back," Meade said. "You're unarmed."

"So we are," Clements said.

They pushed through the brush to within easy pistol range of the Mercers. Harvey and Ed grew uneasy. They kept looking at Ben for orders. He said: "Stand tight. Nothing is going to happen."

"The hell it ain't," Harvey growled. "That Meade got a pistol from the nigger."

"Nothing's going to happen," Ben said. He stood there, smiling.

"You're going before a miners' court, Ben, to answer for all the hell you've caused," Meade said.

"String 'em up!" Sammons yelled.

There was an angry muttering in the crowd of miners, but Meade thought about half of it was Southern sentiment against Sammons's cry. Meade knew he could not outface Ben Mercer and let him talk, for Mercer would find the words to drive a wedge between the Yankees and the Southerners.

"String 'em up!" Sammons yelled again.

Harvey and Ed clutched their rifles nervously. They shrank a little closer to Ben, and edged toward the rim of the gulch where the thick willows began. A fear grew in their eyes.

"That's what we're going to do, Harvey," Meade said. "You and Ed lied about what Creston said. . . ."

Ben took a couple of steps backward. "Meade's bluffing," he said. "Don't let him crowd you into anything."

"We're bluffing?" Bland said. "You see Clements with us, don't you?" He hammered at the weak spot, the fear in Harvey and Ed. "You'll hang."

"No!" Ed cried.

Clements broke them when he yelled: "Grab 'em!" Ben

Mercer had seen how the play was going. He shouted again to warn his half-brothers to do nothing, but Clements's shout had cracked them. They swung up their rifles. Clements already had a pistol out. Billy Bland fired with his hand in his coat pocket.

The Mercer brothers reeled back, half hidden in the trees now, still fighting to bring their heavy weapons to bear. Ben Mercer recognized that everything was lost. His gambler's coldness turned to hate. His hands went toward the Derringers in his pockets, and, as he brought them out, he leaped backward into the trees and crouched down low. He fired once, and then vanished into the bushes.

But Meade had never looked away from Ben. He had seen the guns, and coldly he noted the odds. Mercer was in the woods now, thrashing heavily, but still hidden, a man in ambush. And even with the dream gone, the gold literally shot to hell, Mercer still was a man to fear, a man with a brain. Meade held himself for a minute, a bit of the old fear nagging at him, the knowledge eating away that he had done his job, that he could stand aside and let Bland and Peek and Sammons finish it up. And then he bent low, moving to his left, unthinking now, his hand loosely gripping the gun Peek had given him, hefting it as he ran, heading for the woods at an angle that would—might—bring him to Mercer's side.

Inside the woods he went, parting a bush with his left hand, his eyes searching out the spots where Mercer might be, hoping he could draw a shot. But all he heard was a bird somewhere whistling suddenly through the woods, and away, and then silence.

"Mercer!" he called. "Mercer, here, here." And then Meade plunged two quick steps to his left, gaining the shelter of a bush.

But still nothing. He was up again, moving silently to his left, trying to complete the half circle, hoping desperately he could swing around to Mercer's back, and then make his move. It all depended on how far Mercer had backtracked. If Meade cut his circle too short, Mercer would be on his back, the two Derringers, erratic as they were, still good enough. Even with the sweat now pouring down his back, the muscles along his spine prickled, and a little shudder ran through him. Left, he thought, still more left. But the farther left he went before veering in, the more chance Mercer had of backing clear out. And so, savagely, almost not caring whether the shot came now or later, he cut in and moved to the top of the circle, his eyes peering ahead, trying to guess the lay of the woods ahead, wondering how thick it was, behind how many trees Mercer could be.

Then he reached the imagined point where he had half-circled Mercer, and slowly he started to move straight back toward the center of the circle, his left hand poking as he walked, the right still low, the gun still loose, pointed down. He was nearing the point of the woods now where Mercer had to be, if he was near at all. Meade scooped down and in one motion pitched a pebble ahead of him, looping it through the squares of sun and shade and hearing it land and bounce and scuff some leaves before it came to rest.

Meade froze for a second, waiting, hoping he could bring Mercer out of whatever hole he was in, but nothing happened. The old sickness washed over him. He could still get out of it, he knew. Mercer wasn't there. He had backtracked and maybe he was fifty yards away or 300. But he wasn't in front of him. And Meade could just walk out, and the others would look at him once, and then blast their way in, three, four, maybe ten of them, and Mercer would be full of holes in less than ten minutes. He wavered, and then he thought: *Damn, the job is mine! Nobody else's.*

He would find the man he sought. He turned around to look for him, and found himself looking into Mercer's Derringers, looking into Mercer's cold-hot eyes, and even then, as Mercer squeezed off his shot, Meade was down, hitting his bad rib side and gasping once as gunshot burned by, and rolling, rolling, and then up.

And now the look was all hot in Mercer's eyes, and Meade laughed, once, loudly. The other Derringer fired now, and still Meade hadn't lifted his gun, and this time there was pain in Meade's left shoulder, blazing down to his hip, and Meade laughed again. He had reached the man, he knew. He had stood up to him when everything said he should have groveled or run. From some place inside he had found the answer and this time when Meade laughed there was joy in it, and this time he raised his gun and took an everlasting second to get Mercer in his sights, and then he lowered them once, and shot Mercer in the leg.

Even while Mercer fell, Meade thought: *There'll be a trial now, an honest one.* He leaped forward, and crashed the barrel of the gun against Mercer's temple, and the man screamed once and collapsed, the Derringers spilling at his side. He reached down and grabbed the man's collar and dragged him out to the staking ground.

XII

Meade looked at his companions. "Where'd your guns come from?"

Clements smiled thinly. "There's a dozen more in the bunch behind us, if a man dared search hard enough." He put his pistol away. "I don't think there'll be any further need of them now."

The same impatient Southerner shouted again: "Is this the place, Meade."

"This is it."

There was no meeting or any thoughts of a meeting to work out preliminary details. The crowd broke with a rush, running like madmen into the gulch. They floundered through the brush, yelling, laying claim to the first piece of gulch ground they fell upon. But a couple of them were careful to truss up Ben Mercer before leaving him.

"They'll growl and argue," Clements said, "but we won't have any more trouble . . . if the gold is here."

"It's here," Meade said. "I'll depend on you to help keep order."

"You can." Clements walked away to stake a claim.

One piece of ground here was like another, Meade thought. Some would be richer, but there was no way of telling from the surface. He staked a claim for Ellen, and then two more for himself.

"Since I'm here, and still alive . . . ," Bland said. He staked a claim beside one of Meade's.

They stood together and watched the activity in the gulch. Men were sloshing in the stream, panning furiously. Others were digging at the sides of the creek, running to water as soon as they had gravel in their pans. There would be a thousand details to work out before the camp was settled, but it would be in time a reasonably peaceful place, Meade was sure.

He might have had it all for himself. He looked up at Old Bugle, and he thought of Luke Reardon's words. Meade could not say in honesty that he was overjoyed to see Kansas Gulch full of miners, but he knew he was relieved of a great burden.

"Go on," Bland said. "I'll find some help to do what we can for the dead Mercers."

Meade went back toward Poverty. Before the sun was down, he met Ellen and her son and all the women coming on the broad trail the miners had left.

"Any fighting?" Mrs. Ledbetter asked.

"The Mercer brothers are dead. Ben is out cold." Meade and Ellen looked at each other, until Mrs. Pingree said: "Come on with us, Rip."

Ellen and Meade walked slowly. "There's a lot we'll have to forget," he said.

They came at dusk to the gulch. Fires were going. Men were standing around them, still talking excitedly. In the confusion of staking ground Southerners and Yankees had taken claims side-by-side, and now they were sharing each other's fires.

Ellen said: "Perhaps you've led them toward something more than a gold strike."

"They haven't changed much." Then Meade added defensively: "Neither have I. I was forced into this."

"But you did it." That was obvious enough. Deep inside himself Meade knew that his reasons for giving up Kansas Gulch went far into his being. He had fooled himself for a while, but he knew that he could not live at peace with himself in the midst of hatred and injustice. He was the same man he had been before he rode across the Missouri line so long ago.

"How much can you forget?" Ellen asked.

Their personal problem was bare before them. Meade answered honestly, knowing that he had only himself to blame for some things. "Everything that's necessary."

They walked toward the fires together.

Look Behind Every Hill

I

Vastness was the burden. Its silence was eloquent, promising nothing but time and defeat. From the Empire Mountains to the last dim break of the Spotted Hills the long land miles threw their challenge at any man foolish enough to pit a plow against their lonely bigness. Carmody Steele tried it, with his pretty wife, Faith, and his two children. His shack was an affront to the rawness. The sun hastened to brown the boards and twist them from the nails that held them, and the winter wind tried to tear the boards away.

Lee Hester said the land was fit for cattle only. He was a Northern man, like the owners of Wagon Wheel, the other big ranch in the Spotted Hills. The great log ranch house of the Hesters was in a basin at the head of Pennsylvania Creek—Cloverleaf, they called it. Hester and his ranch neighbors, miles apart, waited for Carmody Steele, the Rebel cavalryman, to starve out.

Steele's daughter was twelve; Vaughn, the son, was sixteen. Because of the women Lee Hester said he would be patient, but he added that there was, of course, a limit to his patience.

Faith Steele was the first to break. She stayed longer and longer each visit at Mrs. Trotter's boarding house on the railroad at Gettysburg. Mrs. Trotter was a Southerner, too, but she lacked a plantation upbringing, so the country did not frighten her. A young conductor who ate every fourth day at the boarding house kept telling Faith Steele that this was a hopeless country for women. His uniform would have looked jaunty beside Carmody Steele's rough clothing, all stained with the red soil of Elk Run. One day Mrs. Steele went with the young conductor, east toward the memory of great rivers and flowers and friendly houses standing close together in countless towns and cities.

She left Nan, the girl, with Mrs. Trotter, and dark-browed Carmody and Vaughn to fight the red earth of Elk Run without a wife and mother. That happened on a raw spring day. Carmody did not know about it for two days. He took Vaughn with him when he went to town to bring his daughter home. Nan was ill with grippe and Mrs. Trotter said it was best to leave her in town for another week or two. "I tried to talk her out of it, Mister Steele." Mrs. Trotter was sincere. Her profanity startled Vaughn.

Carmody nodded. He did not look now like an ex-Confederate major. There was a sag to his body and a lumpishness about him that did not come entirely from his heavy clothes. The glory of the high-riding South was long away. Only the doggedness was left, and the breeding. He bowed to Mrs. Trotter and thanked her. Vaughn stood, silent and wondering. He was a flat-backed youth with his mother's golden complexion and his father's dark hair and eyes. All sympathy ran to his father. Betrayal.

He asked: "When is there another train east?"

Carmody smiled. He shook his head. "We'll go back to the farm, Son." He always called it a farm.

He had stayed until Appomattox. He would be no different now. On the long ride home he squinted at the lonesome land. Snow still lay rotting in the shady parts of the gullies. The wind from the Empire Mountains was cold.

"You can't blame her," he said. "She grew up in a different country. There was always something around her, something at her back for reassurance. Here. . . ."

Vaughn raised his head. Out here the mountains were the only thing a person could put his back against, and they seemed very far away. He had never been to them. They stood in gray and white triangles, unfriendly barriers on the long horizon.

Vaughn said: "What about Nan?"

"She'll grow up with us. She'll stay."

His father had lost one way of life, Vaughn knew. He had seen the promise of another. Maybe it was stubbornness or maybe it was determination, but Carmody Steele would stay forever on Elk Run now, if only to prove that he must have been right this second time.

Hours later the shack began to grow from a dot of yellow-streaked brown. The fields scratched on the surface of the vastness were tiny marks that could disappear after a month or so of neglect.

"Of course, some women would have stayed," Carmody said. That was the only blame he ever laid on his wife.

Lee Hester and Troutt Warner were waiting at the house. Hester was a rangy man, iron gray at the temples. There was a loose mobility about Warner's mouth, a sort of roving lewdness. His eyes were hooded at the outer corners, and the downward draping of the flesh seemed to be part of the bone structure. He and Charley Burgett owned Wagon Wheel Ranch on Pennsylvania Creek.

Steele dismounted. He gestured toward the house. "Won't you come in?"

Hester shook his head. "We heard that you. . . ." Hester stopped. "Your wife. . . ." It was a delicate subject. Steele's bleak, indrawn expression did not help Hester any.

"We heard she ran out on you," Warner said.

"Yes," Steele said. It was both confirmation and a question that edged on deadly politeness.

"You won't be staying here much longer then, I suppose. The little girl and all. . . ." Hester glanced at the house.

"Why, yes, I'm staying."

Warner looked at Hester. His by-passing of Steele was an insult when he said: "I told you, Lee. This waiting for nature to take its course is no good. We'll have to help him move."

"It's like this," Hester said. "We haven't got anything against you in particular, you understand." He was trying to speak with reason, Vaughn realized, perhaps because of what had happened today. Through a growing rage Vaughn realized that fact, but it served only to make him angrier.

He walked toward the house.

"Yes, you have something against me," Steele said.

Hester forgot politeness. "You're a Rebel. That, we might learn to live with, but you're planted in the middle of our land. We hoped you'd starve out. You haven't, so far. You're setting a bad example. . . ."

Steele laughed. "That sounds familiar, considering what I saw in the South after the war. I'm setting a bad example by trying to make a living."

"Somebody else will be encouraged to move in here," Hester said. "You'd best get out, Steele."

Vaughn stood in the doorway with a rifle. "You'd best get out, Hester. You and Warner. Right now!"

"Put it away, Son," Steele said.

Vaughn swung the rifle on Warner's chest.

"No, Vaughn," Steele said, but nothing changed and nothing happened. Across Carmody Steele's face there came the realization that authority was no longer vested in him alone. He stared at his son a moment, and then he said in a tired voice: "Yes, gentlemen, you'd better leave."

The ranchers rode away. Vaughn watched the vastness gather around them. He put the rifle down. There was nothing here to put your back against, nothing here that stood as a shield.

He helped his father take care of the horses, Mitch and Corkey, good riding mounts, Steele's only salvage from a lost war. They were not like the lumpy team that plowed the fields. They represented something that Steele could not seem to find in this country, something that his son thought he himself would never find.

The two men stood together for a moment, looking across the raw fields. "Maybe . . . ," Vaughn said.

His father said: "No. We'll stay here. There are thousands like me out here, Vaughn. The more we run, the more we'll have to run."

Vaughn thought of the weight of all the hostility around them, hidden in the folded hills. He had brought trouble to a point this day. He said: "What will we do?"

"We'll cook supper. We'll do that first, and then whatever else we have to do will come as it will."

They brought Nan back from town the next week. Her father told her that her mother was not coming home, and that there was no need to ask the question, ever. It rode like a puzzled shock across Nan's face. She was losing her chubby look. Her hair, rich chestnut in color, and her long face, were sharp reminders of Faith Steele. But her eyes were dark, like Carmody's, and they understood a great deal when her father spoke to her.

"You'll have to cook," Steele said. "Did your . . . did you ever learn about it?"

"Not much."

"Learn now," Steele said. He spoke with unneeded harshness. Faith Steele had never been a good cook. Now it occurred to Vaughn that his father was associating that failure with others.

"You don't scare me one little bit," Nan said. From the window of the kitchen the country was reduced considerably. Green was springing where the snow had been, and the fields seemed an important part of the whole.

That afternoon, with the red soil coming up in lumps behind the plow, Steele nodded to himself, then said: "She'll be all right, Vaughn. She's not like her mother." A little later he said: "We'll break a hundred more acres than I planned at first . . . there on the other side of Elk Run."

"Fine," Vaughn said. Let his father try to take his hurt out on the soil if he would.

At the far end of the field they stopped a few moments after making the turn. Carmody Steele raised one fist and said: "By God, I'll make this country bloom! I'll grow things here. You'll see."

He shook his fist at the land. Vaughn watched while the cold spring wind chilled his sweating back. The lostness of his father came to him with frightening intensity. Carmody Steele would try to lash the land because it had robbed him, because it had beaten him already.

They ate that night by a smoking lamp. The boards of the shack rattled a little under a light wind rushing from the mountains. On the windows were curtains that had once been in a mansion.

Carmody Steele stared at them. "They're too frilly for here. I've always said that. Change them, Nan."

"There's nothing else."

"Then we'll do without." Steele went across the room and tore the curtains down. He dropped them into the woodbox. He leaned against the wall for a moment, and then he shook his head as if to clear it. He walked outside. They heard his footsteps go into the night.

"Back in Virginia Grandpa used to ride his horse in the moonlight, jumping fences, when he was drunk or mad about something. Mother told me," Nan said.

Vaughn said: "He's all right. You go to bed."

Hours later Carmody returned, walking like a beaten infantryman. He sat at the kitchen table, looking out on the moonlit land. The soft light shafting through the window could not hide his haggard look.

Vaughn came quietly to the doorway. "We got a lot of work to do tomorrow."

"Yes," his father answered. "Yes, I know. Did you ever walk in the moonlight, Son, wondering what happens when something dies in you? No, of course you haven't. You might someday. If you're tough, Vaughn, really tough inside, you won't let anything die in you. Things change, but you won't let anything die."

He rose wearily and went to bed.

They came that night in the dead still hours of slumber. Vaughn felt the house tremble. He thought it was a dream. Something snaked across the boards, as if a small animal were running on the roof. Boards groaned. The house began to move.

Outside someone said: "Downhill, you fool!"

Vaughn leaped from bed. The puncheon flooring struck him in the face. It was utter terror in the darkness for a while. There was no balance in his being. He groped and fell. Nothing in the room was where it should be.

Carmody Steele's voice came sharply. "Get the mattresses around Nan! Keep her on the floor!"

Vaughn knew now. There were men and horses outside. There were ropes on the house and it was being dragged away. He tripped on the mattress he pulled across the swaying room. He found Nan sitting in her bed. "I had a bad dream," she said. She was fully awake but did not realize it yet.

"Hang onto me, Nan." He felt her grab him hard. She knew now that she was not dreaming. He dragged her corn-shuck mattress off the bed. The floor was bouncing now and everything loose was washing around the room.

The stove went over in the kitchen and threw the warm smell of soot through the darkness, and then the kitchen, an unfloored lean-to, ripped from the other part of the house.

Night air swooped in. Someone outside shouted, urging a horse to greater effort. In a moment the walls were creaking in. Roof boards snapped.

Vaughn was covering his sister with the second mattress, but now picked her up and tried to stagger through the open end of the room. From outside there came the heavy rocking sound of his father's rifle. Carmody Steele had already made it through the opening.

A man cried out in alarm. The rifle replied, and then there were scattered shots and cries. The house quit moving. Vaughn put Nan on the twisted flooring, kneeling above her. The rifle boomed once more. A half dozen pistol shots replied. Some of them ripped the broken boards around Vaughn.

Some moments later the night was still, except for the sound of horses trotting in the darkness. Vaughn groped his way outside, calling his father, crying into an emptiness from which there was no echo or answer.

II

Vaughn Steele and his sister stood around the cook stove, warming themselves in the gray dawn. The stove was propped up on wreckage, with a short pipe carrying its blue smoke across the chill land.

Carmody Steele was dead, lying on a mattress, covered with a second mattress. He had been dead when his son stumbled through the darkness and found him. His children stood closely together at the stove, not looking directly at each other.

Nan limped when she stepped away to gather an armful of board fragments for the fire.

"You hurt?" Vaughn asked.

She answered crossly. "No."

The first of the sun touched high on the Empire Mountains with a rosy glow, but here on the lonesome land the cold was sharp.

"We'd better have something to eat," Nan said, "before . . . well, we'd better have something to eat."

Vaughn poked around in the ruined house. He found enough for breakfast.

When he returned with the food in a chipped graniteware pan, Nan was crying. She held tightly to him and sobbed. "Where's our mother, Vaughn? Why did she go away?"

They tried to comfort each other but they had no answers to give each other. Vaughn looked over his sister's head at the mattresses on the damp ground. He thought: *Someday I'll kill every one of them. I'll get them one by one.*

While Nan cooked, he cleaned the rifle, and then he turned over boards and moved broken household gear until he found a handful of cartridges. Guns and horses—Carmody Steele had loved them both. His rifle was here yet, but the horses had been taken, or run off.

They had just finished burying their father in the rich red soil only a few feet from where he had died when Vaughn saw the rider coming with a pack horse. He overbore an urge to shout and wave his arms to attract the man's attention. He knew who it was, Drake Gardner, who lived somewhere against the mountains. On his infrequent trips for supplies Gardner generally stopped a few minutes at the Steele place, seldom dismounting, saying very little before he led his pack horse on toward what Vaughn had imagined must be a mysterious existence there below the tall Empires.

The wrecked shack caught Gardner's attention. He came in faster than usual. He was what Carmody Steele had called a young-old man, a slender fellow with eyes like chips of black stone. One side of his face was scarred and pitted as if flecks of molten iron had splashed against him. On that side the view gave him an evil appearance; the other side was different, the face of a young man, but there were lines already growing in his cheeks and the flesh around his eyes was puckered with little spoke-like wrinkles.

He sat his horse and said nothing, seeing everything in quick, hard flicks of his black eyes. Then he swung down and walked around the grave of Carmody Steele.

"What's the matter with your ankle?" he asked Nan.

The girl shook her head, moving closer to Vaughn.

"Come here." Gardner's tone expected obedience.

The girl walked slowly around some shattered boards, holding her hands behind her back, and stopped in front of Gardner.

"Let me see that foot. Sit down there on the ground."

Gardner felt the ankle gently. He removed Nan's shoe, and a moment later he stared at Vaughn: "Look here."

The girl had stepped on a nail. It had gone through her foot, leaving a tiny purplish mark on top.

"Not nearly as nice as a good clean bullet hole," Gardner said. He stood up. "Did you recognize anybody, Steele?"

Steele. The name carried stature. Vaughn shook his head. "It was dark."

"Naturally." The sun was rising. Gardner looked around at the Spotted Hills. "Where's the horses?"

Vaughn shrugged.

"Have you looked for them?"

"Not yet."

Gardner frowned. He appeared to be facing a situation that did not bother him greatly. His face showed no sympathy for the victims, no hatred of those who had caused the ruin. If there was any expression at all on his face, it was annoyance.

"Your mother's gone back East?"

"She ran away," Vaughn said. Betrayal. It built a savagery in him, not particularly against his mother, but against all else that had happened.

"You have folks"—Gardner inclined his head toward the sun—"back there some place?"

"Virginia," Vaughn said. "They're all scattered now, I guess."

"Yeah." Gardner seemed to understand. He pulled a bridle from a tangle of clothing wrapped around some studding. He dropped it again. "Work that foot with your hands," he said to Nan. "Squeeze it and make it bleed."

"It hurts." The girl's lips were trembling.

"Make it bleed!" Gardner frowned, annoyed. He glanced at his horse, as if he were thinking that he could mount and ride away and save himself a lot of trouble.

"What will you do now?" he asked Vaughn.

"I'll take Nan to Missus Trotter, and then I'll find something to do."

"Will you?" Gardner said shortly. "The big woman who runs the boarding house, you mean?"

Vaughn nodded.

"She didn't cause any of this."

Vaughn blinked. "Of course not."

"Then why bother her with your problems? She's not quite the woman to be raising a girl anyway." Gardner walked away to look at some hoof marks. He picked up a broken lariat. He flung it aside and came back. "I'll take a scout for the horses. Get together whatever you want to take with you." He stood a moment looking at the smoke trailing from the short pipe of the cook stove. "I never saw anything like that."

He ground-hitched his pack horse and rode away, in the direction the night raiders had gone.

"I don't like him," Nan said. She was making a pretense of squeezing her injured foot.

Vaughn did not know about Gardner himself; he had been attracted to the man as a casual visitor, but now he did not know whether he liked him or not. "Here, let me at that foot," he said.

He knelt and began to work the bones. Nan's lips

twisted in pain. Blood began to seep from the tiny hole in the bottom of her foot, to run down the smooth surface on top where the nail had emerged. "Why didn't you say something before?" Vaughn demanded.

"We had trouble enough."

After a while Gardner returned with Mitch. "The other one is dead. Somebody shot it. It was a good-looking horse. The team . . . I didn't look for them."

"Corkey was a good Kentucky. . . ."

"They're not built for this country," Gardner said. "Thoroughbreds of any kind don't belong out here." His face was bitter. He looked at a pile of gear that Steele had gathered, some of Nan's clothes, two saddles and a bridle.

He touched a saddle with his foot. "Is that all you're taking, Steele?"

"And this." Vaughn was holding his father's rifle.

"There was a pistol?"

"Somewhere there," Vaughn said. "A Colt."

"Find it."

Vaughn found the pistol.

"Can you shoot one?" Gardner asked.

"Some. I'll learn in time."

The scarred face twisted a little in a mirthless smile. "No doubt . . . you and that Southern blood of yours."

"There's nothing wrong with my blood, Gardner! We're not asking you for any help."

"Fine, fine." Gardner took a look at the country, at the wrecked homestead. He picked up a saddle and walked toward Mitch. "This beauty doesn't carry double, no doubt?"

"No," Vaughn said.

"Then you can walk, Steele." Gardner saddled up. "If you've got your heart set on town, that's fine for you,

201

Steele, but not for the girl. How old are you, Nan?"

"Twelve."

Gardner cursed under his breath. "Come on. We're going over to the Cloverleaf."

"Hester's place!" Vaughn stared. "He was with the men last night."

"You saw him?"

"No, but. . . ."

"You would have, undoubtedly, if it had been light enough. Come on." Gardner lifted Nan on Mitch. He put her clothes and the extra saddle on his pack horse. "I suppose you want to carry your rifle, Steele, all by yourself."

Vaughn walked beside Mitch, across the rolling hills, through the slushy snow of the gullies, puzzled and half resentful of the will of this strange man who led toward Cloverleaf. Gardner set a slow pace. He did not look around or inquire of Vaughn how he was getting along.

The Spotted Hills went on forever. Now and then Gardner glanced toward the mountains. Although he did not try to hurry, there seemed to lie in him an urgency; he gave an impression of feeling that he was wasting time. Watching him one time when he glanced toward the Empires and then briefly at Nan, Vaughn saw a fleeting smile, half sardonic, half gentle.

They came in the middle of the afternoon to the lower reaches of Pennsylvania Creek, which ran through a wide bottom deep with sod. Lee Hester had been first in the Spotted Hills, and he had made no mistake in picking his spot. There were cattle here, in bunches all along the stream, shorthorns that had wintered well.

Vaughn stopped. "I don't know about this, Gardner. I. . . ."

"I do," Gardner said. "Come on."

They entered a silent yard before a huge log house. To the right, along the hill, there were lesser buildings, a bunkhouse, storerooms, a cook shack. Water carried in the adzed halves of logs ran from an enormous spring and made a sparkling fall to a log trough in the yard.

Vaughn had never been here before. He stared around him, half angry, half envious. Two things happened at once. A girl about Vaughn's age came around the shady side of the ranch house. Her flowered gingham was bright and cool-looking. She wore her hair in pigtails, blonde, shining hair that caught the full strike of the sun when she passed the corner of the logs. There was a startled look upon her face.

At the same time a blocky man stepped quickly from one of the storerooms. He was carrying a long strip of rawhide in one hand and a knife in the other. Now he tossed the rawhide behind him and put the knife away. He stared at Gardner. His hand moved toward a pistol on his hip, and then it stopped, and the man's face was no longer surprised but hard and watchful.

"Well, by God," he said.

It was Anson Dodge, the Cloverleaf foreman. Vaughn had seen him before, riding past the Steele homestead. Once he had stopped, looking long and hard at the two Kentucky horses, grunting when Mrs. Steele had tried to be polite, and then he had ridden across the garden on his way out. Gardner gave the man no attention.

"Well, by God!" Dodge said, louder this time.

Still Gardner gave him not as much as a glance.

The girl in pigtails said: "Hello there, Mister Gardner." She looked at Nan, and then her glance flicked quickly over Vaughn. He felt sharp awareness of his dirty clothing, of the heat and tiredness bearing on his body.

Gardner said: "Martha, you're getting uglier every day." A smile passed with the words and the girl returned the smile.

Martha Hester. Vaughn had heard of her. Her glance brushed him again. The smile that she had held for Gardner died then, and she looked away quickly.

"Won't you all come in?" she said.

Gardner swung down. "Just me and Nan, if you please." He introduced the girls, and left Vaughn standing there, leaning on his rifle. Gardner helped Nan from her horse and carried her to the porch.

A tall woman with upswept hair, soft gray, came quickly to the porch with a question in her eyes. "Mister Gardner, is she hurt?"

"Not bad."

The woman held the door and Gardner went inside, still carrying Nan. The woman gave Vaughn a quick, worried glance, and followed. Martha started to say something to Vaughn. She hesitated a moment, and then she, too, went into the house.

The strangeness of the situation angered Vaughn, but it left him helpless. Partly from his helplessness and partly from odd thoughts about Drake Gardner came the knowledge that he trusted the man. He walked across the yard and took a tin cup hanging from a peg near the log flume.

"Who said the water was free?" Anson Dodge came up behind him, scowling.

Vaughn drank slowly, watching the man over the cup. The water was so cold it set Vaughn's teeth on edge. This Dodge was a burly, ugly man, although no single feature of his face was misshapen, but everything seemed to be crowded into too little space in the center of his head. His mouth was a meager cut; it might drop with cowardice or be tight with cruelty. His face glistened from recent shaving, and on it lay a darkness of anger.

Gardner had ignored him. Dodge was feeling that. He wanted now, Vaughn sensed, to vent his anger on a weaker man. The devil with Anson Dodge. He was probably one of those who had ridden last night to the shack.

Vaughn hung the cup up and turned away. Dodge caught his shoulder and spun him around. The grip was powerful. The fingers dug and the thumb gouged.

"I asked a question," Dodge said.

"I'll ask one, too." Vaughn called the man a foul name. "Where were you last night?"

With his free hand Dodge whacked Vaughn across the mouth. He held him easily and struck again, and then he pushed him into the watering trough, kicking his legs up so that Vaughn was neatly jackknifed in the deeply cut log. The icy water took his breath away.

Dodge kicked the fallen rifle to one side. He stood there a moment, losing interest in Vaughn, apparently more angered by this small victory than he had been before. His glance swung toward the house.

"Hold a civil tongue, if you ever have the bad sense to come here again, Steele." Still glancing at the house, Dodge started toward the storeroom.

Vaughn scrabbled out of the trough. He picked up the rifle. He knelt and put the front sight in the middle of Dodge's broad back. He cocked the weapon.

"Steele!" Gardner's voice was a whiplash across the yard. "Steele!"

For an instant Vaughn was thrown off, and then he sighted again. The first shot from the porch threw dust against his face. He jerked his head. The rifle went off with a roar. He heard another pistol shot after that, while he was fumbling blindly for another cartridge.

When he could see again, Gardner was walking across the yard, a smoking pistol in his hand. Dodge was lying on the ground, with his knees up, moving them from side to side, groaning.

III

Vaughn's first feeling was one of triumph, and then he was sick and frightened; he had gut-shot Dodge. Sure as the world, he had put a bullet from the heavy rifle through the man's stomach. He was afraid to go look.

Gardner walked over to the wounded man. He kicked Dodge. "Get up, you scum! You're scratched across the ribs. Get up and get out of my sight."

A cook came out of the mess shack, hesitant about going near the scene. Gardner hauled Dodge to his feet and gave him a vicious shove toward the cook.

"You'll come once too often, Gardner," Dodge said. "You'll come when. . . ."

"Shut up." Gardner put his foot against the man's seat and shoved him violently. The cook came forward and took the foreman by the arm and led him away.

"That was a devil of a thing you tried, Steele." Gardner walked over to Vaughn and stood beside him. "Come on, we're leaving now."

They stopped at the porch. "Martha and you will have to accept my apologies, Missus Hester," Gardner said.

The woman looked at him with a pained expression. Years before she must have been a beautiful woman, but now there was something haunted in her look, and yet, behind that, there seemed to be a great capacity for calmness.

The girl, Martha, looked at Vaughn with fear and loathing. "You were going to shoot him in the back!"

"Of course," Gardner said. "Why not?"

The quick reversal bewildered Vaughn.

Nan hopped out on the porch on one leg. "Vaughn! Are you all right?"

"He's all right, Nan," Mrs. Hester said. "You come with me and get your foot back in that pan."

Martha stayed on the porch while Gardner and Vaughn rode away. They went down the creek a half mile, and then Gardner cut across the hills, straight toward the mountains.

All at once Vaughn reined in his horse. "That's no place for Nan. I'm going back there and get her."

"It's the only place for her," Gardner said. "It's the only place in the whole miserable country."

"But those Hesters. . . ."

"What about the Hesters?" Gardner stopped his horse. "Are you talking about the women, or the men?"

"Old Lee, I mean. . . ."

"There's a younger brother there you've never seen. Pray to God that you don't. Are you coming with me or not?"

Vaughn rode on. "Where was Hester?"

"In the house."

"Why didn't he come out?"

"He has a bullet through his shoulder, or maybe it was high in the chest. He wasn't cordial enough to explain."

"From last night?"

Gardner said: "I'd say so. It's a fair guess."

Lee Hester then for sure. Vaughn thought of his feelings last night when he had fallen over his father in the dark. He checked Mitch again. "I'm going back there.

"Go ahead." Gardner did not look back. "Dodge would

like it just fine if you went smoking back there by yourself. Try for the front of him this time, Steele."

Gardner's unconcern and the truth of his words threw ice on Vaughn's hot intentions. Once more he went ahead to ride beside the man. "Maybe I shouldn't have tried to shoot him, but I was mad. I didn't care."

"I saw that. There's no particular virtue in shooting a man the hard way. Getting Dodge from the front would be the hard way, too, believe me. There is a code that says murder is all right if done under certain rules. I generally follow it but I don't necessarily subscribe to it, although I do recommend it to those who intend to shoot me."

Gardner spoke carelessly but there was no jest in his tone or words. Vaughn swung his horse around on the other side so he would not have to look at the man's scarred face.

"It's that bad, is it?" Gardner asked. "If it scares a man who would shoot another in the back, think what it must do to a woman."

"It wasn't . . . I didn't. . . ."

"The devil it wasn't my face," Gardner said. "Now let's forget it, shall we?"

There was no understanding the man at all, Vaughn thought.

Gardner said: "He spatted you one and you fell backward into the trough, so that made you mad enough to try to kill him."

"He held me and pushed me in."

Gardner laughed curtly without humor. "Hot Southern blood and ice water. It should have cooled you off. You're a prize now. A Rebel's kid who tried to shoot Anson Dodge, after your father already pinged one through Lee Hester's shoulder. There's seven ranches in the Spotted Hills. Your hide would look good on the stable door of any one of them."

"Don't call my father a Rebel, damn you!"

"Don't tell me anything about the war," Gardner said. "Not one single thing. Make a big fat note of that, Vaughn Steele, and maybe we'll get along fine."

The snow-veined mountains seemed to grow higher as the hills unrolled at their feet. Vaughn had never been this far west before. He twisted in the saddle to look at the enormous red carpet stretching out behind them. Somewhere down there, lost entirely now, was the hope that had killed his father.

Vaughn Steele knew that he would never go back to it. He wished that he had burned what was left of the house, leaving only the long mound to remind him of what he must do someday.

They rode into aspen country. There were no fuzzy blooms upon the branches yet but the trunks of the trees were glistening with new green. Underfoot the leaf mat was thick and damp, spilling in chunks from the feet of the horses.

"Why'd you want to settle 'way up here?" Vaughn asked.

"Because I did, that's all." Gardner stopped his horse suddenly and swung around. He waved his hand at the country below. "It looks like half the world down there, doesn't it? It's nothing. It's too small now. You're looking at a battlefield, Steele. The lines are already drawn. Didn't any of that ever drift over to you on that homestead?"

"No. I don't know what you're talking about."

"You'll find out." Gardner looked doubtfully at Vaughn. "I can get you out of this country, you and your sister, in a few days. Where would you go?"

There was no place to go. All the loneliness of the world

settled down on Vaughn. There was a lump in his chest when he thought of his parents. Here he was, separated from Nan, riding away with a stranger to an unknown destination. In the space of a few days all this had come to him.

"You sure my sister will be all right?"

Gardner spoke with the first gentleness he had shown. "She will. Depend on it."

They came at dusk to a small valley set among the rocks. There was a meadow in the upper part. The long grasses were lying on the ground, combed flat by the recent passing of the snow. A dozen horses, still shaggy from the winter, were grazing in the valley. Where the rocks made an arc at the upper end of the meadow, light was showing in the windows of a low cabin.

Gardner dismounted. "Stay here until I call you in." He took his rifle and went ahead on foot.

Sometime later Vaughn saw his shadow pass a window, and then his call came clearly through the growing dark and cold. "All right, Steele!"

Vaughn caught up the rope of the pack horse and went on in, too tired now and jarred by the events of the last twenty-four hours to wonder much about Gardner's behavior. A man came out and helped them unpack, not speaking. He was tall and moved with a minimum of effort, and that was all Vaughn could tell about him. Gardner called him Brett.

When they went inside, Vaughn saw gear piled against the walls and in the corners, six bunks against the walls, and the general rough set-up of a bachelor house. Brett's face was youthful, a restless face. Tiny muscles not ordinarily used in normal expressions moved in it when he spoke. When they sat down to eat, he took off his hat. His hair was white, thick and straight and shockingly white. Vaughn kept looking at it and at the man's face, not knowing then how old to guess his age.

"What's new around the hills, Drake?" Brett asked. He seemed to have accepted Vaughn's presence as normal.

"Nothing," Gardner said. "Just building up."

"Uhn-huh," Brett said tonelessly. He glanced across the room at Vaughn's pistol and rifle lying on a bunk. "Did you see little Gentle Face this time?"

"Who said I was over there?"

"You were late coming back, that's all."

"My business, Janney. All mine." Gardner looked at Vaughn. "Take the bunk where you left your loot."

Vaughn was drooping in his chair. The heat of the cabin, the long ride, and the drop from tension had loosened everything in him. He stumbled off to bed.

The lamp on the table seemed to burn all night. He half wakened now and then, enough to realize it was still lighted, that the two men were still sitting at the table.

He heard Brett Janney say: "Who is he, Drake?"

"From the shack down there. They wrecked it last night."

"Where does he fit now?"

"Does he have to fit? Does everything have to work out in that cold-blooded mind of yours?"

Janney laughed gently, but it was not a pleasant sound. "I've always said you have a soft spot, Gardner."

"That's my business."

"Up to a point. Then it becomes mine."

"We'll see," Gardner said.

Vaughn went back to sleep, into the sweet darkness of rest where nothing could puzzle him, and no guns could speak to him from the night. When he woke up in the morning, Brett Janney was gone.

Two men had eaten breakfast, for the tinware was still on the table. There was a fire in the stove and hot coffee in the pot. Vaughn cooked a meal and cleaned up the mess. He walked out into the sunrise, surprised to see that the Spotted Hills were visible through the rift in the rocks where the trail came up.

He walked to the center of the meadow. The shaggy horses edged away from him warily. There was a dark stripe on their backs. They were smaller than Mitch or any of the average run of ranch animals he had seen. There was a wiry, tough look about them that said they could winter any place they pleased. He recalled what Gardner had said about thoroughbreds in this country.

The sun swept up the long miles of the Spotted Hills. From here they were beautiful, for this was shelter. Grimly and solidly sat the mountains and they gave a feeling of security that Vaughn had never felt on the open land.

Drake Gardner came riding from the trees that had root-split granite to hold to life around the edges of the meadow. He was a slouching rider, sitting his horse as if it were merely an extension of his own body. For the first time Vaughn saw the man's face as a whole, without the scarred side standing out alone. In a way, it was not nearly as startling as Janney's mobile features thrown in sharp contrast against his snow-white hair.

Impulsively, and not from raw curiosity, Vaughn asked, touching his own cheek: "How'd you get that?"

"A fool threw a bucket of water on the breech of a red-hot cannon while we were waiting for the battery to cool. I was the luckiest one of the whole crew." Gardner stared at the hills. "Pretty, huh?"

"I like it better right here. There's something you can put your back against."

213

"Oh?" Gardner gave the youth an odd look. "Yeah. Living down there on the flats. I see. But you better learn, Steele, that you can't put your back against anything, because there is never anything but yourself behind you. You're sure you don't want to leave the Spotted Hills for good?"

"Not this part of it."

"Why?"

"Someone killed my father. I. . . ."

"Someone killed my father, too, and my mother, and my two brothers. I'd be a damned fool if I spent my life trying to get even over that. There were ten men, at least, in that mob at your shack, Steele. No one will ever know who shot your father. You'd better forget about it."

"Forget about it!" Vaughn cursed. "They might have killed my sister, too. They didn't care."

"Lee Hester wouldn't have been there if he'd known Nan was home. I'll bet he thought she was still in town. He wouldn't have let any of his men. . . ."

"You're pretty thick with the Hesters, Gardner."

"I hate Lee, and I hate his brother, Finlay, even worse."

"You go right to their place and. . . ."

"Shot their foreman. That was your fault, Steele."

"You shot Dodge? I thought. . . ."

"You thought you nicked him with that rifle. I know. I knocked dirt in your eyes with one shot and raked another across his ribs just when he was leveling down on you, Steele. Your shot put a hole in the rooster's tail on the wind vane, I think . . . on top of the barn."

IV

Vaughn blinked. He owed this man a lot. First, for seeing that Nan was taken care of, and then for several other things. If he could not understand some of Gardner's actions, he still was bound by loyalty to him.

With a wondering sort of bitterness, Gardner sat looking down at him. "Get that pistol, Steele. Let's see what you can miss with it."

The separator from a case of crackers was big at twenty paces. Vaughn's grip was natural and loose; his eyes were good and his nerves were young and steady. He slammed his shots fairly close to the middle of the target.

"Try again," Gardner said.

Vaughn let off one more careful shot after reloading. He was aiming when the pistol blasted, almost against him, it seemed. He felt the gush of heat across one ear, the sting of powder grains. His shot went some place and he had no idea where.

Gardner put his own pistol away, his eyes inscrutable. "Got the idea? Men like to shoot back."

In the days to come Vaughn learned to shoot a pistol at a target, not flinching when Gardner fired beside him, no jerking when Gardner yelled wildly, trying to hold steady even when Gardner shoved him.

"I don't know," Gardner said. "You might become too

good at it. You might get the idea that calling out a man and facing him like a gentleman is honorable and good. Someday you might decide it was time to shoot Anson Dodge from the front. Then I could bury you."

"What makes Dodge so tough?"

"Cowardice, and ambition. He also would like. . . ." Gardner stopped suddenly and walked away from the target area near the rocks. "I'll go with you someday to see Nan. Don't ever try it alone."

A rider from Cloverleaf had been to the valley the week before, to carry a message saying that Nan's foot was all right. The courier had been uneasy. He watched the rocks around Gardner's place; he stared at Gardner himself in fear, and he left soon after the message was delivered.

That night across a hot lamp in the low-roofed cabin Vaughn studied Gardner. He liked the man now; he trusted him. He had come to think the thing that Brett Janney had spoken, that Gardner had a large soft spot in him, not weakness, but inherent decency that the man tried to hide with curtness.

"How come you could take Nan right to Cloverleaf and be sure she would be welcome . . . after what the Hesters did to us?"

Gardner frowned. "The Hesters, not even Finlay, take their brutality out on women, at least not by violence."

"I've never seen Finlay."

"That's too bad." Gardner rose and started to undress.

"I want to go see my sister."

"Tomorrow."

Vaughn undressed and got into his bunk. "Who are all these extra bunks for?"

"Anyone that needs a bed."

"No one comes here."

"Not since you've been around, just Janney."

"Who's he?"

"An old acquaintance."

After a while Vaughn said: "You don't ever sell any of those horses you breed."

"The strain is not right yet. Shut up, Steele."

In the dead of night Vaughn heard the hail. He grabbed his pistol and swung out of bed and padded barefoot to the door. There he collided in the darkness with Gardner.

"It's all right," Gardner said. "Light the lamp." He opened the door and called: "All right, Janney!"

There were five of them. White-haired Brett Janney was the only one Vaughn had seen before. They came in like they lived here. A flat-nosed man with a curling black beard tasted the water, then tossed the dipperful on the floor. He looked at Vaughn. "Get a fresh bucket, kid."

Vaughn said: "Get it yourself, or ask in another tone."

Janney laughed. "He learns fast from you, Drake." He looked at the bearded man. "Go get your water, Sloss. You know where the creek runs."

Gardner sat at the table, smoking his pipe in measured puffs. He watched the men cook a meal and wolf it down. Except for Janney, they ate as if they had not seen food for a long time. Janney's hands were long and slender. He cut his bacon up in small pieces. He wiped his lips afterward, looking with delicate distaste at the soiled bandanna he used.

There was little speech, but enough for Vaughn to realize that four of the men spoke with the slurred accent of the South. Sloss's lips were thin and red in his beard. He watched Vaughn thoughtfully at times.

The meal over, Janney took a cheroot from his pocket.

"It's growing a little tiresome on the other side."

"Maybe you'll get used to it," Gardner said.

"I'm afraid not. The men don't like it, either."

"Not a bit," Sloss said. "Not one bit."

Vaughn looked from face to face. They were watching Gardner, and the tension was full and thick.

Janney said: "You haven't changed year mind, have you, Drake?"

"I never made it up in the first piece."

"Ah, yes. I began to suspect that when I was here last. That's why we came again so soon."

"No," Gardner said. "Not your way, Janney."

"What's your way?"

"There isn't any."

Janney smiled. "Let's not say that. Charley Burgett and Troutt Warner don't think so." He yawned, but there was tension even in that. He looked around at the four who had come with him. "Suppose we talk about it again in the morning, Drake, just you and I, without the doubtful benefit of these hairy, drooping ears."

"We can talk," Gardner said. "No difference, though."

"There might be," Janney said. "There always has been where. . . ."

"That's enough." Gardner had put on his pants and boots, and he had thrust his pistol into the waistband of his pants. The lamplight gave his face an evil, waiting look, heightening, rather than softening, the pits and scars on the one side.

Vaughn saw a careful weighing, mixed with fear, in the eyes of four men who watched Gardner, but he saw only a deadly sort of amusement on Janney's face. The muscles of Janney's cheeks and forehead rippled easily when he smiled. For an instant Vaughn wondered if the man could flick a certain area of his skin to scare a fly away. It gave him a queasy feeling to think about it.

Gardner's live dark eyes caught sharp points of light and jetted them. He was sitting sidewise at the table, with one leg braced solidly against it. Sloss shifted his arms casually, placing both hands against the edge of the table on his side.

Gardner's eyes touched Sloss like the tip of a whip. "You wouldn't try to jam me in against the wall, would you, Max? You might need both those hands to hold your guts in if you tried."

"Max was never very subtle," Janney said. He yawned again. "Get up and go to bed, you ox!"

The bearded man came up from the table slowly. His teeth gleamed whitely as he tried to pass it off with a twisted smile. He walked down the narrow room, sat on Vaughn's bunk, and started to remove his boots.

"That's my bed," Vaughn said.

"It was." Sloss grunted as he tugged at his boots. "You can have it back tomorrow."

Both Gardner and Janney were watching Vaughn. What lay on Gardner's face the youth could not tell, but the fixed, waiting set of the man seemed to demand decision.

"Get off my bed."

"You've got a big mouth, son. You've been too long around Gardner."

Vaughn glanced once more from the corner of his eye at Gardner, and then he kicked with his heavy shoe as hard as he could. The toe caught Sloss fully in the beard. It straightened him up from bending toward his boots. His head rapped hard against the bunk above him.

Wide-eyed, he sat there loosely. Vaughn grabbed him by the shirt front and hauled him up, intending to push him toward the end of the room. The man came to life with a grunt. He knocked Vaughn across the room. Sloss shook his head and started after Vaughn.

Once more Vaughn glanced at Gardner. Both he and Janney were still seated, watching but apparently unconcerned.

Sloss hurled himself across the room. Vaughn slid along the wall. The bearded man crashed hard against the logs, bringing down a fine sprinkle of dirt from the roof.

Janney murmured: "I said he wasn't subtle."

Sloss turned, kicking at a saddle that lay across his feet. His eyes were dazed. He hunched his shoulders and started toward Vaughn again. Vaughn raised on his toes and with all his might brought down the stick of aspen wood he had snatched from a pile beside the stove.

It made a sodden sound on Sloss's head. Vaughn struck again while the man was groping toward him. Sloss fell to his knees, shaking his head. He began to rise slowly. Vaughn reached to the wall beside his bunk and got his pistol. He started to use it as a club, and then he cocked it.

"Never mind!" Gardner said sharply.

"Your bed, I'd say." Janney laughed. "Wouldn't you, Max?"

Sloss lurched past Vaughn and sat down on a bunk against the end wall. He twisted his head from side to side, holding one hand spread on the top of his skull.

Janney's other companions moved quietly, preparing to turn in. One of them, a squat man with a baldhead spotted with great freckles, looked across the room and winked solemnly at Vaughn.

"This mountain air does things to a man, Drake," Janney said. The little dips and trenches moved with his smile, but his eyes were bleakly speculative as he looked at Vaughn.

Gardner and Janney talked inside after breakfast, telling the others to go see that the sun came up all right.

Vaughn went to the meadow. Green was rising among the dead grasses of long summer. Vaughn called Mitch, and the animal tossed gouts of earth and wisps of grass from flying hoofs as it galloped to him. Gardner's horses caught the smell of the morning, snorting and kicking as they raced down the meadow.

The world was young, Vaughn thought, and this had been a wonderful place before Janney and Sloss came.

The bald man who had winked at Vaughn left his three companions at the small corral and came out to Vaughn. "Fair piece of horseflesh there," he said loudly. Frog was this man's name. His mouth was wide and puckered, and, if he had any teeth at all, they were not in front.

He walked around Mitch. From the side away from Vaughn he said in an almost inaudible voice: "Don't ever let Max get his hands on you, kid. You would have been ahead last night if you'd pulled that trigger."

"Who are you fellows?"

Frog patted Mitch's shoulder. "Would you sell him?" His voice was normal again.

"Where do you come from, Frog?"

The man glanced toward the mountains. "Well, maybe I don't blame you for not wanting to sell him." He walked back to the corral, where his companions were watching.

Vaughn was chopping wood when Gardner and Janney came out. Janney was not smiling now. There was a cold tightness in Gardner's manner.

Janney said: "Saddle up."

Before the five rode toward the Spotted Hills, Max Sloss licked his red lips and shook his head at Vaughn. Gardner watched until the long folds of the land took the riders. The grass was coming down there now, irregular patches of it against the red, making the pattern that gave the hills their name.

Gardner's face was grim. "Did you enjoy that show you put on last night, Steele?"

"No."

"You wanted to show me you could take care of yourself, huh? How far would you have gone without me around?"

"It was my bunk."

"My bunk," Gardner said. "My land. My slaves. My right, no matter what." He started toward the house. "We'll go to Cloverleaf now."

"What does Janney and those others do?"

Gardner went inside without answering. *To hell with him then,* Vaughn thought. He did not ask any more questions during the morning's ride.

On the creek below Cloverleaf they met Lee Hester riding a long-legged bay. One of his arms was in a black sateen sling. He nodded to Gardner and some inner amusement twisted his face.

"You stayed away longer than usual, Drake." Mockery came with the words, puzzling Vaughn and irritating him. No one seemed to care if he knew what was going on. He kept staring at Hester, trying to feel deep anger against the man, this handsome, arrogant man who had come by dark to the Steele homestead to wreck and murder. It came as a surprise to Vaughn that his feelings did not touch the peak he thought they should. He hated Lee Hester and always would, but he did not want to kill him.

Gardner was watching Vaughn narrowly, and it was because of that steady scrutiny that Hester turned his eyes. He said: "I did not know your sister was in the house that night, Steele. For your further information, my men were all unarmed."

Vaughn said nothing.

"Your white-haired friend has ridden to the Wagon Wheel, Hester," Gardner said.

"A waste of time. Burgett and Warner are my friends."

"Ask Finlay about that. He draws more truth about men from the air than you ever could by studying them."

Hester smiled thinly. "Brother Protector, why don't you move to Cloverleaf? Or could you stand that?" He watched Gardner's face turn white, ashen on one side, hideously splotched against the scars on the other. "No, Drake, I don't believe you could." Hester laughed and rode away. "Excuse me. Spring roundup."

Nan and Martha Hester were working in a flower garden beside the house when Gardner and Vaughn rode in. Nan dropped a spade and came running to Vaughn. Her face was radiant. Whatever blight of uncertainty lay on Cloverleaf, it had not touched her, Vaughn thought.

"Where have you been so long, Vaughn?"

Vaughn nodded toward the mountains. He was glad to see this girl who threw her arms around him, but he was embarrassed by the act. Martha Hester stood at the edge of the garden, watching. Her hair was up today, and the effect gave her a startling resemblance to her mother, without the strained, haunted look of Mrs. Hester.

"I've got a room all by myself!" Nan said. "You'll have to see it. Martha and I . . . you never talked to Martha when you were here before, did you?" Nan pulled him toward the girl. "This is my brother, Martha."

Martha smiled and spoke as if she had not known the fact before. Vaughn dragged off his hat, conscious that his hair was overlong and probably disordered. The heavy pistol on his hip seemed out of place. He bowed without thinking, a gesture that his father had taught him long ago, and now it seemed betrayal of Carmody Steele to be acting so at the Hester place.

Gardner had already gone into the house. Suddenly awkward in his heavy shoes, Vaughn stumbled back and picked up the reins of the horses. "I'd better give them a drink."

Nan chattered at his side while he let the horses drink. He looked uneasily at the house and at the other silent buildings.

"Mister Hester's brother, Finlay, is nice," Nan said. "He sent a man out to put a board on father's grave."

"He did?" Vaughn had thought of doing so himself. *Pray that you don't meet Finlay,* Gardner had said. Now Nan said he was nice. Confused and troubled, Vaughn stared at the house. Martha went up the steps. "I'll start straightening up your room, Nan, so you can show it to your brother."

Mrs. Hester came to the porch. "Put the horses in the corral, if you wish, Mister Steele. You and Mister Gardner will have dinner with us."

"They really do eat here, Vaughn," Nan said.

"Yeah? Are you ashamed of the way we used to live?"

"No, but . . . there's something funny about you, Vaughn. You act a lot older than you used to. It's only been a few weeks, but you're changed."

Inside, the house seemed larger than it did from outside. Two hallways ran from a large living room toward winged Ls on each side of the central area. Gardner was pacing the living room. He barely glanced at Vaughn when Nan rushed him down one of the halls to see her room. It was large and comfortable, and there were furnishings in it that had never been in the Steele shack.

"Mother used to talk about things like this," Nan said. "Isn't it wonderful?"

Vaughn was vaguely dissatisfied, suspicious of what seemed like finery to him. Somewhere in his background there had been finer rooms than this, but all that meant nothing to him now, for he had heard only his parents' talk of days before the war.

Mrs. Hester was talking to Gardner when Vaughn returned to the living room. There was a haunted bleakness on his face, too, it seemed to Vaughn. *Damn, but this was an odd place.*

V

The dinner did not change anything. Vaughn observed that Gardner barely ate. The rest of the time he kept watching Mrs. Hester, his black eyes lifting to her as if he were looking against his will, or without conscious knowledge of the act. They finished in silence.

Mrs. Hester said: "Perhaps Mister Steele would like to see your father's horses, Martha."

"He probably would," Martha said. "Uncle Finlay wants to see him first, though."

"Oh?" Mrs. Hester gave Gardner a startled look.

"Why not, Molly?" Gardner shrugged.

"I'll show him," Nan said. Going down the hall with Vaughn, she whispered: "Uncle Finlay is awful nice, Vaughn. It's too bad about him."

She knocked on a door and a soft voice said: "Yes, Nan, tell your brother to come in, and would you please look once more for the violets there in the damp by the spring. They should be out by now."

The room was furnished in dark oak. A shade halfway down on an enormous window let slanting light rest in a bright wall on the feet and legs of a gentle-looking man who sat in a straight-backed chair near a bed. There was a tray of food on a table beside him.

"You would be young Vaughn Steele?"

"Yes."

"Stand right there a moment and say that again, please."

Utterly puzzled, Vaughn obeyed. Finlay Hester tilted his head, nodding. His face had the pink look of baby skin. His hair was jet black, and his eyes held a patient, seeking look.

"About six feet. Large for your age," he said. "Now walk over to that armchair . . . don't tiptoe, please . . . and sit down."

Once more Vaughn obeyed. He was still halfway across the room from Hester, who sat in his own uncomfortable chair with what seemed to Vaughn to be back-breaking stiffness.

"You must weigh a hundred and seventy-five pounds, Mister Steele."

"I guess so."

"And you fully intended to shoot Anson Dodge sometime ago. Did you leave a pistol outside when you came here today?"

"Yes, sir."

"Are you proficient with it? Oh, never mind." Hester wiped out the question with a wave of his hand. "You would be, of course, being with Drake Gardner any length of time at all. How do you like Drake?"

The man had cocked his head to the other side now. He had the softest voice, the gentlest manner Vaughn had ever known. Gentle Face! That was the name Brett Janney had used. *Did you see little Gentle Face this time?*

"How do you like Drake, Mister Steele?"

"Fine."

"Of course. And Janney?"

"I don't like him."

"How many men did Brett have with him the last time he came?"

"Four."

"They went back over the mountains, as usual, I suppose?"

"They went to Wagon Wheel."

There was a pause as sharp as a flung question. "I see," Hester said. "I would say that you did not care for any of those men." He waited. "Your silence is sufficient. Another important consideration. How do you feel about the death of your father? I mean . . . about the men who killed him."

"I hate them."

"That is natural. You don't realize it, of course, but your father persisted in bringing about his fate. He belonged to a lost group. He was further lost when your mother recognized basic facts that he refused to see. She acted. He clung to nothing. Your sister is a charming youngster, Mister Steele. I assume she is greatly like her mother."

"No," Vaughn said. "She's like my father."

"That can be corrected. I've wandered a little, Mister Steele. Let us move toward a more immediate point. When you started to kill Anson Dodge, was it utter rage that made you act as you did, or were you impelled by the more logical view that the task could be best accomplished without the dragging impediments of code and honor? I refer, of course, to your attempted method."

"You mean was I out of my head, or did I figure I ought to kill him anyway I could get him?"

"Roughly put, but correct. How was it?"

"I don't know."

"Ah! That is encouraging. We have had too much prattle of honor around here for too long." Hester cleared his throat. "Step over there to the window, please. Don't bother to raise the shade. Merely pull it back a little and tell me what you see."

Vaughn did as he was directed. Against the hill was a lattice house covered with vines that were just beginning to unfold their leaves. Drake Gardner was standing there, looking down at Mrs. Hester. She shook her head.

Vaughn Steele's experience was limited, but he had seen his father look at his mother with that same intense, tender expression. He let the shade swing back against the window casing. The one short look had given him a view of a Drake Gardner he did not know at all. He went quickly across the room and sat down.

Finlay Hester had taken the tray from the table beside him. He was eating, lifting his food with overly careful movements, almost dainty in his precision. Vaughn was reminded then of Brett Janney. Suddenly an uneasy feeling began to mount toward fear. There was something strange and evil here, something akin to the crawling sensation that Vaughn had felt when he wondered if Janney could jerk any given portion of his flesh, like an animal.

"You saw. I suppose it must have startled you, Mister Steele."

Vaughn was not Mr. Steele; he was a boy who wanted to get out of this room, into the clean sunlight. But he sat where he was, repelled and fascinated by the erect figure in the straight-backed chair.

"They have loved each other a long time," Hester said. "A man not hampered by code and honor would have taken her from my brother, who did not deserve her in the first place. But not the gallant Drake. Oh, no. He merely sits in his aerie there in the mountains, a slave to puny man-made law."

Hester put his fork down as if the food had lost taste. He

229

set the tray on the table, lifting it high and letting it down quite gently. "I had hopes for Drake Gardner, my boy, but the war brought out a latent defect in him, the stupidity called honor. Now you are different. You have made a good start, although I would have been temporarily embarrassed by the loss of Anson Dodge. You can serve where Gardner failed. There is one man who is a festering sore in the Spotted Hills. When he is gone, things will arrange themselves, with some direction, of course. I mean Bret Janney. Kill him for me, Mister Steele, and you will be rewarded well."

"Kill him?"

"Why, yes. By any means you see fit, as expediently as you would have shot Anson Dodge. Once that is done, return to me here. Believe me, the world will begin to unfold for you in its true perspective then. You will begin to understand that kings are made, not born. As a small start to aid your present limited understanding. . . ." Hester opened a drawer in the table at his elbow and pulled out a small packet. The rectangle of sunlight reached from his polished boots to slender, pale hands that held the packet.

"As a meager start, but important in its way, here is five hundred dollars." Hester flipped the packet across the room. It struck Vaughn's chest and dropped to his lap.

All at once his fear was overwhelming terror. Hester's head was cocked to one side, and his seeking eyes looked at Vaughn with fixed attention. The man was smiling gently. Vaughn stumbled to his feet. He put the money on the chair and started to run from the room.

"Come now." Hester frowned. "Have I made a mistake? Surely I haven't, have I?"

Looking back at Hester, Vaughn flung the door open, keeping his hand on the knob. He jerked when someone touched his arm. Nan was standing in the hall with a tiny bunch of woods violets in her hand. She put her finger on her lips, shaking her head to indicate silence. Stupidly Vaughn stared at her.

"I did make a slight misjudgment, I see," Hester said. "Fear, I suppose, instead of honor, was the deterrent this time. Ah, well. . . ." Hester sighed. "If you see Nan before you leave, please tell her I am waiting for the violets."

She was standing there in full view of him. Vaughn knew then that Finlay Hester was blind.

"I'm here Uncle Finlay!" Nan cried. "And I've got something, too!"

Vaughn watched her dart into the room. She gave the tiny bouquet to Hester. He raised it to his face and his smile was beatific as he inhaled the scent, and all the time the blind eyes seemed to be looking straight at Vaughn.

"Your brother and I just had a most interesting chat, Nan."

Vaughn went quickly down the hall. He startled Mrs. Hester, who was looking from a living room window. Outside, Drake Gardner was leading his and Vaughn's horses from the corral.

"I think Mister Gardner is ready to leave." A bleak, drained expression on Mrs. Hester's face did not change. "Come see us again soon, Mister Steele. Nan misses you a great deal."

Just before Vaughn mounted, Nan raced down the steps and embarrassed him again by hugging him while Martha watched from the porch with an amused smile. Nan said: "Wasn't Uncle Finlay the nicest man you ever met?"

Vaughn glanced at Gardner. "She'll be all right," Gardner said. "Don't worry."

They rode down the creek. Gardner was silent,

brooding. Vaughn said: "That Finlay. . . ."

"I know. He puts a chill on a man. God knows why kids and women think he's fine."

They passed a herd of cattle being held by three men. Anson Dodge was on the ground, tightening his cinch. The hostility of his glance and poise came across fifty yards of space like a shout.

"Finlay Hester's eyes," Gardner said. "Lately they have been corrupted, but Finlay doesn't know it."

There was a black mood on Gardner. When they came to the place where they should have turned to return to the mountains, he rode straight ahead.

"Where we going?" Vaughn asked.

"To town!" Gardner was savage.

He was in love with Mrs. Hester and he could not do anything about it. Vaughn tried to think of what a man should do in a case like that. He did not know. He recalled how his father had come apart after Faith Steele left. Maybe there was good reason for Gardner's mood.

"Nan said he put a headboard on my father's grave."

"Finlay? Sure. He loves to advertise a dead Rebel. Who do you think sent those men out that night, Steele?"

"Him?"

"Yes, him! Cloverleaf is his, not Lee's."

It came to Vaughn how little he knew of anything in the Spotted Hills, how close his bondage to the soil of Elk Run had been. "He offered me five hundred dollars to kill Brett Janney. Why did he pick me? I'm just. . . ."

"You earned it by the way you acted the first time we went to Cloverleaf. He picked you because Anson Dodge isn't man enough, and because I won't kill Janney without an excuse . . . and maybe not even with an excuse."

"I don't know what's going on. I don't. . . ."

"Maybe it's a good thing," Gardner said. "For a brat fresh off a homestead you've done plenty lately. You've attracted Finlay Hester's attention, and you've marked yourself with Janney's gang. You don't seem to have to know what's going on to get into trouble."

Vaughn said in a surly tone: "I don't have to go to town with you, or anywhere else."

"No, you can go back to Cloverleaf and take that five hundred. Finlay's probably laughing now because you didn't take his blood money and walk out with it, without any intention of earning it. That's what he would have done."

"I don't want money made that way."

Gardner grunted.

"Is Lee Hester like Finlay?"

"No. He's the next thing to helplessness there ever was behind a handsome face. He's as dumb about what's going on as you are."

"He's dumb, huh? He wasn't so dumb but what he got the woman you wanted."

Gardner's face turned gray. He shot a wicked look at Vaughn and for a moment Vaughn thought he was going to curse violently.

"Who told you that?" Gardner asked.

"I looked out of the window of Finlay's room. For a dumb brat fresh off a homestead, I still know one or two things when I see them."

"Finlay told you to look!" Gardner cursed Finlay Hester then. He would not talk any more on the ride to town.

Gettysburg clung hard against the railroad, board shacks that drew their sustenance from iron instead of soil. The town was weathered, dirty; it did not have the appeal to Vaughn that it once had offered. When they stabled their

233

horses at Burnett's livery, the train from the east was whistling in the distance.

Gardner said: "The conductor that took your mother doesn't make this run any more, in case you're looking for trouble."

"What makes you say I always look for trouble?"

"Maybe you don't." Gardner's tone was different then. Vaughn realized that the man's curtness from the very first might have been partly from an effort to make him and Nan forget their grief and shock over Carmody Steele's death.

"I'll be here a while," Gardner said. He held two $10 notes toward Vaughn. "Those clodhoppers you're wearing look like hell. So do your pants and shirt. What do you think Nan and Martha must have thought of them?"

"I'll pay you back."

"Pay! Pay! Everybody tries to pay something in this world, even Finlay Hester. He was standing right beside me when that gun blew up. He's been trying to pay somebody for it ever since."

Vaughn made what he thought was a shrewd guess. "Was it Brett Janney who threw the bucket of water on the cannon?"

"Oh, hell! The man who did that got the breech of the piece right through his stomach. Brett Janney was. . . ." Gardner looked sourly at Vaughn. "I'll see you." He strode down the street.

VI

Vaughn bought new clothes. He went to a barbershop for a haircut and bath. Sitting in the chair while the barber clipped and sheared, he watched Charley Burgett of the Wagon Wheel pull up with a spring wagon across the street, in front of the general store.

"I hear you're up there with Drake Gardner now," the barber said.

"Yeah."

After a while the barber asked: "Hear anything of your ma?"

"No."

The barber eased away to more comfortable ground. "Those five men of Burgett's and Warner's at Wagon Wheel sure must be eaters. Now that's the second time this week Charley's been in town loading up with grub."

"Five men?"

"The regular crew. They must eat enough for a dozen men, I'd say."

Brett Janney's bunch had gone to Wagon Wheel, Gardner had said. They must be staying there. What then did that mean? All the shreds of half statements and his own guesses swirled in Vaughn's mind, but they would not coalesce.

"How does Lee Hester and Wagon Wheel get along?" Vaughn asked.

"Well," the barber said cautiously, "there's some feeling there, I hear." He watched Charley Burgett and a clerk lift a barrel of flour into the wagon. "Charley's a good customer of mine. Yup, there's some feeling between the two ranches." He glanced at Vaughn's pistol belt hanging on an elk-horn rack in the corner. "What does Drake Gardner think about the situation, Steele?"

"I don't know."

"He's pretty thick with the Hesters."

"Is he?"

"I hear that," the barber said quickly. "You know, a person can hear most anything."

The barber watched Vaughn from the sides of his eyes while the youth strapped on his pistol belt. "Going home tonight?"

"Next week."

Vaughn stood on the street a moment. There had been a chance to find out a great deal of gossip, but he had become disgusted and cut the barber off short. It was too much like peering from the window at Gardner and Mrs. Hester. Still, there were many things he would like to know.

He walked across the street. Burgett was tying a tarpaulin over his supplies. He was a tall man with sloping shoulders and heavy wrists that ran far beyond the cuffs of his linsey-woolsey shirt. His eyes were deep-set beside blistered cheek bones. He wore a pistol in his waistband. There was rust upon the hammer, and it looked as if the rust might extend on down to seal the hammer into the frame.

"Lots of visitors at your place, Burgett?"

"What makes you ask?"

"I wondered."

"Uhn-huh." Burgett rubbed red stubble on his cheeks. "Been around the homestead lately, Steele?"

"The last time was several weeks ago, at night."

Burgett nodded. His gaze kept wandering up and down the street. He did not know exactly where Gardner was.

"Were you there that night, Burgett?"

The rancher stared. The sharp directness of the question laid guilt across his eyes.

"There's a lot of hills out there, Burgett. They dip and rise, and there's rocks and trees. If I were you, I'd clean the rust off that pistol."

"By God, you've tried to put on weight since you took up with Drake Gardner."

Vaughn said: "I never had reason to before. Look behind every hill you come to from now on, Burgett."

"You're just a kid!" Some of that was surprise and much of it was fear and wondering.

Vaughn Steele learned quickly wherein the marks of cowardice lie. Burgett was afraid of him. It gave Vaughn a heady feeling. Let the man ride forever with the fear that a bullet would seek him out from ambush someday. He had fired in the night at rifle flashes near a lurching shack. Let the memory of that and the words Vaughn had spoken feed the worms of fear in his brain from now on.

Vaughn learned much, but he learned too little. He turned and started down the street. Instants later he heard Drake Gardner say: "No, Burgett, no."

Gardner was standing in the doorway of the store, his pistol in his hand. Burgett's pistol was half drawn, and he was looking at Vaughn, and his face was twisted.

"Go home, Charley," Gardner said. "Tell Janney and Warner anything that comes to mind."

After Burgett drove away, Gardner walked down to Vaughn. He gave the youth a savage look. "You see what it feels like, what you started to do to Dodge?"

"I was bluffing him. I didn't think he. . . ."

"You wear a pistol. You lack ten years of experience in knowing how to use it. Go to Missus Trotter's boarding house, Steele, and go to bed. I'll come there after you when it's time to go home."

Vaughn said: "Yes, sir."

Mrs. Trotter hugged him. She smelled of cooking grease and sweat. "I've been worried sick about you and Nan. I can't understand how she ever went to the Hesters."

"The women there are all right."

"By hell, how could they be? Look what them Hesters done to your pa, boy."

Before he finished eating, Vaughn learned another thing: Gardner had been right, a railroad boarding house was no place to raise a girl. But neither could he leave Nan at Cloverleaf forever; he did not know what to do.

The room Vaughn went to held an odor like a day coach after two nights of being crowded with passengers. A dusty heat came in with the night wind from the railroad yards, and then the framing members of the building began to creak when late coolness spread from the hills. Vaughn tossed on a lumpy mattress, thinking of his bunk at Gardner's place, thinking of the cool wind brushing curtains in the dainty room where Nan slept at Cloverleaf.

He wondered what Martha's room was like, and he wondered if she would notice his new clothes the next time he rode to Cloverleaf. Finlay Hester's gentle face and the press of evil in the darkened room where he had sat were all mixed up with the blotched, murderous expression on Charley Burgett's face when he would have shot Vaughn in the back.

Rest had barely come to Vaughn when Mrs. Trotter shook him, standing by his bed with a brass lamp in her hand, in a shapeless sleeping dress, with her hair all wild about her face.

"Get Drake Gardner out of town," she said. "Did you tell anyone you were going to stay here a week?"

Vaughn could not remember, and anyway the question seemed to have no point. He swung out of bed, groping for his pants.

"There's talk. By daylight men from Wagon Wheel are coming here for Drake. It might be later but that makes no difference. Get Drake and go home. He's in the back room of the Spotted Hills saloon. Now get to hell moving, Vaughn."

The town lay dead. There was no light in the Spotted Hills saloon. Vaughn shivered in the pre-dawn cold. A friendly dog came out from a bed in a pile of manure and huddled against his legs, thumping the ground with its tail.

"She said the back room," Vaughn muttered, and the dog took the words as approval and thumped the ground more violently. Vaughn went to the livery stable. A sleepy hostler cursed and said: "Two dollars, and get them yourself, at this hour. You people never come or go at a decent time."

Vaughn paid. A dirty lantern made a cavern of the stable as he went along the stalls. He passed the rump of a sorrel horse, and then he turned and went back, moving in an empty stall beside it, holding the lantern high. The sorrel was warm. It rattled its halter when it swung its head at him nervously, and then he recognized the blaze mark. Brett Janney's horse.

Vaughn ran back to the stairway and called: "When did that sorrel come in?"

"Just before I went to sleep the last time, fifteen minutes ago."

"There's two more dollars here under the lantern. Saddle mine and Gardner's and bring them to the Spotted Hills saloon right away."

He heard the hostler sigh. The man's bare feet came down with a *thump* on the loft floor. "I guess I was never meant to sleep."

The dog leaped beside Vaughn's knee as he ran down the street. He went behind a row of buildings, stumbling over cans and broken bottles. And then he slowed to a walk and felt his way to where a dim light showed at the back of the Spotted Hills. There was a grayish scum upon the glass and the corners of the window were rounded with spider webs.

Gardner was sitting at a table under a Rivers lamp. Brett Janney sat across from him, his hat pushed back on his white hair. There was a whiskey bottle and one glass upon the table. The scarred side of Gardner's face was toward Vaughn. He saw the sweat on it.

". . . the difference you asked about . . . I can trust you if you give your word, Drake," Janney said. "I can't trust Burgett and Warner and Anson Dodge. I have their word and they have mine. . . ."

"And none is any good," Gardner said. He poured a drink and took it slowly.

"That's right." The creases ran on Janney's face.

"I told you how it was yesterday."

"I don't believe you. You'll get everything you want out of it. How can you turn it down?"

"I am."

"He stole her, Drake. Lee knew you weren't dead. He talked to a man who saw you in the hospital. He let her believe the report and stole her."

"Damn you, leave her out of this."

"I can't. She's all you want, Drake."

"I'm not in it!"

"You are. It was in your mind when you came here. That's why you built those extra bunks in your cabin, and told us to drop in anytime. Even dumb Max Sloss caught on. Who are you trying to fool, Drake? Take another drink."

Gardner drank automatically. He shook his head at Janney. "No." There was no force in the refusal.

"If I thought you'd take her and leave, I wouldn't worry, but I know you won't. You're against us, Drake, if you're not with us. I'll have enough to handle all the rest, without that. You planned it. You planned it from the first."

Gardner put both hands on his forehead. His elbow knocked over the glass. It rolled in an arc toward the edge of the table. Janney waited until it fell. He caught it, refilled it, and set it before Gardner.

"You had it in mind to drive Lee into the ground and take Molly," Janney said. "What's wrong about that?"

"I changed my mind," Gardner mumbled.

The admission startled Vaughn but his loyalty to Gardner was not affected. The sight of Janney, smiling, twisting the barbs of his words into a helpless man brought a fearful rage. Vaughn drew his pistol and aimed at Janney's chest. Things that Gardner had flung at him stopped him. He let the pistol drop to arm's length at his side. It struck the dog and brought a tiny yelp. "Here, Sport," Vaughn whispered frantically. The dog leaned into his legs, brushing the ground with its tail.

"I made a long ride," Janney said. "The others are coming, but they won't stop to talk, not after that deal the kid forced you into today. Tell me I'm right about you, Drake, and I can handle Warner and the rest."

"You're wrong. Get out of here!"

The loose motion of Janney's smiling face was far worse than Gardner's scars. Janney shook his head gently. In that moment he was everything to Vaughn that Finlay Hester was. Janney rose, stepping back. "I taunted you about that soft spot, not believing it myself, but now I know. In a way I'm sorry you've forced me to do this, Drake. It makes me admit that I was completely wrong about you."

Almost casually Janney reached toward his pistol. Gardner made no move. He sat tightly against the table, with his elbows on it, staring at Janney.

Vaughn raised his pistol. He sighted fully on Janney's chest and pulled the trigger. Glass shards spewed across the room. With his gun in his hand Janney fell forward against the table, then rolled to the floor. The dog at Vaughn's feet let out a startled yelp.

Vaughn felt his way along the building. His pistol barrel struck the thin panel of a door. He threw it open and stepped inside. Gardner was still at the table. Janney was sprawled, face down, with his white hair spilled over his forehead on the dirty floor.

"You," Gardner said. "You earned five hundred." He put his head down on the table.

Vaughn shook him by the shoulder. "Get up! We've got to beat it!"

"Go away."

Vaughn put his pistol away and tried to lift Gardner to his feet. The weight was loose and shifting. "Come on!" Vaughn cried. The sight of Janney, lying there, was driving panic into him. He could not lift Gardner.

He was still trying when a fat man came into the room, still fighting his arms through suspenders. His loose jowls were gray. There were pockets under his eyes and the eyes themselves were sagging toward half moons of redness. Vaughn let go of Gardner and reached for his pistol.

"You fool!" the fat man said. "I run this place."

He turned Janney over, grunting when he saw the sheet of blood smeared in the white hair above Janney's ear, on down to the jaw. "Who's he?" the saloon man muttered to himself. "I left Drake here alone."

"Brett Janney. Five hundred dollars." Gardner's drunken laugh was a rasping sound.

"Dead?" Vaughn tried to swallow, but the muscles of his throat knotted.

The saloon man knelt. "Hell, no. He's bullet-scorched along the side of his head, that's all. Where did he come from?"

"York, Pennsylvania," Gardner said with drunken gravity. "He was a guerilla leader once."

"One of them, huh? A stinking bushwhacker." The fat man stepped across Janney and took the bottle of whiskey. He drank, cleared his throat, and spat on the floor. "You did a miserable job of shooting, bub," he said to Vaughn. "I could beat that, and I've been three-fourths drunk ever since the war."

Janney lay like dead. Vaughn glanced at the broken window. His nerves jumped when the dog outside whined and scratched at the door. "I've got to get him home right away. Janney wasn't the only one."

"Five hundred dollars." Gardner laughed.

"How you going to move him?" the fat man asked.

"That's what I want to know." Gardner hit the table a slow, deliberate *thump* with his fist. He reached for the bottle. "Did I pay you, Tubby?"

Vaughn knocked the bottle off the table. He struck Gardner on the head with his pistol barrel. Gardner's hands and arms shot out across the table and his face went down in the whiskey rings.

"By God!" Tubby said. "That was short and sweet. Where's your horses, kid?"

"In front." Vaughn hoped so.

The saloon man took Gardner's feet and Vaughn held him by the arms. Tubby stumbled over Janney's legs and kicked at them when he regained balance. They carried Gardner out. Vaughn felt a great relief when he heard Mitch snort at the hitch rail.

The livery hostler's voice came carefully from the darkness. "What's going on, Tubby?"

"We just murdered four men and we're taking them out to bury them," the saloon man said. "Now you can go to bed in peace, Fellows."

VII

They put Gardner across his saddle the only way he would fit, belly down. Tubby tied him there. It was well he did. Both horses crow-hopped in the morning cold before Vaughn got them lined out. The friendly dog went along.

Gardner began to groan and curse when the first dawn light touched the red hills. They were then a mile out of town and Vaughn had wandered off the trail into a scrub oak thicket. The whipping of the branches had stung Gardner back to life. He fell out of the saddle while Vaughn was trying to hold him and untie him at the same time.

Still utterly stupid, Gardner was on his feet when Vaughn saw the five riders trotting toward the town. His eyes went from them to the far dim breaks in the direction of Pennsylvania Creek, where Wagon Wheel lay.

"You've got to ride," Vaughn said.

"Sure! I'll ride a nice fat battery horse up the hill, and we'll plant the pieces there, and, if they come at us in columns, we'll string their intestines from tree to tree! And don't throw any water on the cannon this time, men!"

"Don't you remember anything?" Vaughn asked desperately.

"I remember falling out of a duck boat once when I was a boy." Gardner laughed. He leaned against his horse. "Now there's a fine-looking dog. Where'd you get him?"

Vaughn helped him mount. Gardner raked his foot aimlessly, feeling for the right stirrup. His horse went out with a lunge. Gardner found the stirrup automatically then and habit made him bring the animal under control.

At last Vaughn got ahead of him. He led toward Cloverleaf, and then he remembered that Anson Dodge had been mentioned with Janney's other men, and the owners of Wagon Wheel. He cursed the fact that he still knew little of the tensions and the undercurrents of the Spotted Hills, although he was involved.

Anxiously he kept looking back. There seemed to be no pursuit, but Gardner was most unsteady in the saddle now, and getting worse. Another hour of riding and the sun was hot. The dog was panting, the horses lathered.

Gardner was still completely fogged with drunkenness, jerking from side to side every time he dozed and started to fall off his horse. As much as possible Vaughn kept to the troughs of the hills. The skyline offered nothing but waiting vastness, more hostile because there was no threat in sight, but the little valleys gave a feeling of security.

It was in one of them, between two sandstone hills, that Gardner half dismounted, half fell from his saddle. He muttered: "Far enough." He sprawled on the ground, asleep as soon as he struck. His pistol was gone, Vaughn noticed.

For a while Vaughn did not unsaddle the horses. He sat on a rock, waiting. The dog lay at his feet. When he decided that Gardner might sleep for hours, Vaughn stripped the saddles off and picketed the horses. He took his rifle and climbed one of the hills. He could see well in three directions but the hill across from him cut off his view toward Cloverleaf.

Danger would come, he told himself, from one of the visible areas, but after a while the thought did not satisfy

him. He went to the other hill. Except by standing exposed
on the very top, he was confronted with another blind spot
caused by the rise he had just left. He went back to the hill
he had left and positioned himself.

Time passed.

Very low and deep the growling came from Sport.
"Quiet, quiet," Vaughn whispered. Sport stopped growling,
but he was stiff, with his heavy muzzle pointed across the
little valley.

Oh, God! They're sneaking in on us!

But there was only one man over there, a burly man
coming down through the rocks with a pistol in his hand.
His boots were off. Vaughn saw the dun color of his socks
as the man's feet tested each rock as carefully as a cat would
move its pads when stalking a bird. It was Anson Dodge.

"Dodge!" Vaughn yelled down to Gardner.

For a tick of time Dodge hesitated. He fired into the
valley at Gardner. The next bullet came at Vaughn, now
standing shoulder high above the rocks. It sprayed fragments against the side of his neck. He did not flinch or lose
his aim. Gardner had pounded that much into him. He shot
across the little valley and saw Dodge fall. Loosely the
Cloverleaf foreman rolled down the hill with his bootless
feet scraping warm sandstone.

"Vaughn!" Gardner's cry carried concern that must have
been jarred from deeply inside him.

Vaughn raced down the hill. The dog took it as fun and
leaped beside him, barking. Gardner was haggard and his
eyes were red, but they were aware.

"I was kind of awake," he said. "When you yelled, I
rolled clear. Was he alone?"

"I guess so."

Gardner with difficulty went over to Dodge. Vaughn

stayed where he was. When Gardner took the man's pistol belt, Vaughn knew Dodge was dead. He did not want to see him.

When Gardner returned, he asked: "Where are we?"

"Three or four miles from Cloverleaf, I think."

Gardner ran his hand across his forehead. "I can't remember much of anything. What's happened?"

Vaughn told him.

"Let's get out of here. We'll go home. Maybe there's a day or two left." Gardner looked at the dog. "Where'd he come from?"

"Town. Last night."

"I wish I could remember something."

They rode toward the mountains.

Suddenly Gardner ripped open his shirt. He turned his horse toward Vaughn. "See that?" His chest was splashed with white scars. "I got that when I got my face. I was two years in a hospital. She married Lee Hester, but he knew I was alive. Martha is my daughter. I never saw her before I came out here to ruin Lee Hester. I don't blame Molly. She thought I was dead. She married again. Martha thinks Lee Hester is her father. She loves him. The Hesters always had a way with women. When Molly saw me, fourteen years after I was supposed to have been killed, I wished I'd never let her see me. I settled up there against the mountains. Sometimes I walked the meadow all night, trying to figure out what to do. I decided to grind Lee Hester into the earth and claim what was mine. Janney knew it. He's as shrewd as a rat. He's always been on the fringe, waiting to dart in and snatch something. All that time I wouldn't let Molly make a clean break. I said it was because of Martha, but it was only because I wanted to torture Hester. It didn't work. He's too cold-blooded. He tortured me, instead." Gardner shook his head. "I made everything worse. When I found out where Hester was, I should have come out here and killed him, or I shouldn't have come at all. Now the whole thing is tangled up in another mess. Did you hear anything Janney told me last night?"

"Yes," Vaughn said reluctantly. "I heard some things."

"When Janney first showed up in this country, I talked it over with him. I was going to smash Cloverleaf. Lee Hester doesn't own it but it means as much to him as if he did, because everyone thinks he owns it. Janney was going to take the ranch. There's no legal filing on any part of it. All I wanted was revenge, and my wife and daughter. Janney began to set his sights higher. He decided to take the whole Spotted Hills."

"The whole country?"

"It's nothing, compared with what men have taken in Texas and farther West. Smash Cloverleaf and Wagon Wheel, and there's only a few small men left to fight. That cold devil, Finlay Hester, decided to do the same thing. All he had to do was break Wagon Wheel. Lee wasn't big enough to do it, so Finlay tried to use Dodge." Gardner cursed. "You know what he promised Dodge, besides being foreman of the whole country? He promised him Molly. Dodge had been in love with her for years."

"I'm glad I killed him, then," Vaughn said.

Gardner began to button his shirt. The sweat and whiskey odor of him was strong in the still, warm air.

"Janney got wind of how Finlay was trying to use Dodge. Janney never misses anything. Stack a blind man sitting in a dark room, no matter how strong his will may be, against the clever talk of Brett Janney, backed with three ex-guerillas, and you can understand how Janney won Dodge by promising him the same things Finlay offered."

There are at least four, not three, with Janney, but the point does not matter now, Vaughn thought.

"You know what was supposed to happen when Wagon Wheel and Cloverleaf came to your shack that night? Finlay planned it. Charley Burgett and Troutt Warner were supposed to have been wiped out in the dark. Dodge couldn't do it. Before the men left Cloverleaf, Lee made them leave their guns. Dodge sneaked a pistol along, all right, but your father put up such a scrap Dodge never got a chance to get at Warner and Burgett. He did crawl in and shut the rifle down. I know that, because he told Janney about it."

Dodge then. He was dead now. That was enough for Vaughn. The knowledge that Anson Dodge had killed Carmody Steele would help, in time, to dull the tight, sick feeling Vaughn felt each time he recalled a rifle shot across the little valley of the two red hills. The vow he had made, to kill everyone who took part in the night raid on the homestead, was a childish thing to him now.

"I drew Janney into the plan," Gardner said. "I've got to live with that mistake, no matter what happens. He played it two ways, like he always did everything. He went to Wagon Wheel and told them there that Cloverleaf could be ruined and taken. The idea grew on Warner and Burgett, especially after Anson Dodge testified that Finlay Hester was planning the same thing against Wagon Wheel. You see what I started, Vaughn?"

It was clear enough to Vaughn Steele now. Brett Janney had needed Gardner because he feared him, and because Gardner's desires did not conflict with Janney's. But now Janney was done with Gardner. He would use, instead, the force of Wagon Wheel.

"Charley Burgett is a sneak," Gardner said. "Warner, I believe, could be made to live in peace here. He'll be the first one Max Sloss or Janney will kill after they have used him up against Cloverleaf."

Dodge was dead, taking much from Finlay Hester's strength, even though he had been a traitor to Hester. Lee Hester had laughed about the threat of Wagon Wheel; he had said Burgett and Warner were his friends. There would be then, Vaughn reasoned, no trouble coming from Cloverleaf. It would come the other way. But without Janney to foment it . . . ?

"How bad did you wound Janney?" Gardner asked.

"Tubby said it was a bullet scorch across the head."

"He won't be worth anything for a few days. There won't be any trouble until then, at least."

Vaughn went on with his reasoning. It was simple, if you had the stomach for it. Kill Brett Janney. Finlay Hester had a strong point there

Vaughn said: "Kill Brett Janney."

"No!"

"Why not? It will stop what you started."

"No!"

"You said once you might not kill him even if he gave you an excuse. Last night he was going to shoot you. Why don't you want . . . ?"

"He's Molly's twin brother."

When they reached Gardner's horse ranch at sundown, Gardner swung down wearily. He stood for a moment looking down at the Spotted Hills, and then he went in and climbed into his bunk with his clothes on.

VIII

Drake Gardner was gone when Vaughn woke up. On the top of the cold stove was a note: **Stay here**.

He did not think of the dog until after breakfast. He whistled. The horses in the meadow pricked up their ears. The whistle rode away to silence. Sport was gone. Maybe back on the hill chasing rabbits. Why would Gardner take the dog with him?

Vaughn went scouting on the hill, pushing through rose thickets, whistling now and then. There was no use. Sport was gone. It left Vaughn more uneasy than ever. He went back to the cabin.

"Hello, kid."

Vaughn's muscles jerked. Frog was standing near the stove, his thumbs hooked into his pistol belt, his puckered mouth grim, turned down at the corners. Vaughn squinted, trying to adjust to the sudden change of light.

"Where's Gardner?"

Vaughn went for his pistol. His hand was on the butt grips when Frog's weapon was clear, pointing at Vaughn's stomach.

"Take it easy," Frog said. "You trying to get killed, kid?"

Vaughn eased his hand away from his pistol. He glanced behind him, expecting to see Sloss stalking in, licking his red lips, expecting to see Janney's deep-creased face all rutted in an evil grin.

"I'm alone," Frog said. "Promise not to get the drop on me again if I holster up?" His lips twitched.

"You scared the hell out of me. What do you want?"

"Where's Drake." Frog put his pistol away.

"I don't know."

"You sure?"

"I don't know where he is."

Frog considered. "My horse is down in the trees. I'm going to get him and take care of him. I'm not with Janney any more. That good enough for you, or will I see a rifle looking at me when I come back?" He grinned.

"I guess it'll do."

"You'll never buy a wooden nutmeg, will you?" Frog walked out and went toward the trees below the cabin. He came back in a few minutes with his horse. Vaughn put the corral bars down. When they went into the cabin again, Frog sat down as if he were weary. "No idea where he is, huh?"

"Maybe Cloverleaf," Vaughn said cautiously.

"Yeah." Frog nodded. "I reckon. You mind if I have something to eat? Been up all night." He began to unstrap his pistol belt. "Funny thing, I thought I was done with guns when the war ended. It didn't work out that way."

"Guerilla?" Vaughn asked.

"No, by God. You know about Janney, then?"

Vaughn nodded. He began to cook breakfast for Frog. "How is Janney?"

"He's got a thousand-dollar headache. Every time he makes a quick move he closes his eyes and cusses."

"How soon will he be all right?"

Frog shrugged. "I've seen men die from little bullet cuts

across the skull. Brett won't, though. You tried to crease him thataway?"

"I tried to hit him in the heart."

"That's a pistol for you." Frog drank three cups of coffee before he began to eat. There was an insouciant good humor about him. "Know who killed your pa?"

Vaughn nodded.

"He won't hear the dogs bark no more, will he?"

"You saw Dodge?"

"In my prowling around I sort of cut your tracks." Frog glanced at Vaughn's rifle laid on pegs on the wall. "I buried him. Any man ought to get that. I'll bet Finlay Hester still thinks he's the fair-haired boy."

Vaughn dumped bacon into a tin plate. "What's going to happen?"

Frog shrugged. "I ain't remaining to see. If Gardner comes back before dark, I'll speak a word or two, and then . . ."—Frog grinned—"I've got a cousin out in Oregon, or some place such like, that I ain't seen in years."

Vaughn asked a question that had disturbed some basic feeling in him for a day and night. "How can one bunch of men just kill off some others and grab everything they own? How can that work out?"

"You stayed mighty close to that plow, didn't you, Steele? Your pa could have answered that. You ought to be able to answer it yourself, seeing as what happened one night to your house down there on Elk Run."

Vaughn supposed he had known the answer all the time; it was just that knowing was a shock. The things you learned at home didn't fit the pattern of the world around you, maybe.

Frog puffed his pipe. He did not sleep.

Sport arrived, bursting into the cabin.

"He'll be down there in the trees," Frog said. "He'll be wondering about the tracks of my horse. Save him the scout in, Steele."

Vaughn found Gardner easing toward the cabin through the edge of the trees. "Frog's horse made the tracks, Vaughn. Was Frog on it?"

Vaughn nodded.

"I told the dog to stay here," Gardner said. "He caught up with me about two miles away. Now that's a habit you'd best break him of."

Frog was still on the bunk. He sat up and knocked the dottle from his pipe on the side pole, studying Gardner's face. "No luck, huh? I'd say you went to Cloverleaf."

"Lee is a crazy fool," Gardner said. "He wouldn't believe that such a thing could happen. He still thinks he's in Pennsylvania. He also told me that I was trying to make a hero of myself before his wife, and then he laughed in my face."

"Little Gentle Face?" Frog asked.

"I had bad luck there. He sat there weighing what I'd told him with that dreamy, creepy look. I'd left my pistol on the porch. That blamed carved orangewood handle on Dodge's gun caught Nan's eye. She called clear across the yard to Martha . . . 'Why, Mister Gardner's got Mister Dodge's gun, the one with the big stars on the handle.'"

"A man ought to have two pistols," Frog murmured. You didn't turn around when you walked out, I see."

"I remembered. He used to go out at night with that knife, looking for Rebel pickets. He was an artillery captain, Frog, but he went out alone, and, when he came back, grinning, he would say . . . 'You know, the nights grow quieter around here all the time, Gardner.' No, I didn't turn my back, Frog. I opened the door and stepped against the wall of the room, inside. The knife went stomach high through the doorway. When he heard it hit the wall in the hallway, he shook his head. He said . . . 'Toss it over toward my feet, Drake, so the children won't see it. I might have known you wouldn't trust even a poor sightless man.' "

"Crazy?" Frog said in a hushed voice.

Gardner shook his head. "A Hester, that's all."

"Yeah," Frog said. "I've heard of the cousins."

"When does Janney start it?" Gardner asked.

Frog grinned. "When I get back from scouting to see if Lee still has everybody out on spring roundup."

"Would you take that chance and go back? Maybe we could fix up something for them to ride into."

Frog shook his head. "Not for the biggest farm in all Ohio, Drake. Brett has been smiling at me too easy ever since the time I sneaked in here alone last spring. I've got a cousin that needs seeing. He may be in China now."

"No, you can't go back," Gardner said. He felt the coffee pot, and then poured himself a cup. His eyes showed that his mind was working now with all the webs of indecision cleared away. Vaughn was pleased, and scared.

"There's women there," Gardner said. "They wouldn't leave, not Molly and Martha, at least."

"I'm marked," Frog said.

"I wouldn't promise you a thing."

"I didn't ask."

"Not a single thing."

"I'll be in the pass by morning," Frog said.

"You've gone this far."

"Just on my way out, Drake. Brett ran thin on me a long time ago, but I'm still afraid of him."

"The kid was afraid of Dodge, too," Gardner said.

"I know. I came by that place." Frog grinned. "Steele

started to draw on me, too."

Gardner groaned. "I'll leave you home, Vaughn, when we ride away from here."

"We?" Frog asked. "Who said . . . ?"

"Would you like to see Sloss loose with those women, Frog?" The scars on Gardner's cheek were livid.

"Next to Janney, I'd like to see Sloss dead," Frog said. "But. . . ."

"Two days after I enlisted, bushwhackers killed my whole family," Gardner said. "It wasn't Janney's bunch. This was in Missouri. I've never tried to get even with the breed. Don't you think it's time? I need help, Frog."

Frog rubbed his broad baldhead. "That's getting it sort of down to where I can understand it. By morning I should be in the pass. . . . How do I know I could ever get through the country on the other side, anyway? They're looking day and night over there for anybody that ever rode with Brett."

Now there were three of them, Vaughn thought.

Gardner asked: "When will he try it?"

"Dawn. Noon. Dusk. Brett never got in no rut thataway."

"I'm not long on ammunition," Gardner said.

Frog grinned. "It so happens that I borrowed a scad of cartridges of various kinds just before I left the Wagon Wheel. I thought, Drake, that you might put up some kind of hard luck story to make me change my mind. I'm not fooling, though. My intentions were ninety-eight percent to go over the hill."

IX

Lee Hester paced his brother's room at Cloverleaf. "No," he said, "you're wrong, Finlay. For all that Brett is no good, he still wouldn't do it. And Gardner has a soft streak. He's a weak fool. That cannon burned more than the face off him. No man with any guts would have put up with what I've given him."

"Dodge is dead, Lee. Gardner killed him."

"Oh, hell. Dodge said he might be gone several days when I sent him out to ride the south breaks. This is a big country, Finlay. You can't realize. . . ."

"I see it better than you do," Finlay said softly. "You didn't send Dodge to ride for cattle. I sent him to find Drake Gardner and kill him. You've never sent Dodge any place, Lee. When are you going to understand that?"

"Your stinking money!" Lee said savagely. "What good is it to you? One day you'll misjudge the steps when you start out to the lattice house. . . ."

"Be quiet, Lee. I can't see your face. I can't see that handsome shell you use to impress the people of this country. The whine in your voice is enough for me, even if I did not know you. I want you to go to Wagon Wheel and talk to Troutt Warner. Patch up a peace some way. Show him that he can't trust Janney. Get me some time, Lee. I'll send for men I know, men that I can trust. Get me time,

258

Lee, and then I'll take this whole country."

Lee Hester stopped pacing. "What do we want with the whole country? You don't mean . . . ?"

"I've been patient with you, Lee. I've tried to teach you certain facts about our neighbors. They hate us. Their voices have told me that. They would do to us just what I've planned to do to them."

"Warner and Burgett?" Lee's voice was loud, incredulous.

"Close the door, please, and lock it." Finlay listened carefully while his order was carried out. "Burgett particularly," he resumed. "He's a coward, Lee. Warner is not, but neither is he ruthless. I think he can pull Burgett out of this thing, at least for a time. That leaves Janney. Drake Gardner can stop him. Talk to Warner, then see Gardner. Tell Drake that you have decided to give up Molly, that you have realized she loves him."

"You're crazy, Finlay!"

"Tell him that Molly loves him, and that you have realized it at last. That will appeal to the softness in Drake. Add, of course, that you must have Gardner's help to smash this threat against Cloverleaf before you can release Molly."

"That would be a filthy bargain. She doesn't love him. She's sorry for him, that's all."

"Your poor, blind fool," Finlay murmured.

There was a long silence. "What makes you think she does?" Lee asked.

"She loves him, be sure of that," Finlay said. "Martha is the only reason that she has not left with him long ago. I recall the first day Gardner came here, from the dead, Molly thought. My ears see coloring in speech and hesitations. You wouldn't remember how Molly acted. Your own voice was trembling with fear that day, until you realized that

Gardner had not come to kill you."

"Damn you, Finlay."

"Ah, the truth is at last blooming."

"No. You've made it up, sitting here in the dark."

"I see no dark, Lee, you do." Finlay took a glass of water from the table at his side.

"There're food stains all over your shirt and on your lapels," Lee said. "You're filthy. I suppose you can see that, too."

Finlay shook his head. "Now I know there are three children who come into my room, and you are more child than the other two. It's a pity that I must use you to do the work of a man, but it must be that way for a while."

Lee tried to make his voice crisp, decisive. "I've got to get back to the men on the range." He walked across the room and let the shade up viciously. The sunlight struck on Finlay's pink face, but he did not flinch or turn his head.

"So you did not order the men back here, as I told you to do?"

Lee was looking at the lattice house. "No. I saw no need. You can ride out and do that, if it's so vital. You'd look good on a horse, Finlay." He strode over to his brother. "I'll take that precious knife of yours, I think." Leaning past his brother, he opened the drawer in the little table.

"A quarrel is never good," Finlay said. He put his left hand on Lee's shoulder, gripping gently. His right hand pulled a pistol from under his coat. He shot Lee Hester in the side of the head at point-blank range.

The pistol was in Lee's hand where he lay sprawled beside an overturned table when Finlay unlocked the door in response to Molly Hester's knocks and calls. Finlay caught her shoulder as she started to go past him.

"Lee shot himself, Molly. He realized at last that you were still in love with Drake."

He could not see the horror on her face, but she did not start or gasp. Her silence told him what she believed. She whispered: "You killed him, Finlay." She tried to thrust past him into the room.

"Go get the cook," he said. He pushed Molly Hester from the room. "Get the cook, I say!" He heard the girls running toward him. He closed the door behind him.

"Mother, what . . . ?"

"Don't go near him!" Molly cried.

"Martha, Nan, come here." Finlay groped for the wall. He knew exactly where it was. He heard Mrs. Hester run from the house.

Nan asked: "What happened, Uncle Finlay?"

"Nan, do you know where the men are?"

"I heard Uncle Lee say they were hunting cows in the cedar breaks on Kincaid Creek, but I don't know . . . I heard a shot, Uncle Finlay. What . . . ?"

"Tell her where the Cedar Breaks are, Martha. Go there, Nan. Tell the men to come back here at once. Martha, ride to Drake Gardner's place. Tell him to come here immediately."

There was silence. Then Martha said: "What was wrong with my mother, Uncle Finlay?"

He read hostility that had never been in her voice before. In a way it pained him, because he respected women as gentle, loving beings. That had always been a Hester weakness, and the Hesters were proud of it.

"She will tell you when you return," he said.

Martha said: "I won't go unless my mother tells me to. And neither is Nan going any place."

Mrs. Hester returned with the cook.

"I have told the children they must go do certain errands, Molly," Finlay Hester said. "Please add your approval."

"Yes, go," Mrs. Hester said. "Go now!"

When the front door banged shut, Finlay stood back and extended his arm toward his room.

In late afternoon Brett Janney lay on warm grass on a hill a mile from Cloverleaf, with his hat shading his eyes. Charley Burgett sat near him. With one hand Burgett kept pulling blistered skin from his cheek bones; with the other hand he pulled blades of grass, rolling them between his thumb and forefinger before he dropped them. His deep-set eyes drifted frequently to Janney.

Four men waited near the horses, two riders from Wagon Wheel and two of Janney's men.

"Nervous?" Janney asked of Burgett.

"Yeah. About Warner."

"When it's done, he'll have to go along."

"What about Gardner?"

Janney sat up. "He's paid for. Him and the kid." He looked at the men squatted near the horses. The two from Wagon Wheel were not much, according to his way of thinking. His own men, Rance and Sloss, would do, but a gang wore out. It was best to make frequent changes. Sloss was a sore spot. It was best to get him killed, if it could be arranged. Sloss couldn't remember that the old guerilla days were dead. He would run wild among the women at Cloverleaf and that would not do out here. With a wondering sort of detachment Janney thought that one of the women was his sister, and another his niece. Yes, Sloss was worn out as far as Janney was concerned.

Burgett kept watching Janney uneasily.

It was possible that Charley Burgett would also get killed in the fight. As the brother of the woman whose husband had owned Cloverleaf, Brett Janney would feel rather badly about the raid Wagon Wheel had made. Once he was well set up at the ranch, he would have to see that Wagon Wheel paid for killing his brother-in-law.

"What are you grinning about?" Burgett asked.

"About living like a king, after all the years of abuse I've taken."

"The little ranches . . . we won't have to get so rough there, will we?" Burgett asked.

"They'll run, if we work it right. Half their range for me, half for you, with whatever happens to be loose on it. That's all right, isn't it, Burgett?"

"Yeah." About one fourth more of the Spotted Hills. Burgett could move then, make the break with Warner, and then he could lay other plans. Everything else was all right, except. . . . He looked uneasily at Janney again.

"This is the worst of it," Janney said. "After that, we'll move more subtly. You and I can own the hills, Burgett. We need each other. We'll have to get along, won't we?"

They did need each other, but Janney's stating the fact seemed to color it a little. White-haired at his age. Maybe he had taken a lot of abuse from the world. Cloverleaf would seem like a lot to him, and he ought to be satisfied with it. But that damned crawling grin of his. . . .

One of the Wagon Wheel men said: "There's a horse coming, Burgett."

Burgett took some assurance from the fact that the man had addressed him, and not Janney.

Piney Bauman rode in a few minutes later. He was a wiry little man with a pinched face, and he could smell out loot in a poor white shack. He was the only one of Janney's bunch that Janney trusted. A gold bracelet, a few rings, and a gambling game were enough to satisfy Piney Bauman. He rode directly to Janney and swung down.

"The hands are still away, Brett, all but the cook. On the way back I scouted the house. The two girls. . . ."

"What about Gardner?"

"They skipped," Bauman said. "All three. You was right. Frog had been there."

"How do you know they skipped?" Janney asked.

"They took everything in the cabin that was worth a dime. They druv the horses ahead of them and lit out toward the pass."

"How far did you follow?"

"Two miles, I reckon. They never let a horse get away, Brett." Piney took a chew of tobacco. He offered some to Burgett, who shook his head. "They skipped, Brett. They wouldn't bother with the horses, otherwise, would they?"

Janney chewed his lip. His eyes narrowed. He was so full of tricks himself he could not trust the news.

"That helps," Burgett said.

Bauman ignored him. "I burned the cabin."

"You fool!" Janney said. "I could have used that as a line camp." Almost in the same breath he added: "Me and Burgett could have used it."

"I didn't know." Bauman's hand was on a broken watch in his pocket, the nearest thing to any item of value he had been able to find in Gardner's cabin.

"You couldn't dig out any loot," Janney said, "and that's when you always start pouring coal oil."

"No, Brett. . . ."

"What was it you started to say about the girls?" Janney asked.

"The big one rode toward the mountains. The other one

went skimming off to the south a while ago. I just seen one man, the cook, around the ranch."

"Lee's there," Janney said. "I saw him myself a couple of hours ago." Finlay would be there too, of course. The idea of shooting an afflicted man disturbed Janney more than he would have admitted. That would be a job for Sloss. He rose. "We'll ride in just like any visitors. How long ago were those tracks made above Gardner's place, Piney?"

"Sometime yesterday . . . early."

"I'd like it better if they'd been made today."

While the group was mounting, Janney had a few quick words with Sloss alone.

X

From an aspen thicket on top of Buffalo Hill, about two miles from Cloverleaf, Gardner, Frog, and Vaughn watched the last of the smoke die against the mountains.

"I'll build it again," Gardner said. "This time without the extra bunks."

The waiting built up terrible pressure in Vaughn. "Hadn't we better get on down there?"

"Not yet," Gardner said. "Wait until we see which direction Bauman takes."

The little rider on a powerful claybank had passed sometime before, going toward Cloverleaf. Gardner had said nothing would happen until after he went back to report to Janney. Frog agreed, but Vaughn wondered how they could be sure. He kept patting Sport. He kept thinking of Max Sloss.

Vaughn was the first one to see the rider streaking toward the mountains. "Oh, oh," he said. It came out a whisper, although the rider was a quarter of a mile off.

"That's a woman," Frog said.

"Martha." Gardner looked at Vaughn. "She might be headed for my place. Go after her, Vaughn, and then stay with her. Stay clear of Cloverleaf, too."

"You didn't want me along in the first place."

"That's right. Don't come near Cloverleaf until you

know for sure how things stand. Go on now. She's running the legs off that sorrel."

Gardner and Frog rode on. Vaughn hesitated. Gardner did not look back, and that more than anything convinced the youth that he must follow orders.

She rode all the faster when she saw him coming. It was a long chase before he got within hailing distance and she recognized his voice. Her face was pale and sweating and her hair was in disorder. "Where's Drake Gardner?"

Vaughn jerked his hand toward Cloverleaf. "Have they come in yet?"

"They?"

"Oh, hell! I'm sorry. I mean . . . what do you want with Drake?"

"My uncle wants him. I think. . . ." She slid down from the saddle and leaned against the sorrel and began to sob. "Something's happened to my father! I know it. Something awful is going on at home!"

She took him by the shortest route to Cloverleaf, and they let the horses stretch out. He left her and Sport and his horse in a scrub oak thicket.

He saw then why he was not too late. Two riders were coming from the south toward a group of men on a hill. Janney must have sent scouts toward the Cedar Breaks before he came to a full decision. From the ranch house the group upon the rise would not be visible. Vaughn watched the scouts report.

Only three men came down the hill, riding casually. By the black beard, one was Max Sloss; another, tall, slope-shouldered, was Charley Burgett. The third one Vaughn did not know.

Vaughn held to the trees until he reached the lattice

house. He crawled from there to the back door of the ranch house. It was locked. He dared not risk the pounding and shouting it would take to attract someone's attention. He ran through the soft soil of a flowerbed to Finlay Hester's window. The shade was fully drawn. The window swung back when he pushed. He hauled himself astraddle the sill and eased inside. It was gloomy and the hallway door was shut. He was tiptoeing across the room when he saw the sheet-covered lump upon the bed.

Every nerve jerked in his body. He half turned to run back to the window, and then with icy sweat on his brow he saw Drake Gardner standing on a chair, peering from a narrow casement window near the fireplace in the living room.

Terror gave way to normal fear. He ran down the hall. Two pistols and a rifle trained on him. There were four men—Gardner, Frog, the cook, and Finlay Hester, who said: "Ah, the clodhopper boy I would judge by the steps."

Gardner jerked back to the window. "At the cook shack now. Where's Martha, damn you, Steele!"

"Hidden."

"They see there's no one here," Gardner said. "They're riding into the yard. Don't shoot. We've got to have the whole bunch, or the surprise is worthless."

"It ain't no surprise, or he would've come down hisself," Frog said. "By God, what'll we do?"

Max Sloss hailed from the yard. "Hello, the house! Anybody home?"

"If any of us goes out. . . ." Gardner looked at Vaughn and Frog. He glanced at the cook. The man was sunk in terror now. He clutched his rifle and kept looking toward the kitchen.

"Is they anybody home?" Sloss called.

268

"That's a Southern voice." The calmness of Finlay Hester's tone did not conceal hatred. "I'll bring those others into range for you, Drake. How many in the yard?"

"Three," Gardner said. "They'll kill you if you step out there."

"They wouldn't shoot a blind man. Are they near the porch steps?"

"Just getting off their horses," Frog said. "Sloss would shoot his mother, mister."

"Oh, I think not." Finlay Hester walked to the door. His fingertips touched the edge of a small table on the way and that was the only guidance he used. He took a cane from a hat rack. He opened the door, calling: "Just a moment, gentlemen! Who is it?"

Vaughn was on his knees near Frog, peering from between a lace curtain and the casing of the window. He saw Finlay lose his steadiness. The man went out on the porch feeling with his cane ahead of him. He groped for the banister of the porch and found it.

"Blind as a bat," Sloss said. All three of them were on the ground, at the foot of the steps. Sloss's hand was near his pistol. He relaxed a trifle. His red lips blossomed in his beard as he grinned.

Finlay leaned on the banister. He hooked his cane over it. He was not bearing much weight on it, Vaughn observed. "Would the rest of you gentlemen speak up please?" Finlay asked.

"Burgett. You know me."

"Ah, yes, of course. You came to see Lee? He isn't home right now, but won't you come in, anyway?"

"Well. . . ." Burgett looked at Sloss.

"There's three of you. Would the third gentleman please speak?"

"I'm just a rider for Charley," the third man said.

"Burgett," Finlay said.

"What?"

"Sloss?"

"Yeah?" Sloss scowled, puzzled.

"You rider, what's your name?"

"Leason."

Finlay's head had moved just a trifle as each man answered. Watching, Vaughn felt a fearful force of cunning evil in the man. He saw exactly what Finlay was doing.

"You alone here?" Sloss growled.

"Oh, yes." Finlay's weight had not been on the rail at all. His right hand went under his coat. He fired with the pistol close to his body, guided by the uncanny wisdom of his ears. He fired as they had spoken, from left to right.

Sloss reeled back with both hands on his stomach. Burgett doubled in the middle and dropped on the steps. Leason, the Wagon Wheel rider, saved his life by not trying to fight back. He was near the rail. He jumped aside. The bullet meant for him went under the belly of a horse.

The third shot sent back to Finlay's ears no brutal impact sound. The plunging of the horses ruined his aim. He made a guess as to which way Leason had jumped; he fired, on the wrong side. Leason touched his own pistol, and then in panic he ran to his horse and leaped on. Finlay heard part of it, but he made another mistake. He killed a horse ten feet from Leason. The rider steadied then. He took careful aim from his saddle. He fired. Finlay Hester dropped his pistol. This time it was no pretense when he leaned upon the banister. He sank to his knees, still clinging to the railing, and then he spilled over on his side.

Leason spurred away.

Vaughn started to run toward the door, his only thought

to get a shot at the fleeing man. Frog tripped him. Gardner leaped across the room and wrenched the cook's rifle from him, just as the man, standing now, was steadying to fire through the window at Leason.

"You're trying to ruin it!" Gardner cried.

The cook and Vaughn steadied then, looking shame-faced at each other. The cook was a fully grown man, Vaughn thought, he should have known how to control himself.

Frog winked at Vaughn. "No hard feelings for this trip?"

Vaughn shook his head. It would take a lifetime to learn anything.

"That did it," Gardner said.

"They're coming now."

"That Finlay almost made a sweep," Frog said. "Didn't that chill the red-hot vinegar in you?"

Gardner cursed. "Janney's holding back."

Frog said: "He always does."

One of the men at the foot of the steps gave a bubbling groan. All at once the cook was as sick and as frightened as before. "Will Missus Hester be all right alone in the cellar?"

Frog laughed. "Sure, pothook."

Only two men came into Vaughn's sight, Bauman and Leason. Janney was not trusting the evidence on the porch, what Finlay had said, or the silent house.

Gardner looked at Frog and pointed toward the kitchen. "Take the cook with you."

Frog and the cook crawled across the floor and disappeared.

"Leg shots," Gardner said. "Take Bauman."

The two men in front were on the ground, with pistols drawn. Remembering how Leason had rested his gun across his arm to shoot down Finlay Hester, Vaughn disobeyed another order. He aimed at Leason's leg as the man came toward the porch.

The big window came apart. Black powder smoke from his heavy rifle swirled back and blinded Vaughn. When he could see, Leason was on the ground. Bauman had ducked like a weasel under his horse and now he was running beside the animal, with it between him and the house.

While Vaughn was trying to reload, Gardner jumped to the chair at the narrow window by the fireplace. The window blew out in his face. He fell back on the floor with blood running from his forehead.

Vaughn dropped his rifle and ran to him.

"Hang onto your gun," Gardner said. He wiped his arm across his face and got up. "That was Janney, from the corner of the cook shack."

A rifle and a pistol roared in the kitchen. Frog said: "Too bad, Rance." An instant later bullets crashed into the partition between the living room and kitchen. The cook cried out in pain.

"Oh, hell," Frog said, "use the other arm."

"I can't see Janney now," Gardner said. "I think he got past the cook house and came this way."

There was utter silence. Vaughn's face was white as he watched Leason out there in the yard. He wanted to go out and help the man, but he knew he would not.

Frog yelled: "Bauman's skipping!" His pistol sounded twice. "Hang that Piney! He's no bigger than a flea." He shot once more. "He's clear. I always said he could duck a bullet."

"Stay here," Gardner said to Vaughn. He walked out the front door. For a moment he stood looking at Finlay Hester, and then he went down the steps.

Leason heard the sounds. He raised his head a little.

"Will somebody help me now?"

Gardner went past him, carrying his pistol at his side. He did not slow down when the corner of the house no longer obscured his vision of the end wall. He turned that way to go around the next corner.

A heavy bay horse, dragging its reins and shying sidewise, started up the hill from somewhere near the corral. An instant later Brett Janney broke from behind a building and ran toward it. The second Wagon Wheel man was escaping on foot.

"Janney!" Gardner called.

Vaughn shot the horse through the neck as Janney was reaching to catch the reins. The white-haired man, still half crouched from his attempt to grab the reins, turned toward Gardner.

Vaughn watched the running out of something that affected him like the chilling flow of Finlay Hester's voice, but he knew there was justice in this present act, somewhere.

Gardner kept walking with his pistol at his side. Janney leveled his own pistol, holding it, not firing. The attempt to rush Gardner backfired on Janney's nerves. He backed up a few steps, as if he would suddenly turn and run.

Gardner kept pacing toward him. He would get killed! Vaughn fumbled for a cartridge, but his eyes were on the hill, and he tried the wrong pocket.

Suddenly Janney dropped to one knee. He fired three times as fast as his pistol would work. Drake Gardner never broke stride. He raised his pistol slowly.

Vaughn cut his face on a shard of glass as he jerked when the rifle blasted beside him. The cook was kneeling at the window, and Frog was standing behind him, and Vaughn had heard neither of them come into the room.

Brett Janney seemed to sink into the ground. He rolled over on his face, and Gardner let his pistol drop until it was pointing toward the ground again.

"I got one of them!" the cook yelled. "And me with a bullet in my arm!"

Troutt Warner came in with Nan and the Cloverleaf riders an hour after sundown. His big mouth was loose and startled when he heard the story. "I won't lie," he said. "I figured to squeeze the Hesters out, but not like Janney and Burgett planned. When I found out what they were up to, I streaked like hell to find Lee's crew. Lee's dead, too?"

Nan began to cry. Vaughn took her to the cook shack. There were a lot of things here that were none of his business. Let her think that Finlay Hester had been a kind and gentle man, let Martha mourn Lee as a father, until Molly and Gardner told her otherwise, if they ever did.

About the Author

Steve Frazee was born in Salida, Colorado, and in the decade 1926–1936 he worked in heavy construction and mining in his native state. He also managed to pay his way through Western State College in Gunnison, Colorado, from which in 1937 he graduated with a bachelor's degree in journalism. The same year he also married. He began making major contributions to the Western pulp magazines with stories set in the American West as well as a number of North-Western tales published in *Adventure*. Few can match his Western novels that are notable for their evocative, lyrical descriptions of the open range and the awesome power of natural forces and their effects on human efforts. *Cry Coyote* (1955) is memorable for its strong female protagonists who actually influence most of the major events and bring about the resolution of the central conflict in this story of wheat growers and expansionist cattlemen. *High Cage* (1957) concerns five miners and a woman snowbound at an isolated gold mine on top of Bulmer Peak in which the twin themes of the lust for gold and the struggle against the savagery of both the elements and human nature interplay with increasing, almost tormented intensity. *Bragg's Fancy Woman* (1966) concerns a free-spirited woman who is able to tame a family of thieves. *Rendezvous* (1958) ranks as one of the finest mountain man books, and *The Way Through the*

Mountains (1972) is a major historical novel. Not surprisingly, many of Frazee's novels have become major motion pictures. According to the second edition of *Twentieth-Century Western Writers* (1991), a Frazee story is possessed of "flawless characterization, particularly when it involves the clash of human passions, believable dialogue, and the ability to create and sustain damp-palmed suspense." *Black Diamond* will be his next Five Star Western.